WEST INDIES,

from the Lateſt

IMPROVEMENTS.

ATLANTIC

ATLANTIC OCEAN

BAHAMA ISLES

Guanahani or Sᵗ Salvador
Watlings I.
Little I.
Rum Key
Long I. Atwoods Key
Exuma
Bahama
Crooked I.
Mayaguana
South Key
L. Inagua
the Cayos
Turk Iˢ
Handkerchief
the 3 Keys
Silver Keys
Old C. Francais
Hogsties
Mulas
Inagua
C. Maize
Yago
Torridas
Monte Christe
Samana
Sᵗ Nicholas the Cape
HISPANIOLA
Marin
Port au
Prince or Cᵗ Engano
Gonave St DOMINGO
C. Dona
Sᵗ Louis
Abac
Domingo
Cape Beata
Bell Rock
GREAT ANTILLES

WINDWARD PASSAGE

Mona
Portorico
Sᵗ Juan
Serpents I.
Sᵗ Thomas
Crab I.
Santa Cruz
Saba
Sᵗ Eustatia
Sᵗ Kitts
Nevis
Monserat
Guadeloupe
les Saints I.
Aves

VIRGIN ISLES
Anegada
Sombrero
Gorda
Tortola
Sᵗ Johns
Anguilla
Sᵗ Martins
Sᵗ Bartholomew
Barbuda
Antigua
la Desirade
Mariegalante
Dominica

LEEWARD ISLES

CARIBBEE ISLES

C. Monant
Royal

BBEAN SEA
CARIBBEAN SEA

Martinico
Royal
WINDWARD
Sᵗ Lucia
Barbados
Sᵗ Vincent
Bequia
Granadines
ISLES
Grenada
Tobago

LITTLE ANTILLES
Monges
Aruba
Curacao
Bonair
Roca
Blanca
Orchilla
Margarita
Testigos
C. de la Vela
Lᵗ Piedro
C. Coquibacoa
L. Curacao
Avis
Sᵗ Martha
enas
Sᵗ MARTHA
Gulf of Venezuela
Sᵗ Felipe
C. Coden
Salt Tortuga
C. 3 Points
Leon de Caraccas
Cumanagote Cumana
CUMANA
Maracaybo
Tenerif
Lake of Maracaybo
Truxillo
Gibraltar
VENEZUELA or CARACCAS

PARIA
G. of Paria
Trinidad
Mouths of the Orinoco

CARTAGENA
R. Cauca
Rio de la Magdalena

Rio Orinoco
Sᵗ Thome

TERRA FIRMA

SOUTH AMERICA

CONGO JACK

CONGO JACK

A NOVEL

by

ROGER NORMAN BUCKLEY

Pinto Press
Mt. Kisco, New York

Book design by Dale Schroeder, Synergistic Data Systems

Publisher's Cataloging-in-Publication
(Provided by Quality Books, Inc.)

Buckley, Roger Norman, 1937
    Congo Jack: a novel / by Roger Norman Buckley.
    p. cm.
    Preassigned LCCN: 97-65343
    ISBN 0-9632476-5-4

    1. Great Britain. Army—Colonial forces—West
Indies, British—Fiction. 2. Soldiers, Black—West
Indies, British—Fiction. 3. Mutiny—Dominica—
Fiction.   I. Title.

PS3552.U3554C6646   1997   813'.54
                          QBI97-40263

9 8 7 6 5 4 3 2 1
First Edition

Pinto Press

Mt. Kisco, New York

In memory of my cousin

Charles "Sunny" Mapp

Artist
Dreamer
Sorcerer

CONTENTS

Illustrations & Maps

Map of the West Indies, 1800 (C. Cooke,
London) Endpapers

Inset map of Dominica (A. Muñoz, New
York) Endpapers

View of Portsmouth Harbor and Cabrits from
Lt. Colonel Alexander Whaley Light's *Views
in the West Indies 1811-1814*, courtesy of the
Public Record Office, Kew, Richmond, U.K.,
MPH III. Title Page

Acknowledgments

A book is always the work of many people. This book, which tries to sense what it was like to be a stolen African, is no exception. I owe an enormous debt of gratitude to writers of all kinds, living and dead, from whom I have gained knowledge and inspiration. Because this is a work of fiction, I have omitted several hundred footnotes from the text. Nonetheless, to those who read this book, the scholarly and literary lineage may be evident. So, following the good advice of my Trinidad-born mother to "give credit where credit is due," I acknowledge my indebtedness to Robert Ardrey, Philippe Ariès, Thomas Atwood, K.M. Buchanan, Philip Caputo, Richard Collier, Philip Curtin, Leslie G. Desmangles, Bakomba Diong, Charles Douie, Guy Endore, Erich Fromm, Mohandas Gandhi, Eugene Genovese, Margaret George, James Grant, Carl Hoffmann, George Lamming, T. E. Lawrence, Jacques Maquet, Paule Marshall, Philip Mason, C.K. Meek, Carleton Mitchell, Margaret Murray, Orlando Patterson, George Pinckard, J.C. Pugh, Santha Rama Rau, Satyajit Ray, Thomas Reefe, Thomas Reide, Bruce St. John, Janet Schaw, William Sumner, Douglas MacRea Taylor, Michael Thelwell, Robert Farris Thompson, Yi-Fu Tuan, Victor Turner, George F. Tyson Jr., Alexander Tytler, James Vaughan, L. Lewis Wall, Richard Wheeler, H.C. Wylly and Paramahansa Yogananda.

PROLOGUE

Somewhat more than three quarters up the western coast of Dominica is a dramatic vista that seems almost theatrically contrived. A spectacular land mass juts suddenly out from the northwest coast of this lush West Indian island to form Douglas Bay on the north and Prince Rupert's Bay to the south. When viewing this peninsula from Pointe Ronde, a small promontory four miles across Prince Rupert's Bay, you are quite unprepared for its closeness. The peninsula across the bay is laid out before you in intimate detail. It almost seems as if you are looking at an island, so low in the pellucid, blue-green water of the Caribbean is the land connection. And then the narrow finger of land rises abruptly to form the two nearly symmetrical domes of the Cabrits hills.

At a distance the Cabrits give the image of a lush garden. However, upon closer inspection the range of green is disappointingly limited for a West Indian island. Scant rainfall and a blazing sun blanket the hills with a dry forest vegetation. The foliage is everywhere an exhausted green, which gives the appearance of crisping to old age. Closely barricaded all around by a wooded solitude, the precipitous slopes of the Cabrits hills plunge sharply into the Caribbean. The Outer Cabrit, 670 feet high at the end of the peninsula, rules the Inner Cabrit, which rises only 462 feet above the surrounding sea. Clouds frequently sweep low over the domed hills, masking a tyrannous sun and trailing a slate gray curtain of rain. Their passing reveals Dominica's tallest peak, the towering Devil's Mountain, a sinister, yet mysteriously inviting, volcanic massif. Between the humps of the hills runs a long, sharply marked valley now full of brushwood and stones that crashed down from the heights. This narrow place is also home to a continuous wind. The valley is a lonely place and the wind's never-ending howl makes it seem even more desolate.

Beckoned toward something mysterious and unknown, visitors see that the hills and valley are patterned with ruins. Amidst the screen of trees, in the hidden crannies of the steep slopes of the hills, is an impressive military complex of more than fifty major structures. Most of the construction of these buildings was undertaken by the British during the eighteenth century to protect shipping in Prince Rupert's Bay and to defend Dominica from an attack by the French colony of Guadeloupe, a few miles to the north. The sprawling site comprises gun batteries, hospitals, cisterns, barracks, officers quarters, and ordnance storehouses. The most prominent structure is Fort Shirley, a squat, irregularly shaped construction of gray masonry standing guard over Prince Rupert's Bay at the southern exit of the Cabrits valley. A few of these structures have been restored, others stabilized, but most are ruinous. At a distance they appear toy-like, absurd little stone houses, dirty-gray and lonely among the many trees.

At this remote site in 1802 a fury broke. A surplus of bitterness and fear drove a regiment of African soldiers to mutiny and turn their guns on their British officers. Mutiny strikes at the very heart of the military system. For that reason it is a capital offense. Many mutineers in history crouched in their final hiding places, intending to fight to the end like cornered animals before they died. They knew instinctively that there would be no pitying comrade, no commiseration, no mercy. Yet, soldiers mutiny. It is not difficult to understand why. There are primal human longings and needs—like freedom—that run deeper than a soldier's oath to obey a stranger. To these urges men truly dedicate themselves. Surveying the Cabrits from Pointe Ronde, one can imagine the fear, the enraged soldiery, the violent deaths, the passions that tell the story of the Cabrits mutiny. (The air is also pregnant with some message too faint to be heard at the distance. But it beckons us with the promise of hearing a soldier's voice muted for centuries in deep forgetting.) We have only to journey across the placid waters of Prince Rupert's Bay to the Cabrits and there set free the imagination to conjure up a universe. A stroll among the ruins and through the forest reveals that the Cabrits hills hold time as well as belongings. Here and there, in the matted grass and foliage, lie musket balls and tunic buttons, shattered clay pipes and earthenware plates, evidence of a bitter conflict. We can easily imagine that some of these relics once belonged to our soldier. And if we look at them with the help of an intoxicated imagination, they will bring him out of the dark of silence and tell us of his private ordeal.

Chapter 1

The British Army Camp at the Cabrits,
Dominica, West Indies
12 April 1802

The Trial Begins

Through the bars of the window of my cell I could see the first peep of the dayspring. The rising sun silhouetted the brooding mountain, leaving it black against the gold of the clouds at its peak. The sun climbed higher in the sky to color the clouds pink and the mountain a light purple. The brilliant sun was now shafted through the piled morning clouds. Light poured in through the lone window throwing the shadow of the bars across the floor and walls. The sun would soon make the wet foliage steam. It would warm the water, warm the air, encourage the rough grass, coconut, sugarcane, and coffee to grow. It would excite the fish in the many streams into action, the colorful birds into song. Look, there! The sun had already begun its play of light and shade and two-tone greenery on the brooding mountain and the swaying palm leaves. My cell was suddenly bright. The scent of coffee drying in the sun reminded me of my first visit to the interior of the island. The great High God, the creator of the world and mankind, could not have fashioned anything more beautiful. This dreamy peace of a new West Indian day almost took possession of me. Almost.

I rose and donned my fatigue dress. It was a very simple dress, having none of the richness and vitality of my fancy main uniform. *White linen trousers and short white tunic!* After my capture all of my other regimentals had been taken from me on the main parade ground, the same area where I learned to double march and perform the infantry drill. Gone was my musket. Gone was my fine, shiny-black shako with its black leather cockade, white and red plume, and gold-like plate decorated with power pictures of military banners, a mighty lion and the crown of the English king. Gone, too, was my splendid red jacket with its gray facing and white tape, and a thin red, yellow and black stripe in each buttonhole loop. It was these simple bits of colored tape that made the regiment special. We of the Eighth West India took great pride in our uniform, for no other regiment in the whole of the British army had the same facing and decorative tape!

The day I received the thick woolen clothes that made up my uniform was a day I shall never forget. The red tunic fit very tightly under my arms and it had a high firm collar. An even stiffer black-leather neckstrap or stock, worn behind the collar, prevented me from ever lowering my chin. The white breeches hugged my backside and legs like a second skin. My uniform, in fact, encased me like a musket ball in its paper cartridge. So it proved to be an experience for me to be dressed in this manner as I was accustomed to wearing only a strip of light cloth around my loins. Yet that day, dressed in a uniform which made no concession to the sun and comfort, I felt inviolate. I delighted in its rigid embrace. And with each move, its stiffness reminded me that I was a warrior, that I appeared rock-like, that I had authority, that I was indestructible. Martial zeal flared in my soul with incredible force, and I instantly began to dream of the ways I could prove that nothing in this world could conquer me.

But in a flash I had lost it all—my authority and my feeling of indestructibility. And now I was overwhelmed by emotions I could not resist. The tears in my eyes betrayed the sorrow in my heart. On top of that my mind became oppressed with fear and grief and my very soul turned cold. If I ceased to be a soldier, what was I? *A mafa, a slave?*

"ESCORT, HALT! LEFT TURN!" A loud command beyond the cell door ended my thoughts. The subaltern's guard was here! So, it was come: the start of my trial, my ordeal. I had prepared for this day, but I now began to feel the dread effects of panic steal over me. The order, comfort, high standing and even safety of my position as a soldier these last few years were in great peril.

"Good morning, sergeant. I have a warrant for yet another one of your prisoners."

"May I see your orders, sir?" said another. "They are in good order. Thank you, sir," said the same voice, after a pause.

The sound of the rattling of the key in the lock reminded me of the opening and shutting of the hatches on the slaver. I became cold. The large studded door creaked open heavily. A young subaltern and a corporal of the Sixty-eighth Regiment entered my cell, each bowing low to clear the lintel. The rest of the escort, large men of the same regiment, grenadiers all, stood outside, flanking both sides of the door in cool silence. Their red coats provided some warmth to the chilly dimness withinside the guardhouse. Before he uttered another word, I could plainly see that the subaltern was a Johnny Newcome in these parts. His skin was still pink and he used up much too much energy in his motions.

"Private Congo Jack?"

"Sah!"

He looked startled. "I take it, Private, that although an African you have some facility with the English language?"

"Sah!"

"Good, then. You will place yourself in my custody. Refrain from speaking to anyone while you are in my charge. I will not permit it. Is that quite clear?"

"Sah!"

"Right, then, Corporal, let's be off."

The corporal was the first to leave the small cell, followed by me and then the young subaltern. As I emerged from the cell the rest of the escort came to attention, turned and flanked me closely.

"ESCORT, RIGHT TURN! QUICK TIME!" snapped the subaltern. I walked stiffly.

The blast of daylight hit me full in the face, and I stepped awkwardly forth from the guardhouse. I blinked. We headed for the main gate of Fort Shirley, a few feet away, down a gentle slope paved with rounded stones. We clattered over the stones and through the gate and along the path passing the bake house on the left. Along the route, on both sides, were small groups of gaping people: fort negroes, slaves, black and white regulars, sailors, and hard-faced white militiamen.

Not far beyond, the path divided and we bore to the left to enter the narrow valley. On we went, passing a line of huts and workshops for the engineers. They were all constructed in a single straight line that ran in the same direction as the main road through the valley. Behind these low, squat structures were a number of other buildings used by the military and civil departments of the ordnance. How odd that I never had any reason to visit these buildings in all the time I served at the Cabrits. In fact, I did not recall having ever taken notice of them back there before today. As I glanced up at the top of the Outer Cabrit, to my left, I could plainly observe the heavy timbers of the barrack roofs.

Straight ahead I could see the open space of the sprawling main parade ground. We moved in quick time along the line of more huts and workshops for about a quarter of a mile into the middle of the valley. I recalled the old drill sergeant's bellowing voice as he attempted to explain the quick time to me and the other recruits soon after we had joined the regiment.

"Quick time consists of 108 steps in a minute, by which the distance of 270 feet is gained in that space of time. All filing of divisions from column into line or from line into column are performed in this time.

"A quicker time consists of 120 steps and gains 300 feet in a minute. This time is used in doubling up of divisions, wheelings to the front, diminishing or increasing the front division in column." Divisions? Wheelings? Minutes? Column? Line? It was all a meaningless confusion of sounds to me and my new comrades, and the old, white drill sergeant, who seemed to take no notice of our ignorance of these matters, had it not in his power to make us understand.

In a short time we reached the last of the huts and workshops of the engineers. Ahead lay the smith's forge and directly opposite, on the right side of the main valley road, was the large, stone provision storehouse. "ESCORT! RIGHT WHEEL!"

Going into the storehouse I entered a long, bare room. I looked quickly about me. From the floor halfway up to the beamed ceiling, the walls were painted dark green all round, a sign in some parts of Africa of fertility, vigor, newness. Yet the top portion of the walls were stained brown, the color in some regions for mourning the dead. The floor was formed of long wooden boards, which, when passed over, sent back the sound of heavy footsteps. At the other end of the room, in solemn silence, behind a long, heavy table, stood the members of the court. They were twelve in number. The president, a thin and bony field officer of the Sixty-eighth Regiment, stood erect in the middle of the line. The other officers of the court arranged themselves on the right and left hand of the president, the closest to him being the most senior officers. They all had complexions of dark nut-brown except two nervous-looking young subalterns of the Royal Artillery.

Standing close together along the wall to my right were the other prisoners, my regimental comrades, Manby, Lively, Cuffy, Genus and Pedro. There was Hussar, too. On this day he wore his tunic over his shoulders, partially concealing his mangled left arm in a sling. Even in his prison dress he cut a handsome figure. Little wonder women threw themselves into his arms, and he was always prepared to receive them. He was tall and thin with appealing brown eyes and an open face. His large, sensuous mouth fitted well with his lusty nature. But it was his movements that stirred up the emotions. He moved with the oiled actions of an animal that women (and even some men, I suspect) delighted in watching. He took great joy in peacocking his lusty nature in his too-tight uniform. He was beautiful and he knew it. Yet these gifts were often wasted. He detested thinking, which frequently got him into difficulties. He believed that to ponder over something would only cripple his speed in action. And so the rash act and the hot-tempered nature were mated in him. *Live quickly. Love quickly.*

Trust to impulse. Life should be an adventure, mysterious, an entrance into the unknown. This was the law by which he lived. Despite this feature of his nature, he was sensitive, soft-hearted, innocent, simple, kind, all of which made him the idol of many of his comrades. Because of this it was impossible not to love him. And I never resisted it, but gave him my loyalty, friendship and love without hesitation.

I felt comforted seeing them all. I nodded discreetly in their direction.

And there was Souvarine Petro, our *defender!* When I had first noticed him among a new batch of recruits for the regiment, I thought that in some way our destinies were linked. How odd, for our paths did indeed cross and now I despised him. He alone thought he knew what was best for us. It was he and those he had duped in the grenadier company that had brought us to this ruin, I was certain of it. How well I recalled that he had insisted on keeping his own name—*which was not even an African name*—when he joined the regiment in the same manner that I entered. He even had his way in this matter, for "Souvarine Petro" appears in all the regimental books! What overbearing pride! See how majestic he stands there without apparent concern or embarrassment for his undoubted role in the mutiny. Why should I be here and he goes free? He was not even a good and faithful soldier. In fact it was never his intention to be a soldier. I was certain of this. See how poorly his uniform fits! But how did he come to be a grenadier? I am taller and sturdier than he, and yet I was posted to an ordinary battalion company.

I continue to believe that Petro came to this island intending mischief. I never discovered the circumstances surrounding his arrival in Dominica nor from whence he came. "Discovery only leads to further mystery," was his constant way of pushing aside my attempts to learn something of his background. Everything that surrounds him remains a troubling secret. It is said in the regiment that he came here from the north, from Haiti, and that he is in the service of Toussaint L'Ouverture, the black general whose name and exploits are constantly on the lips of every soldier in the regiment and every slave on the island. Words from his own mouth seemed to confirm this suspicion. When he drank too much he would boast that one day soon Haiti would be rid of all white devils. He was fond of quoting one of Toussaint's black generals who had decreed that the end of white rule in Haiti would be written "using a white man's skull for an inkwell, his skin for parchment, his blood for ink and a bayonet as pen!" This was not an idle boast, he would insist. Smiling smugly, he would talk with intense feelings—his reddened eyes glowing like hot embers—of a free nation of Africans being forged at that very moment by the great Toussaint and his black generals and the need to light a "Haitian spark," as he put it, under slavery *wherever* this evil existed. (Was the mutiny to serve as a spark in Dominica?)

See him now: calm, his fiery spirit dampened as though it were asleep in dreamtime. I despised him. Did he not deceive us and destroy the regiment which was my home, my tribe? Yet, I did admire him. I admired him for his book learning, his eloquent English, the smartness of his mind and the very many things he knew of distant places like Haiti and the events going on there. But I admired and, again, despised him most because he possessed a vision, a vision of a free new world for Africans. I had no such vision. I was rooted in the here and now of slavery.

Standing directly opposite my comrades, across the narrow waist of the room, was the judge advocate, a little man with a stare. He was very orderly and precise in his appearance. He stood alongside a small table upon which he had placed a neat pile of white papers and several important-looking books with thick brown covers. I noticed him constantly arranging these papers and straightening his uniform. He eyed me carefully as I entered the room. According to the *Articles of War*, I was to be on *my* trial, but truly speaking it was the colonel of the Regiment who should be on *his* trial. I saluted the court smartly and took position next to Manby. "Backside, Jack!" said Manby out of the corner of his mouth. "We in trouble plenty!" "Hush it," I whispered. But Manby, simple, loyal Manby whom God denied the gift of eloquent speech, was right and I was very frightened.

We were made to stand under close guard. The soldiers were many. In fact, there were three guards for every one of us! How humiliating it was now. To have been a warrior. To have worn a red tunic. To have carried arms. To be looked up to by black *and* white people. For me there was no other life. Soldiering had become my existence. Yet now I was reduced to a common criminal and watched over by the white members of my new tribe, men I had high hopes of joining one day as an elite warrior. Not even the *culprits* serving in the white regiments, those hardened white men recruited in English prisons for military service in the West Indies, received this kind of humiliating attention.

I felt at that moment that my fate had been decided. My heart was filled with great pain. I felt myself capable of stuffing my mouth and nostrils with dirt and thereby ending my life right there. Absorbed in these sad reflections, I did not hear the court as it began to call out our names in order for us to approach the bar. The movement of one of the guards caught my attention and wrenched me back from my mournful thoughts.

We were called to the bar, each by name. When it was my turn to enter the enclosure, which resembled a fenced pen for animals, all the eyes of the court fixed on me in a sudden stare. I felt humiliated. I felt alone. I felt like a criminal. Quickly I grasped the true purpose of this strange ritual: to intimidate and threaten. What kind of justice requires the degradation of the innocent? How can one defend himself when weighted down by shame and fear? Alone and frightened, I stood there staring at the court. I then had a sudden dread: I was going to die.

"This court-martial is convened this day, 12 April 1802, by virtue of a warrant from His Excellency the Honorable Sir Thomas Trigge, Lieutenant General, commanding His Majesty's troops in the Windward and Leeward Charribbee Islands, Guyana and South America." The unexpected voice was that of the judge advocate. Under the law of the British army the judge advocate was supposed to assist the prisoners in their defense. It was also his duty to prosecute them in the name of the king. What arrogance on the part of the English to suppose that someone—an Englishman, of course—could play God and devil at the same time! For that reason I saw the judge advocate as the enemy. I felt afraid beholding him. Alarm was also etched on the faces of my comrades. They too were suspicious. After all, our lives were at stake.

The judge advocate, in a calm voice, continued to read the warrant calling for the court-martial. "By virtue of the power and authority in this warrant, I do also hereby confirm the appointment of Lieutenant Colonel Owen Watson of the Sixty-eighth Regiment of Foot as the president of this court. The following officers, Captains Coggins, Codrington, Durant and Hancock of the Sixty-eighth Regiment, and Morris and Cribbs of the Fourth West India Regiment; Lieutenants Gaffney, Ashford, Dowrich of the Forty-fifth Regiment of Foot; and Subalterns Rogers and Patterson of the Royal Artillery are the whole members of the court. The members of the court are desired to take their places according to their rank in the army and dates of their commissions."

There they sat. There was no outward toughness about these twelve men, no look of anger on their faces, no weapons close at hand. Yet they were as intimidating as if they each pointed cocked muskets at my breast. Their menace was the warm threat of the bullet wrapped in an icy bearing. If it was intended to stun, it succeeded. Unlike the judge advocate whose table was covered with papers and books, the long table before these men was empty. There they sat, cold, composed, enthroned, ready to concentrate and judge. Their stiffness would never melt away. They would judge every instant and would in the end weigh my life as indifferently as an army butcher measures off a piece of meat. Shaking, I seized hold of the railings to steady myself.

"You, the prisoners at the bar," shouted the judge advocate, "the honorable members of the court are those gentlemen who are to pass between His Majesty the King and you, upon the trial of your several lives. Do you have any objections against or challenge to make of any member of the court? If you do, you must challenge them before they are sworn and you shall be heard."

A long pause followed. In the silence I heard the buzzing of a sawyer fly. I imagined the insect cutting down a branch with its horny bill.

"Sah! I do so object to de presence of Captain Morris as a member of dis court-martial." It was Hussar! *May your stupid tongue recoil on you*, I told myself. *Have you learned nothing?* It is said that only in the middle of his life is a man truly a man. At the start and finish he is a child. Brave and handsome Hussar, the delight of women, was not at the start or the end of his span, but he was still a child. He never knew when to silence his tongue. Now was not the time to show disrespect to that officer. But Hussar continued and my heart leaped into my mouth.

"A fortnight pass, an' me tek de slave women Suckie, employed 'ere 'bout as fort negro, from de Captain's arms while 'im was preserved in rum. Wen 'im wake 'im vexed so at not making merry wid Suckie. Private Manby, who did duty dat night, 'im overhear de Captain say to de corporal of the guard dat 'im see to it dat me would do hard time in de black hole. Sah! I am certain dat Captain Morris 'im has a interest in dis case since I prevent he from havin' he way wid Suckie. I fear dat 'im has it in for me an' dat in order to do me harm, 'im will be led to wish de condemnashun of me."

Silence. For a long moment no one replied. It was as if no one had heard Hussar. Then there came a rasping sound from the mouth of the president of the court.

"The invidious and lubricious efforts of the prisoner to tarnish the reputation of Captain Morris as an officer and gentleman is evident and will not be countenanced in this court. These charges are baseless, of course. The impunity with which a certain class of white men enter into illicit liaisons with native women is an infamous custom and is well known in these islands, but as a practice it is limited to creole whites only. There are, I am very sure, regulations in clear and distinct language which caution His Majesty's officers against the establishment of close associations with local black women. If by some mischance these rules are not distinctly enumerated in the body of regulations which govern the conduct of His Majesty's troops, then I have no doubt that propriety and station would dictate the proper mode of behavior. I would therefore urge upon the prisoner to avoid further intemperate speech and wild accusations. Pray let these proceedings continue."

What lies he spoke. No sooner do our white officers arrive here when they become children of the sun and are quickly surrounded by a swarm of black and brown house-keepers, as they style themselves. Every officer, though he be in debt, has one or more of these mongrel wenches who lay themselves out for their white lovers. These whores are a common sight at the Cabrits. As sunset approaches they stream noisily into the Cabrits, waving their passes, which are signed by the commanding officer and the local magistrate. When this horde of public wives reaches the great causeway wall it divides. The younger women, some mere girls, peel off to the right and head for the Cabrits Valley. There they connect with the common soldiery who either drop their seed on the spot or outside the camp in the Cabrits swamp. The rest of the whores, women of sexually mature years, gaily climb the Outer Cabrits to the officers quarters where they sell their sexual favors.

You also meet these wenches in Portsmouth. They are easy to recognize by the showy manner in which they tie their turbans and the inciting way in which they stroll and lounge about. They gather at the several rum shops which line the main street. They are noted for their insolence and troublesome ways. You cannot affront them more than to say they are dull and unskilled in the use of their bottoms. But be wary if you do. They are a rough-and-tumble lot. One soldier did just that and made a jokingly rude comment to one. She leaped up and grabbed his private parts through his pants and shook him violently until the pleading soldier made excuse for the offense and admitted defeat.

In truth, sexual contact between our officers and black and brown whores is the order of the day. And such is the constant sexual appetite of our officers that virtually every woman living within walking distance of the Cabrits is a whore. The president of the court must live with his head well up his horse's arse not to see that which appears too plainly. As for Captain Morris, he had a furious appetite for black lovers. His quarters atop the Outer Cabrit were a whorehouse, well stocked with young girls. Many a night, while on outpost duty, I observed his hired boy and old woman slip away to scour the Cabrits and Portsmouth for a black wench. And if they returned empty-handed they were flogged. He craved sexual pleasure to its furthest bounds and exhausted it.

If an early finish was on the mind of the president, he was disappointed. Hussar's challenge brought the judge advocate to his feet. He addressed the court warily knowing that what he was about to say would anger them. "I am ever mindful," he began in his uncomfortable position, "that the court's time is precious. Yet I must advise this honorable court that since one of the prisoners has raised an objection against a member of the court, the president and members must order the court to be cleared and deliberate on the validity and import of the challenge."

"Is this not a legal nicety?" the president lashed back. His cold and severe face had suddenly turned bright red. He glared at the judge advocate and for a few moments said not a word. Then he spoke again. "May I remind you, Captain Mapp, that the day wears on very quickly and that it shall soon be three o'clock!"

"The law is quite vigilant of the perfect impartiality of each juror of the court," replied the judge advocate politely but strongly. "As a result, the law is precise on this point!"

There was a long pause before the president broke the silence. "Clear the court of the prisoners!" he roared like an angry leopard.

Outside, Hussar talked like a river, telling anyone who would listen his best stories of the women he had made love to. One, he claimed, was a young buckra girl whose fair skin had never been touched by the sun. He sucked his lips with the pleasure of this particular victory, as he called it. Since I felt humiliated by my position as a common criminal for all the world to see, I was in no mood to listen to Hussar's bawdy tales of whores. I was shaken by the trial and wanted nothing more than to lay quietly in the warm morning sunshine for as long as I could. I looked up at the sky. Except for the usual ragged blanket of cloud sitting on top of the mountain, it was cloudless. The sun blazed down, making Dominica an island of beauty. The trees were still dripping from an early morning shower. Amid the sounds of falling drops of water low voices could be heard coming from withinside the courtroom. I strained my ears to hear, but it was all a low whisper. Then there was silence. A few moments later a door creaked open and then, without warning, came the pulse-quickening command of the white sergeant of the guard. "RETURN THE PRISONERS TO THE BAR!"

"The prisoner, Private Hussar, has suggested hostile enmity towards him on the part of Captain Morris, a member of this court," said the judge advocate, rising from his table. He turned his head in our direction without looking directly at any of us. It was as though we did not exist. "The prisoner contends," he continued, "that this malice resulted from an alleged altercation of a . . . personal nature which occurred in the recent past. The prisoner's concern is that Captain Morris's alleged . . . private interest in this case will lead to his condemnation. Suspicion of prejudice or malice is indeed one of the most valid causes of challenging the integrity of a juror. *The law is precise on this point.* Captain Morris has denied the cause of Private Hussar's objection under oath. It is of consequence to point out, however, that Private Hussar's challenge rests on the corroboratory evidence of Private Manby, one of the prisoners! May I remind the court that the right of challenging is mutual to the prisoner and to the prosecutor. *The law is precise on this point.* There may be sources of prejudice in favor of the prisoner as well as against him, and pressing motives that may well tend to acquit as well as to condemn." He sat down looking smugly pleased with himself.

This speech seemed to make no impression on the court, who met these words with a coldness. They showed no hostile attitude towards us. I leaned forward in my chair, hoping silently that Hussar's challenge would be successful. Some instinct told me that the court would not want to be burdened with a tarnished officer. He would be dismissed from the court, I was certain of that. The English, after all, pride themselves on the appearance of things. This I have learned about them during the years I have been in their service. Thus I was stunned when the court disallowed Hussar's challenge.

"Captain Morris will retain his seat as a member of the court." The voice of the president was cold and unemotional. As he issued his decision there was a silence in the room. His words sickened me. I was furious. My face flushed hotly, and I felt the sudden urge to scream out and bang the table with my fist. I did neither. It was useless. It was done. Hussar sucked his teeth in disgust at this setback. It is true what a wise man once said: "When lies abound, he who tells the truth will be judged the greatest liar."

The oaths prescribed by the *Articles of War* and the *Mutiny Act* were then administered to the members of the court by the judge advocate, and the president in turn administered them to him. The oath was taken by each officer holding his right hand upon the *Evangelists* (a holy book for white people) and finally kissing it. This was done by each, man with an expression of cold dignity.

The president removed a piece of paper from his tunic pocket bearing a statement charging each of us with the crime of mutiny. He cleared his throat to draw attention. All were silent. He then spoke in the same cold unemotional voice. "The court, now being regularly constituted, desires the prisoners listen to the charges exhibited against them, to wit Privates Manby, Lively, Genus, Cuffy, Hussar, Pedro and Jack, all private soldiers of His Majesty's Eighth West India Regiment, did excite and join in mutiny on and between the 9th and 10th instant, and did aid and assist in the murders of Captain Alexander Cameron, Lieutenant and Adjutant William MacKay, Lieutenant Edward Wastenays, and Sergeant Major William Broughton, all of the Eighth West India Regiment; and Mr. William Lang, the Commissary, Sergeant Gordon Mackay, Second Battalion, His Majesty's Sixty-eighth Regiment of Foot; and gunner Robert Gill of the Royal Artillery. Are the prisoners guilty or not guilty of the matter of accusation?"

It is written in the rules that govern the actions of the British soldier: "The essence of a crime is the intention with which it is committed, and the malignancy of that intention is the measure of its atrocity." The law was fair and straightforward and would assure me justice. I was not a mutineer. I always did my duty and never did I once question an order! I fired my musket in self-defense, only after we were fired upon in the very act of grounding our arms as ordered by Governor Johnstone. That is the truth of the matter! In fact, it was in the act of placing our muskets upon the ground that one of the balls struck Hussar who stood in line next to me. I was greatly tempted to make a statement of justification in my plea of not guilty. I wanted to explain immediately why I fired. But I was reminded that the plea must be simple, an absolute denial without any qualification. It was difficult to stand firm in this resolution, but I succeeded, somehow. "Not guilty, sah!" I shouted, almost in desperation.

We all pleaded in the same manner.

"Captain Mapp," the hollow voice of the president broke in almost at once, "have you provided the prisoners, previous to the start of these proceedings, with a list of witnesses you intend to examine in support of the charge?"

List? What list? What is this all about? I turned to examine the usually expressionless face of the judge advocate. His eyes caught my staring but he kept his face turned towards the court. Still, I could see most of his face. He had been taken completely by surprise by the question. His sweaty, crimson face was proof of that. "The *list*, Captain Mapp," demanded the president, "have you supplied the prisoners with a list of your evidences?" The judge advocate sat stone still and said not a word. All in the room were silent, expectant of what was to come.

Finally, the judge advocate came back to life and stirred in his chair. Then, as he pushed his chair back from the table and began to rise as if to speak, Souvarine Petro took action. It was evident that something had angered him, for he assumed a way of standing reserved for those moments when he was irritated. He walked to the front of our table and stopped abruptly. His feet were set apart. His right hand was coiled inside his tunic, at his breast, like a snake ready to leap out and strike at some unsuspecting prey. But it was the fire that flashed in those terrible black eyes that expressed his determination to speak out.

"The judge advocate has deviated in the correct performance of his duty," he began, his deep and strong voice carrying easily the whole length of the room. Pointing to the judge advocate with his left hand, he continued. "He has *not* provided us with the list in question. We have not, therefore, had time to deliberate on any objection that may work against the admissibility of these witnesses or to counter their testimony with contrary evidence. Your law is not silent on this matter. It is, as the judge advocate knows only too well, precise on this point. I object to the illegal conduct of this . . . business," and he waved his right hand in the air like a sword.

He spoke this last word with particular force as if to show his disgust with the trial. I admired his cunning ways with English words while despising his double-dealing person.

"Is there foundation to this charge, Captain Mapp? Have the prisoners not been provided with a list of witnesses prior to the start of the proceedings?" The voice of the president was firm and deliberate.

"Sir," replied the judge advocate, his unsteady voice hinting of embarrassment, "I had it upon good authority from local white gentlemen that the Eighth West India Regiment, including all the other black regiments raised by government for service in these islands, were recruited and maintained with what is locally termed *raw* Africans, that is, blacks purchased straight off the decks of slavers, who were thus ignorant of any European language. Possessed of this knowledge, which was confirmed by my own personal observations of the generality of blacks serving in the West India regiments, I saw no need to provide the prisoners with the list in question. To have done so would have been an unnecessary nicety."

The president, who had been sitting back in his chair, gave a shudder of disgust and heaved himself forward on the long empty table before him. There was a moment of silence, then he spoke. "Am I to understand it, sir, that you were guided in the performance of your solemn duty by hearsay, the source of which were local planters and merchants? Are you not aware, sir, that these same gentlemen were and remain critics of government's decision to raise the black regiments and that their natural ferocity against the measure continues to be inflamed by an ignorant zeal? Evidence of this is seen in their wildly inaccurate statements regarding the alleged barbarism of His Majesty's African soldiers. Yet a number in each of the West India regiments are acquainted with the English language, as shown here today.

"But to return to the question before us, any deviation from the immemorial conduct of a British army court-martial merely serves to introduce perplexity and confusion in these proceedings. May I remind you, sir, that an important part of your official duty as judge advocate is to assist prisoners in their defense. This solemn charge is more especially obligatory on judge advocates in those cases where prisoners have not the assistance of professional counsel to direct them, which generally happens in trials of private soldiers who, lacking all advantages of education, must stand greatly in need of guidance in such hardships as are sufficient frequently to overwhelm the smartest intellect. Whether *raw*, as you put it, sir, or *cooked*, negroes serving as soldiers in the British army are subject to the rules and articles for the better government of His Majesty's troops which must be *strictly observed*! You shall, sir, do justice to the cause of the prisoners by providing each with a copy of the list of your witnesses immediately. And in order to allow the prisoners full time to deliberate, the court is adjourned till 14 April at the hour of eight of the clock in the morning."

Never once did the judge advocate look the president straight in the face as he spoke; he lowered his eyes and fidgeted with the silver buttons on his tunic. Looking pained and disappointed, he uttered a weak "Yes, sir."

"*Backside*, Jack!" said Manby excitedly. He laughed and slapped one of his large thighs. "Souvarine Petro, big mon 'im. 'Im too big, too broad. 'Im too *baad*. Is where 'im learn fuh speak so? No matter, 'im too *baad* fuh de buckras dem."

"Yas," I replied, although I was tempted to argue the point with Manby. One cannot deny that Souvarine Petro had handled his first clash with the judge advocate very well, one might even say with surprising ease. With almost studied casualness he exposed the prejudice of the judge advocate and his willful wrongdoing. It was a triumph and it tasted sweet as cane juice. I was thankful for it, but it was a small victory in a struggle that carried life and death with it. We were not outside the reach of military justice yet. Souvarine Petro's run with glory thus far had been short.

Chapter 2

"Let Me Speak"

The decision of my comrades to allow Souvarine Petro to lead us in our defense, and thereby speak for us at our court-martial, made me bitterly resentful. I hid my unhappiness from the others as best I could, but this wrong (I felt it was a wrong even though Souvarine Petro was the only one capable of speaking for us) boiled withinside of me for a long time. In my Margi homeland I had been recognized for my gifted way with language and deemed by many as a budding man of words. Before the time of my fall into slavery, my father began to train me as a memory man. At the time I was stolen I was capable of extensive oral testimony. When speaking of the Margi royal dynasty, for example, my testimony could last for upwards of two hours of unbroken recitation! What is more, I could easily recall the complete story line of many of the ancient Margi folktales.

All of this was accomplished without the use of a single memory board! It was not at all unusual for revered memory men to make use of boards as aids. These devices consisted of small white shells and variously colored beads arranged in special patterns on one side of a flat piece of wood. Thus, a curved line of green beads would bring to mind waving papyrus reeds growing along the banks of the great Benue River. It was along these steep banks that the Margi people made rafts to cross the Benue at Yola in the long ago time. I, however, did not have to rely on these devices. My memory aids—proverbs, colors, numbers, place phrases and praises—were all stocked and neatly arranged in my head. And I was very, very proud of this.

But my powers of language and speech went far beyond the mere ability to remember countless past events in detail. More important than my quick and retentive memory was the way in which I was able to use words. There were few if any young Margis who grasped, as I did, the many fine shades of action words, which are the most fascinating and complex part of the Margi language. I could also do special things with those words that denoted the quality of things named. These modifiers were fairly numerous and were considered a special part of our speech.

And I could do more. Like many of the other languages spoken in the region of Nigeria where I was born, Margi is a tonal or musical language. Each sound in a Margi word has its own pitch or tone level, either high or low. In addition, there is a rising sound which is really a combination of a low tone with a high tone. Thus, when I spoke my words danced with the vital aliveness of music and motion. The Fulanis and other outsiders, who attempted to secrete themselves among us to do harm, never did pay enough attention to the proper use of tones. This inevitably led to their quick discovery and punishment whenever they assaulted our language by trying to speak it.

My proven abilities of speech all vanished the moment I was stolen and transported to the West Indies. Here, in this land, where strange and unfathomable languages prevailed, I felt as though my tongue had been cut from my throat, leaving me voiceless. In trying to speak English I was reduced to crude, simple expressions lacking in imagination and refinement. (I received no instruction in English during my service in the regiment; what I learned was limited to a few words of command which I memorized as ordered.) Thus, it was a constant and seemingly losing struggle to share with others what I knew, what I had experienced, what I felt, who I was. Because of this, speaking exhausted me both physically and emotionally. I was ever frustrated. I felt dumb. And yet my mind was swarming with thoughts and emotions which piled up in my head as I had no speech ways of giving them life outside of my mind. Only reluctantly did I speak, and when I did, the sounds—hard, flat, dreary, dull, strange English sounds—were pitiful reflections of what I was capable of. Me, a budding Margi language maker, a namer of things after their essence!

There were in fact two of me. There was the old-world me that enjoyed words and sounds, the me that enjoyed speaking simply for itself, the me that liked to be heard, the me that loved debate, the me that rejoiced in my intellect. And then there was the new-world me: the unintelligible me, pidgin me, slave-like me, muted me, dumb me—the only me that everyone saw and remembered.

Whenever I spoke it hurt. Every time I opened my mouth to speak I was painfully reminded of the me that was lost and the me I had become.

Yes, Souvarine Petro had extraordinary speaking powers and there would be much less of a gamble if he spoke for us.

Still, it hurt. If desire was all that was required my speech ways would have been eloquent. But desire was not enough. Whenever I tried to speak English my brain went numb.

Chapter 3

The Mutiny

That afternoon, after the morning of the first trial day, the racing patterns of clouds cast shifting shadows across the gray walls of Fort Shirley and on the far wall of my cell. I gazed contentedly for a while. Yet the pleasure did not last long. Somehow the quietness of the long moments deepened the menace surrounding me. Suddenly the painful memories of the mutiny flew upon me like a shrieking cannonball and I thought back to that horrible night when my world fell apart.

SHOTS! The sharp snapping sounds of musket fire coming from down in the valley shattered a sweet dream of Jubba Lily and woke me from my sleep. More shots, random shots. "The French have landed," I thought. French Guadeloupe was a few hours sail to the north. You could easily see the island from the top of the Outer Cabrit on a clear day.

But there was no volley firing and no big boom of the cannons to be heard. I jumped up from my crib in time to see the shadowy figures of my comrades leaping up from theirs. There was no time to light the candles in the lanterns. A mad rush as we stumbled over each other in the dark in our haste to grab our boots, our ammunition pouches, our pantaloons, our tunics. Confusion and angry voices at the far end of the barrack room where our muskets had been neatly stacked and where ball and cartridge were stored in large wooden crates. More random shots! The French? But still no volley firing, no alarms, no shrill sounds of French bugles, no big boom of the cannons. "An insurrection of the field negroes?" I thought. They hated us with a passion, but they dared not attack us. They were cowards, broken and despised wretches. But, then, where did the Haitians get their arms and courage to attack the French buckras? That slave Hamlet and his miserable friends attack us? It was unthinkable. Still, Haiti?

Curses and angry shouts as we wrestled to clear our muskets from the wooden stand and grab a handful of cartridges, which we stuffed into our ammunition pouches. A tangle of arms and bodies everywhere. A lone drummer beating the assembly. Sporadic, random shooting from the direction of Fort Shirley down in the valley. But still no signal from our alarm posts, no drum beats, no bugle calls.

The lone drummer still beating the assembly.

I stumbled out of the barrack and made straightaway for the adjacent parade ground. The grounds, which overlooked the now-darkened sea, were thick with milling soldiers. "Where are our officers?" I thought. Screams coming across from the Inner Cabrit followed by silence. I looked across in that direction and wondered.

Over the babble of our excited voices the familiar, soothing words of command pierced the warm, thick night

air. "NUMBER FOUR COMPANY! OVER HERE! FALL
IN!" The deep voice of Sergeant Major Bostonian, the hidden king of the regiment. A pause. "CLOSE ORDER!" We
quickly fell in and formed the customary three ranks as best
we could in the dark. "PRIME AND LOAD!" It was all so
routine even in the dark, the product of a thousand drills. I
grabbed a cartridge from my pouch and bit off one end.
Some saltpeter entered my mouth and scorched my tongue.
I poured a little of the powder into the flashpan and closed
the cover over the pan to keep the powder in place. The rest
of the powder was poured into the long barrel. The ball was
then patched with the paper, and patch and ball were placed
in the mouth of the muzzle. Sharp metallic sounds rent the
night air as a hundred ramrods rammed patch and ball down
the barrel. Several smart strokes of the ramrod and my
musket was loaded. "MAKE READY!"

*The crash of volley fire coming from the direction of the
Douglas Battery at the north end of the valley!* So the French
had landed after all. Yet, no boom of the many big cannons
that lined that powerful battery. Still no alarms from the
forward posts. Where were our officers? What was happening? We stood there in silence, our back to the sea, our front
towards the path leading down to the valley floor. What was
happening down there? The moon suddenly broke free
from the clouds and cast an eerie yellow light over the whole
scene. "FIX BAYONETS!" Another metallic rattle as we
locked our long knives on to the muzzle of our muskets.
The tips of our bayonets flashed in the moonlight. "STAND
READY!" Then a hush fell.

A single musket shot followed by a piercing scream. The
sounds seemed to come from the direction of the main
parade ground in the valley. Then—nothing. An eerie silence took over the Cabrits. I strained my ears to pick up

some evidence of human activity. Nothing. It was as if nature had yielded to death and abandoned the Cabrits.

"PRIVATE JACK AN' PRIVATE HUSSAR! FOLLOW ME!" It was the voice of Sergeant Major Bostonian again. "We is goin' down der to see what dis is all 'bout." The command pierced me like a sharp bayonet. I didn't want to go down there into that fearful darkness. Standing out here was bad enough. The light of the moon helped a little. I cleared my throat. "Yas, sah!" I finally replied.

Hussar merely shrugged as if it did not matter that he was going into the unknown. He pulled and tugged on his uniform as if he were preparing for morning inspection. But I didn't believe that gesture. I knew Hussar. I knew he was afraid like me. This night reconnaissance was a mad idea. Why was the Sergeant Major doing this? Ah, of course! He is a creole black man; he is born here on this side of the great salt sea. His life in the shadow of slavery has shorn him of his African soul and respect of the night as surely as a sacrificed cock is plucked of its feathers. How terrible it would be to die in the dark. My soul would surely become lost and would wander forever. Had not the great High God ordained in the long ago that man should retire to the safety of his compound at night? Even the British king's flag, with all its strong colors and magical signs, is taken down and retired at each dusk.

"FORWARD! AT DE QUICK!" came another command from the Sergeant Major. Regardless of my fear I had to go. I was a warrior. I looked back at my comrades. There they stood, their faceless dark forms silhouetted against a large pale-yellow moon. Because no light betrayed their faces, they looked like they were almost ghosts, the living near death.

We set off quickly toward the center of the hilltop and the single-gun battery where we picked up the narrow path leading down into the valley. In a short time we had slipped silently over the edge and followed the path as it ran towards Fort Shirley. I had gone but a short distance when I stumbled over something soft in the path. I fell forward, dropping my musket, but quickly scrambled to my feet fearing that I would be left behind by Sergeant Major Bostonian and Hussar, whom I trailed. I didn't know what I tripped over and had no interest in discovering its identity in that fearful, silent darkness.

Suddenly, the dark mass of Fort Shirley loomed straight ahead of us. We halted and then moved forward cautiously, our muskets at the ready. Silence. My eyes swept the fort for some sign of life. More silence. Then—voices—coming from withinside the fort. A few words, spoken briskly, drifted over to us: "Corporal . . . Toussaint . . . black man . . . Douglas Battery . . . victory . . . grenadiers . . . fortnight . . . ."

Toussaint L'Ouverture. That name again. Was that little negro coming here, to . . . ?

My thoughts of Toussaint were interrupted by the noise of Hussar's musket striking the hard ground. While adjusting his tunic he had let go his flintlock. The stillness of the night air made the rattling noise sound like thunder. I held my breath and braced myself for the worst.

"Who goes der?" A frightened voice coming from within the fort. Then, without warning, the heavy crunch of soldiers' boots running along the stone embankment, the clatter of accouterments, the sharp clank of muskets hitting the parapet, the bowel-loosening squeaking sounds of cocks being pulled back against their springs. I felt as if every musket was aimed at me. "Who goes der?" That same frightened voice.

45

A pause. "What is de parole?" The frightened voice again. I could hear Sergeant Major Bostonian cursing in frustration.

"What is de parole?" said the frightened voice, only louder and very angry.

"Black man!" I replied. Another pause as everything fell silent. My bowels were about to open. I closed my eyes and again braced myself for the torrent of ball and shot that was about to tear open my body. I waited—on the edge of eternity.

Nothing happened! No thunderclap announcing my beginning as an ancestor. Only silence. Then . . .

"Enter thru de main gate." The same voice, only less nervous.

Instantly upon hearing those words my whole body went limp. I had to steady myself with my musket for fear of falling over. My crotch went wet. I had soiled myself. But I would live! I would live!

The harsh grinding noise of the heavy front gate swinging open caught my attention. A lone grenadier, his tunic open, his feet bare, suddenly appeared in the opening. He beckoned us to enter quickly. "See," he exclaimed excitedly, as we squeezed our way through the small opening and stepped inside the fort, "all we enemies dead dem." It was the soldier with the frightened voice!

What greeted my eyes terrified and sickened me. I blinked in horror. Hussar shied like a horse. I glanced over at the Sergeant Major. He was rigid with shock. All jumbled up together and scattered about in wild confusion as if struck by a summer storm were bits of clothing, regimentals of all kinds, papers, company books, broken weapons and mess kits. And here and there amidst the confusion were dead bodies—all of them buckras! One poor fellow had been hacked to pieces outside the guardhouse. His wide-open eyes stared into the black Caribbean sky, a look of amazement frozen into his looks. Had he been astonished at the identity of his attackers? His shirt and undress jacket were torn open revealing that both of his collar bones had been cut through.

Up ahead I came across an officer sitting against the high wall that enclosed the main cistern, his head thrust back. I had seen torn and mangled bodies among the French lines at St. Martin, but few wounds equaled the horror of this scene. Both eyeballs dangled down on his cheeks. Although wrenched from his face, each remained connected by a single slimy, twisted rope that ran into the gaping, empty sockets. A bullet had passed clean through his head from one temple to the other. His mouth was frozen wide-open and clotted thickly about. He sat in a widening puddle of his own bright red blood which streamed out of his ears and down his neck before seeping through his breeches and collecting on the ground. I ventured closer to this body. As I did I noticed the singed rim of the bullet hole in the side of his head which told me how close to this poor creature his assailants had been. He had been executed! *It was Captain Cameron*! I instantly drew back . . . I had seen enough.

I fled from this scene of horror only to stumble upon another. It was the wife of a buckra soldier. She was lying on her back along the path leading to the kitchens. Her skirts had been pulled over her waist and the ends stuffed into her mouth. She was completely naked from the waist down and was covered in congealing blood where her thighs met. Her stomach bore the marks of repeated stabbings.

Casually milling about, unmindful of the disorder, desolation and death that surrounded them, were the grenadiers of my once-proud regiment. They had thrown all discipline down and all ranks were leveled. Sergeants drank rum with corporals, and privates were everywhere behaving as the equals of any man or soldier!

I quickly departed the fort and the dark and disgusting business that had taken place there. Once I stepped beyond the main gate I fell heavily to the ground as if struck down. All seemed barren, savage, blasted. I swallowed hard, again and again, to suppress the burning vomit from forcing its way into my mouth. Loss and despair filled the air all around me. The Cabrits had turned into a landscape of fear. It felt like a huge grave—all dark and cold and enclosed by earth.

I was unable to explain this savagery. War brings forth pain. Yet the rules of war are designed to take away many of its unnecessary horrors. So this barbarity was simple madness, evil. Those responsible had to pay for the breach of the rules of war. There could be no treating with those who had threatened the life of the regiment.

The thing that amazed me is that only the grenadiers caught this contagion. But why? Do they not have the honor of guarding the colors when they are retired? Do they not have the honor of being posted on the extreme right of the regiment when it is drawn up in line? Why, then, such unthinkable behavior from the best and best treated in the regiment?

And Souvarine Petro. What hand did he have in this filthy business? His words, his voice, his gestures were all poison. True. He had a quenchless inner flame which burned for a new and strange world order. Correct. He was so transparent. Yes, yes. But he was not always like that. When we first met he seemed to tell the truth about all the unimportant things. Did he do that merely to deceive us with the needed authority when it became necessary to lie about something big? Where was he?

Had we not had a reasonable plan? It seemed so full and just in all its particulars. We had planned to take our con-

cerns directly to Captain Cameron, who would then inter-
cede on our behalf with the high command. That was the
correct way to make known our fears. Was it not? Why did
they have to put him to death? Damn them!

The regiment, our once proud home, had been dealt a
serious wound. Would it, we, survive? As a stream once
divided becomes less, so, too, were we now divided and
become less. Still, all must be done to save our home, our tribe,
our world. I could not let it die, for if it did, so did we.

I had to be smart, maybe even clever.

Wordlessly, Sergeant Major Bostonian, Hussar and I
made our way back to the top of the Outer Cabrit. As we
trudged up the long narrow path, the mountain that dominated the camp suddenly loomed out of the darkness with
the help of the first gleam of light of the new morning dawn.
The suddenness with which it bolted out of the darkness
momentarily startled me. In a few seconds the shape of its
huge bulk was in full sight. In the faint morning light I could
still make out its lovely greenness of every shade, tone and
texture. At that moment a brief shower drifted down from
the overhanging mountain before the sun finally broke
through to flood everything with its brilliant golden light.
The morning thus saluted me with encouraging brightness.
I enjoyed this precious interval between the carnage down
below in Fort Shirley and the uncertainty that awaited us up
above.

It was dawn when we finally reached the crest of the
Outer Cabrit. On our arrival at the top we found what
remained of the regiment gathered in one of the soldiers'
barracks. There were not more than a few hundred men in
the long gallery. In the dim, flickering light I saw mostly
white shako cords and white-over-red plumes of battalion
company soldiers and a few green cords and plumes worn

by the Light Infantry. But I saw not a single shako of white cords and white plumes. The Grenadier Company—to a man—was nowhere to be seen. As we approached, I expected some protest, some outburst. Nothing. Only a tense silence greeted us. They sat as a defeated crowd of unpitied slaves about to be exposed to the hammer of public sale. Only a short time before these same men had exhibited not the slightest personal apprehension with respect to their fate as soldiers. They were confident to a man and their simple imaginations saw only the forms of success before them. That bright picture, colored with honor and bravery, came to dramatic life at St. Martin. *Ah! St. Martin. A warrior's dream*. Now, they sat huddled together, as if awaiting a dreaded blow. On the face of each was the same pitiful expression, a mixture of anxiety, dread and desperation.

They had every reason to despair. A few miles distant from here a storm was gathering. Soldiers were assembling in superior numbers to take back the Cabrits. Some were men from our own regiment. We could expect no quarter from any of them. In their minds, we who wore the now-defamed uniform of the Eighth West India Regiment and remained in the Cabrits must all be mutineers, the lowest form of life to any loyal soldier. Our eyes could not be shut to that possibility. Suddenly, we were a menace to men who but a few days ago embraced us as warrior-brothers enlisted in the same cause. You could almost hear them swearing and vowing revenge, for there were those among them who hated us because we were Africans, because we carried guns, and because we were proud of ourselves as black men and warriors.

My concern mounted. Surely we could come to terms with the officers of the relieving column. But what if we could not? Death and destruction would certainly follow. And for those who somehow survived the carnage, a trial awaited. They would be exposed and accused and then ritually put to death before the whole tribe. They would die a traitor's death, as miserable and shameful a death as could be designed. But this must not happen. Clear, reasonable heads must prevail. For every human problem there was an honorable and peaceful solution. We must reach some accommodation, some understanding, with those who held power. If only we could get them to open their minds and hearts.

I made my way through the long room but hung back from going directly to the open area in the center, lest they thought I was to speak to them. *But I should address them.* Someone had to propose a plan to get us out of this terrible mess. The plan must include, however, some device that preserved our honor and station as soldiers. I was not yet able to speak to them. I was too near despair but dare not show it.

My comrades thirsted for someone to rescue them. I could see this in their eyes and feel it in their tension and apprehension. As I waited there, swallowed up in doubts, I became aware of voices growing louder with excitement.

"Give no more to de army!" shouted someone in a high-pitched, excited voice. "We mus' head fuh de mountains an mek we stand dere!"

"Is where yuh learn such foolish idea so?" said another soldier. His voice was deeper and seemingly wise.

"If yuh run away buckras dem will believe yuh fe a mutineer fuh so. An yuh tink buckra cyan't find yuh in doz mountains? Yuh talkin' foolish. An what yuh, a coastal man, know of mountains? Yuh stave dead de first day out. Yuh doan ha' fe worry, breddah, we is innocent. Everyting will arright."

"How can yuh trust de English dem?" demanded the first soldier in his high-pitched voice. "Yuh blind cause yuh

51

head is up yuh ass along wid yuh eyes. Don't de Englishmon shoot white navy mutineers in 1797? An' don't he shoot Irish mutineers in 1798? If de Englishmon shoot he own kind, he will shoot we Africans quicker. If we stay here an' play de Englishmon game of words we is goin' to we grave, I tell yuh."

"Yuh talkin' like yuh guilty," answered the second soldier. "Dem sailors an' Irish were guilty dem. Dat is why dem were hung an' shot. We is innocent, I tellin' yuh. All we mus' do is tell so an' everyting will arright. De Englishmon is a hard mon when he frighten'. But 'im believe 'imself to be just an' fair an' 'im quick fe want uddahs to believe dat he is. 'Im also believe dat 'im own justice is de most perfect dat ever existed an' dat it could nevah be surpassed. So, tings will arright, I tellin' yuh."

"Wen buckra frighten' like 'im now, 'im become inhuman." It was the first man again.

"True. Buckra gets frighten' when tings mash-up dem," replied the second soldier still calmly, "but 'im frighten wid sense."

"Wid sense? Yuh jokin'. Yuh truly mad, sick mad fuh trus' de Englishmon," thundered back the first soldier.

"Tek yuh head from up yuh ass' an' open yuh eyes. See how Englishmon 'im treat slave who rebel from slavery. Dem is shot, dem is hung, dem is burnt alive. Dem always wind up dead done. We is rebels an' we is slaves. What fuh can we expect but shootin', hangin', an' burnin'?"

"We is no slave," shouted the once calm second man, his voice now brimming with anger and fear at the notion that he might be a slave.

"An' if we is slave, de king is goin' fe give us free."

I sided at once with the second soldier. He believed in the holiness of the regiment and the army. In this I was completely with him. Still, still the first soldier asked penetrating questions. I moved closer to the speakers to better hear them, when there came a great shout.

"IF YOU BELIEVE THE ENGLISH KING IS GOING TO MAKE YOU FREEMEN," snapped a familiar voice, "YOU CAN BELIEVE PISS IS COCONUT WATER." It was Souvarine Petro. Of course! Once again he had reappeared on our horizon at a critical moment. His appearance and the timing of his coming were so familiar. But the remembrance of his fiery words brought no excitement as before. He was greeted with a heavy silence from the huddled soldiery who believed, as I did, that they had been deceived and betrayed by someone in their midst. Unmoved by the hostile stillness that greeted him, Souvarine Petro walked fearlessly and evenly toward the center of the room without once slackening his advance.

"Clear the way," he ordered and made his way through the crowd of startled soldiery in the way a sharp knife passes through flesh and divides it. He came on and nimbly mounted one of the cribs. Once again a burning passion lit up his face. You could see that he was in full contact with his powers and some burning vision. He was there to sweep away all resistance to his plan and so launched into his speech once he caught and held the attention of all in the room with that hard, penetrating look. He strained forward as he spoke, with his veins, cord-like, standing out on his neck.

"Some have their nostrils split open!

"Some are subjected to the exquisite pain by thumbscrews, till the blood gushes forth out of the ends of their thumbs!

"Others have their teeth beaten out!

"Still others are routinely hung up and stabbed to death!

"Young girls are tortured with cayenne pepper in their sexual parts for being found pregnant!

"Holes are dug in the earth to hold the extended bellies of pregnant female slaves about to be flogged in order that the children might not be killed in the commission of the punishment as this would bring financial loss to their owners!

"Children are exposed to sale, naked, without respect to any circumstance!

"Those who dare to rebel are roasted to death in the most lingering manner!

"Are these accounts of the savage and obscene barbarity with which Africans are treated by profit-crazed West India planters and slave dealers false or exaggerated? No! These examples, and many thousands more, can be proved beyond contradiction. Each of you has personally witnessed the most horrid tortures inflicted upon the slaves of this island. Can you ever forget your first guided tour of Dominica, when you saw for yourselves scenes of unimaginable human misery?"

As Souvarine Petro spoke I sensed an increasing tension between him and us soldiers. At this point in his speech he suddenly launched into a bitter denunciation of us.

"Your eyes have been open all along to the robbery, cruelty and murder of slavery. How happens it, then, that you defend bloody and abandoned villains who denuded your ancient homelands of their peoples, wronged your mothers, raped your sisters, sold your children, and deemed you a brute creation? I give you notice that by your presence in the army you have plunged the slaves, as well as your-selves, deeper into the frightful abyss of slavery. I give you further notice that by your presence in the army you be-come the enemy of liberty and honor. How can it be other-wise? Can the army control your brothers and sisters in the fields without you? No! Can slavery flourish without the army? Again, I say no! The army is the bulwark of slavery. Without the army there would be no slavery.

"You have only to look at your officers to see this truth told with simplicity. They race to marry the rich daughters of the planters. Many are owners of plantations and slaves. Some even sit in the assembly of this island and assist in the murders of our people by writing and enforcing the hated slave code. The death of that officer Cameron is nothing; he was merely another officer of murder in the business of grave making. Your officers are one with slavery! This evidence, too, can be proved beyond contradiction.

"It lies, therefore, with you, my brothers, to break openly and cleanly with slavery. But to break with slavery you must break with the army. The regiment is not your tribe—it is your prison! It is a vital part of the life-rhythm of the evil that is slavery!"

Souvarine Petro had opened a deep wound in all of us with that savage attack. He depicted us as traitors in the pay of the slavers. What he said hurt. But how he said it was also painful. He could persuade a goat to crawl inside a leopard's den. Then he proceeded, cleverly, to mend what he had purposely torn. There was a way to save ourselves (as he put it) from drowning in the filth of slavery. He continued:

"If you ask what you can do, I answer that there is a sure way to regain your honor and end this detestable system of slavery. This very night a brave and honorable band of men of your regiment, men who yearn to be free, men who yearn to die with guns in their hands rather than submit any longer to tyranny, seized power from their buckra officers. By their brave and honorable action, the Cabrits are now in our hands. But these valuable hills will not remain in our possession unless we crush the evil host now assembling to wrest them back. Join with your brave and honorable brothers to destroy these devils who threaten your freedom and honor.

"Do not be afraid! You have the numbers and courage to revolt and be victorious. Recollect that you and your African brothers and sisters are numerically twenty to one against the buckras. You are a powerful engine of fearful consequence. Did not the battle of St. Martin demonstrate this for all to see? Yes! And they know it. Know this simple fact yourselves and act upon it. Take action and shape your own lives and your reward will be another Haiti. Be what destiny has made of you—*the death warrant of slavery*!

"You, my brothers, are the vanguard of a unique revolution. Former revolutions have done no more than determine which of the privileged classes should govern next. Like the great revolution now underway in Haiti, you fight for nothing less than liberty, equality, land, honor and peace."

He concluded his speech with more provocative words. I hated them with unreasoning hate. They were so powerful, direct and, possibly, true. Damn him. Damn him for his insights.

"You have no cause with the rich who are rich because you are slaves. There is no turning back; the revolution has already begun. The structure of slavery is cracking all through its foundation. The revolution in Haiti is the first crack. Widen this irreparable breach and follow those who cut the path for you. Action is dignity!

"History is watching. Destiny stares you hard in the face. Be decisive; catch this opportunity to take back your freedom, your honor. You have the means! Burn out the evil of slavery!

"LONG LIVE LIBERTY, EQUALITY, HONOR! LONG LIVE THE SPIRIT OF HAITI!"

His words leaped from his soul like a mighty force as elemental as a storm. They hit hard. They even made a certain sense. And they awakened something in me, something chilling, exciting, but something unknown, a thing without a face. In his head he possessed some map of the future from which he spoke. All creation, the world, seemed to be on that map. Most people have only a dull, narrow road of the world in their heads, along which they are for-ever doomed to travel, never veering off to the right or left where lie truth, wisdom, great sensations and experiences, universal clearness, God. Most people are road-bound. Thus we live simple lives. But Souvarine Petro, he was a map person, a been-to man, a man who has been to the top. He also saw things that he believed in and called them by what he believed to be their true names. I admired him for this. As he spoke and stabbed at the air with his fingers, I could not help feel the pull of this powerful personality. His last sentence made me shiver with cold despite my heavy uni-form. Those words told me I was starved for something that I could not put a name to.

Despite the ravages of his words, his speech had missed its mark by a wide margin. We would not follow him into revolution, nor would we allow the odious and accursed mutiny to continue. When I rose to speak against his false scheme, I knew then that my life was at a crossroad. What I said could mean continued life or painful death.

In broken English I exposed Souvarine Petro's fiery words for what they were: brave—no—foolish, dangerous words which held bloody consequences for us should we be so unwise as to heed them. Why, I asked my comrades, should we die for an experiment we did not understand? Why should we trust to an incomplete victory in Haiti—and it was unfinished, something Souvarine Petro never denied. Precisely how were we to act in concert with the slaves and our saviors, the Haitians? What proof was there that our deaths would end slavery and move humanity forward? I even laughed at destiny and history. Why should we go to our deaths in order to satisfy and entertain future generations? History would not be affected; it would merely move relentlessly right along on its own predetermined path, whether we raised a rebellion or not.

No. Revolution and mutiny were not necessary. Revolution was to be avoided, for it merely opens the door for all forms of madness. There was still time to make peace with the army. We must treat with the officers, it is our only hope, I exhorted my comrades. We will meet them, not behind the cannon-studded walls of Fort Shirley, lest they doubt our sincerity, but on the open, sloping ground before the fort. There we will await them with our colors unfurled.

My speech, like Souvarine Petro's, was greeted with silence, but not a stillness born of seething hostility. Many nodded their heads in silent agreement when I finished my speech. I felt relieved. This troubled time of fear, confusion and indecision was over, at least for the moment. We had an honorable plan.

When Souvarine Petro saw that his scheme of revolt had been rejected, he gave me a brief, withering look of contempt and withdrew to the shadows.

I, too, cared for the downtrodden slaves. There were strong feelings of indignation over injustices in my heart. I knew from experience that a slave was under heel at every step. But there is no evil without good. Captain Cameron was dead, but there were other reasonable officers who would listen to us. They would recognize truth when they heard it and they would act accordingly. Of this I was certain as I was in the rightness of my stand.

Later that night a deputation from the grenadiers arrived from the fort and agreed to join us in our effort to reason with the army. They insisted that we should treat with the army with our muskets primed and loaded with ball cartridge. We agreed to this, believing that it was an unnecessary precaution. Let them have this small victory.

Grenadiers, being chosen men, were always in the habit of getting their own way. What mattered now was that they were with us. The regiment, injured though it was, was still united.

In the early afternoon the next day the regiment was drawn up in line, two deep. Forming up the regiment fell to the sergeants and corporals, as our officers either had escaped, were lying dead or were the prisoners of the grenadiers. We formed front, facing down the gentle slope of the esplanade, in the direction of the main road leading into the Cabrits. We turned out in what I can only describe as perfect good order. Our shoes were well blacked, stockings clean, buckles as bright as gold, black gaiters and clothes all correct. Our arms and accouterments were well put on. We turned out in special good order because it helped to damp the pain and tension we all felt.

Sergeant Major Bostonian then ordered the colors to be sent for. The grenadier drummers and fifers instantly beat and played the drummer's call. The Grenadier Company then peeled away from the right of the line. They returned a short time later with the colors, the drummers and fifers beating and playing "The Grenadiers March" all the while as though on parade. As the color party neared we presented arms. The drummers and fifers came on, now beating and playing "A Point of War" and "God Save Great George Our King." It all seemed so ordinary, normal. As the colors approached the center of the line, the music and drumming suddenly ceased.

The order to stand at rest cracked up and down the line.

The air seemed strangely oppressive, deadly. There appeared to be no life in it. Not a single drone of a mosquito in search of a bloody meal.

And all the while the sun, unveiled, blazing, cooked us in our uniforms until there arose that familiar odor of thronged soldiers—the breathtaking, tart pungency of woolen clothes dampened too often with piss and sweat.

Yet another ugly thought entered my mind: the *Articles of War*! I had listened to them on the many occasions they were read. They were at best mere words, words that would never be put into practice. Now I was faced with the realization that the code might be exactly enforced against me. This came as a great shock. For a moment I imagined myself as killed.

Suddenly all these thoughts were swept away; the relieving column was in the Cabrits. A chill came over me at that moment and my feelings of hope began to die. From where I stood on the knoll I could see the column's every movement. It wound its way snake-like along the main road. The head had reached the thick, cannon-proof wall through which ran the down-sloping causeway to the wharf and sea. The rest of the long column stretched far back and then disappeared around a sharp turn in the road. As it coiled steadily along, it seemed to quiver like some serpent with suppressed excitement. This visible tremor caught Hussar's attention. "De column dem got violence stamped upon it," he whispered, not taking his eyes from the oncoming red wall of marching men. I didn't want to reply that I agreed with him, so I remained silent. But I thought to myself, yes, the distinctive forward surge of those quick bodies betrayed their sinister purpose. A chill ran down my back with this discovery and admission.

Ahead of the column, skirmishers, in strained silence, spied out the land. They were pretty to look at at first—small, but agile, determined men coming on in perfect open order at the double.

The fitful movements of the skirmishers attracted the attention of a band of our sharp-eyed Cabrits dogs who immediately gave a furious chase. Amidst much yelping and barking, they challenged the skirmishers for control of the road. Shrieks of laughter rose from our lines at this farce. My face just managed a weak smile. But this distraction lasted only a moment. Several shots rang out and instantly a number of dogs fell dead like dropped stones. The rest darted wildly for cover among the dry brush where they vanished from sight. With the sound of those shots a distinct low groan was heard in our lines. Those dogs lived with the regiment and to kill them was to harm the regiment. We shook our heads disapprovingly, and our light-hearted joking quickly turned to hostile distrust.

The skirmishers then continued to scout the way against an invisible enemy for the silent tramping men behind, who never paused in their determined march forward—toward us! I watched and waited. But despite the fear, I was impatient of waiting longer to settle this thing.

Suddenly, the crowd of skirmishers melted away, their work apparently done. The column, in fours abreast, slipped through the crowd of skirmishers and wheeled sharply to the left, abandoning the road which continued on a little distance before ending at the main gate of Fort Shirley. A command rang out in a hoarse voice from somewhere in the column, and it quickly formed into two long lines at the bottom of the slope. Another hoarse order and the wall of men tramped up toward us with a firm regular tread, muskets shouldered. On they came in a dead silence until, when not more than fifteen paces distant from us, they ground to an abrupt halt. We gave them a smart general salute which they returned.

The secret of the uniform is to take a crowd of men and give it singleness, to make each man impersonal. At this distance, however, that power was shattered. Each man was an individual, distinct. They were tall, thin, short, fresh-faced, leather-skinned survivors of the climate, and some shriveled and torn with the pox. They were also old men, mere boys, young men; and they were privates, sergeants and officers. But all had waxy, knotty faces working with excitement, for this was a fearful moment.

Above all I saw many black men wearing the uniform of my own regiment! At that distance there was no mistaking the distinctive gray facings on their red tunics. Lapels, collars and shoulder straps were all stepped boldly in gray. There were about a hundred of them, a full company. Standing in the middle of the second line, they were flanked by buckra troops.

"*Dem is we own!*" It was the charged voice of Hussar. He, too, had noticed them. I watched him as his eyes swept nervously up and down that line of silent standing black men before us. He shook his head. "Dem der fe one reason, fe prove dem loyalty. Dem ready fe kill we fe live."

"It well looks so," I replied.

It was degrading and humiliating that my regiment should be divided like this and on the verge of making war on itself. I became sick at heart as I looked at them, and I wished fervently that they were nothing more than a mirage of heat. Their faces were stained and haggard and possessed the same waxy quality as the buckra soldiers. I stared at them in silent unbelief. Could they bring themselves to kill us? Did they, who care for nothing outside the regiment, view us as loathsome mutineers? I refused to answer my own question. Why did I have to be here? I wished I could simply close my eyes and when they opened all that was now before me would vanish. More of this and my nerves would snap. It was enough.

A painful silence, like a wall, lay between our lines and theirs. No one spoke. Not a sound broke the total silence.

I looked to nature to distract me. But the air continued breathless, prisoned without relief by the Cabrits. And the staring sun, now high in a blazing sky, pitilessly hammered the earth. Nature provided no escape. What was to be, would be.

In the midst of these thoughts I noticed a mounted officer. I recognized him at once as Colonel Johnstone, the Governor of Dominica and our own commander. A tall man with a long face and hollow cheeks, he was covered with dust from his ride into the Cabrits from Portsmouth. Wearing his customary large white hat with a wide brim—the kind worn by the planters of the island—he rode slowly along the front of the troops. And when he reached the center he turned the horse to face us and stopped abruptly. He gave us a hard look and in a loud voice, knife-sharp in the dead-still air, he talked briefly of how much he loved the Eighth West India Regiment, how he remembered with pride our great victory over the French at St. Martin, and how he had hoped to see his regiment win further honors on the battlefield. But, he added coldly, the regiment had been shamed, and because of that he would now ask us to show our loyalty by laying down our arms.

Lay down our arms!

Except for a few stifled groans, an eerie hush fell over the parade ground.

I rebelled at the thought of surrendering my musket. There is nothing more important to a soldier than his musket. How could I ever forget that moment when I first took it into my hands, a musket of my own. The ancient excitement of power raced through my limbs, my heart pounded in my chest, and for a long moment I was rooted to that spot. I felt dangerous. Even hard-faced buckras sensed this.

They took respectful notice of me whenever I carried my musket. Until that supreme moment, the limit of my power (such as it was) was the length of the shadow cast by my body. Now, the range of my power could be reckoned in the hundreds of yards—the firing range of my musket. Not even our colors possessed such powers. Of course our silken flags were very important to us. They were colorful emblems of our military honor. They were sacred. If we lost them in battle we would suffer considerable dishonor, but we would still be soldiers capable of great potential harm, because we were yet armed. But to give up our muskets by laying them on the ground was another matter. Without them we were as air, lacking substance. Without them we were a toothless, clawless leopard. Without them we were reduced to the level of slaves. What else could a black man without a gun be under slavery?

And yet, to disobey, to refuse the order to ground our muskets, was unthinkable. Obedience was the salt of my service as a soldier; it was at the heart of my oath of enlistment. The first time I looked death in the face as a soldier, the bullets and shots that hissed about my body whispered to me the secret of the glory of the British army. Now was the time to be loyal to that secret, to be faithful to the salt one has eaten. We must show them that we were honorable men and that we were not afraid of British justice.

Colonel Johnstone's voice then carried clearly in the dead air: "Soldiers of the Eighth West India Regiment— SHOULDER ARMS!"

There was a momentary wavering hesitation and murmur through the ranks, but we quickly recovered our bearing and our bayonet-tipped muskets jerked upwards as one.

"GROUND ARMS!"

The wooden stocks of our muskets stabbed downward as one. I stooped down and tenderly laid my musket on the ground. As I did I told myself that there was nothing else I could do.

"STAND FROM YOUR ARMS!"

I stepped backward three paces. As I did I looked over at the silent wall of watching men. Suddenly I felt disgraced, humiliated.

"LEFT FACE! QUICK . . . ."

A disturbance on the right of our lines cut Colonel Johnstone off. I could hear angry shouts coming from that direction, where the grenadiers stood. I glanced around uneasily.

"GRENADIERS, GROUND ARMS!" Colonel Johnstone's angry voice raced through the air.

I strained my ears to pick up the sharp, metallic rattle of bayonet-tipped muskets hitting the iron-hard earth. But nothing happened. The grenadiers had refused the order to lay down their arms. Now I was truly frightened.

The angry shouts continued. Occasionally a few of the words drifted down the ranks to me: *"Stand firm . . . freedom . . . Haiti . . . cut the path for you . . . liberty . . . fire! . . . fire! . . . fire!"*

"Damn them! Fire on the niggers! Give them a volley!

Nigger? I am not a nigger! My mind shrieked it. I am not a nigger! I am not a *mafa*!

Instinctively I ran back to get my musket. At that moment the dull boom of orderly musket fire burst from the right of our lines; the grenadiers were volley-firing by sections. This was immediately followed by a louder crash and instantly a furious gust of killing lead tore into our ranks as we were in the act of grabbing our muskets. Everything fell apart. Men went down heavily on both sides of me. Hussar dropped to his knees clutching at his left arm. A bullet had smashed it just below the elbow. I fired my musket without thinking to aim it.

"PRESENT!" roared someone somewhere. Another voice, as though in response, answered "FIRE LOW! FIRE LOW!" Suddenly I heard a rolling noise like thunder, and immediately another gust of bullets smashed into our ranks.

A bugle blared the "advance" followed quickly by the "double." The firing ceased. I looked hard through the thick gray smoke to see a wall of men, their faces locked in grim determination, surging up the slope. As they came on they broke into groups of three as we had all been taught to do. The center man lunged ahead with the bayonet, the two others supporting him from the left and right. As they rushed us I bent down to get Hussar to his feet. As I did I received a terrible blow to the back of my head. I saw a confused trampling of feet and the sky wheeling over me, faster and faster. "Perish here!" repeated over and over in my mind were my last thoughts as I sank, stunned and senseless, into a timeless void.

I have no idea how long I lay senseless. When I awoke I found myself stretched upon the ground, surrounded by a small group of badly bruised and dejected comrades. Everywhere were armed white men who eyed us nervously. Every button had been torn off my tunic. My regimental identity, which gave notice of my special place in the army, was no more. I resembled the pitiful fort negroes who went about their mean labor in stripped-down, cast-off army clothes.

Chapter 4

The Nightmare

Thinking about the mutiny asked too much of my body. Exhausted, I lay down, trying desperately to sleep as a way of rendering my mind vacant. But when I finally did drowse off I was swallowed up in a dream.

A white soldier, his face a grinning mask, handed me a chalk-white execution uniform. I put it on, but it was too big and kept slipping off. It hung on me grotesquely.

I was escorted by twelve black soldiers of my own regiment. They were to shoot me. It was early morning of a ripening day, a day for living. We did not reach the Cabrits Valley until the sun was straight up, so slow was our progress.

Only a few people gathered along the route—my family who turned their backs to me, an old female slave, and Hiali the Carib.

Standing alone, writing in his little brown notebook, was the hidden king of the regiment, Sergeant Major Bostonian. He never looked up as I passed by.

Souvarine Petro came. "Private Jack. You fool," he whispered. "Unless a man believes there is something great to do in his life, he will do nothing great." Then he faded away into a tree or the sky, I could not tell which.

And Jubba Lily came. She moved towards me, looking as she had the last time we embraced. "*Please*, Madu, stay with me. *Please!*" Her voice was mournful, sorrowful beyond description.

She began to melt. "Wait!" My voice was desperate. I held out my hand to touch her, but as happens in dreams I could not reach her. She then melted into that hateful slave, Hamlet.

I reached a place where a large body of soldiers had formed up in three sides of a square, facing inward. At the open end of the square were seven freshly dug graves. And in front of each was a single wooden box. The firing party came wheeling in to take post in perfect formation a few feet in front of the graves. The sun glinted off the tips of their muskets.

Six other black prisoners joined me. One by one they were taken to a wooden box and made to kneel on it facing the firing party. As one man mounted his coffin, he turned slowly towards me. The eyes in his head were pure red and glowed like hot coals. "You cannot command what you cannot control," he cried. "You have betrayed yourself."

The black features of each man faded into a ghastly hue, and were distorted by pure animal fright. A ringing volley and each man fell backward dead. Bright red blood spurted from the chest of each man with his final heartbeats: throb, throb, throb . . . slower, slower . . . stillness.

My heart was pounding. I tried to press myself back, wishing myself invisible.

Suddenly a towering figure appeared far back among the wall of soldiers. It glittered and shimmered in the sunlight. He came closer, closer. I could see every detail of his dress. We faced each other. I feared him. It was the king of the Margi Dzirnu! He squeezed my hand with his cold fingers and pulled me to the remaining coffin. "Your life has been a lie." His voice was ugly. "I claimed you first and now you shall work again on my terraces."

"Lies! Lies! The crime I never committed was . . . mutiny." I jerked out the words. "I do not deserve to die!"

I pulled myself free from his icy grip and ran into a guinea-corn field or a cane piece, I cannot remember which. My head was swirling, muddled. When it cleared I saw a lowly field negro, a man, eating the charm vomited up out of the belly of a witch. The charm was black, red and white— a rainbow assortment of evil. This negro, whose face I could not see, first became a witch, an eater of souls, and was then transformed into a wild animal. It stalked me to catch and kill my soul. In an effort to escape, I ran farther and farther into the field. Thinking I had eluded the creature, I suddenly fell groaning to the ground, bleeding from my eyes and vomiting blood. The witch had caught me and had taken my soul to its compound to eat.

"At last death has caught up with me," I thought. With a sigh, I prepared myself for ritual slaughter. The witch was about to gorge itself on my soul, when, lo! I awoke sitting upright on the cold floor of my cell. I could hear my heart pounding in my chest. It had all seemed so real . . . .

With the corporal of the guard soaked in rum, and no one to overhear me, I cried. Back and forth I rocked, breathing in and breathing out to convince myself that I was alive, that I had escaped death. I laughed aloud but my heart was not comforted.

A white execution uniform . . . on the edge of horrible deaths . . . the Margi king . . . the substance of evil in the colors of my beloved uniform . . . a lowly slave . . . dread . . . flight. What did it all mean? Was something about to befall me? Was it an omen? Was I to be found guilty of mutiny by the court-martial and then shot dead by members of my own regiment? Enough of this madness. In looking back at one's life, all things, even small events, could be claimed as signs, messages. But what a horrible way to live: all life would become one enormous omen and one would be paralyzed. A stubbed toe here, a fallen leaf there—where would it all end? No. I must not let myself think of life in that way. The dream was just that, a dream, nothing more, nothing less.

What was real and unchanging was the fact that I was a British soldier. This was the wish of God. As a soldier I lived in a small, sealed world of certain virtues: loyalty to comrades, courage under stress, faithfulness to a solemn oath. Soldiering conferred on me the opportunity for honor and dignity. It gave me back my self-respect. I would sooner bleed to death than lose my self-respect. I took soldiering seriously. It was all that shielded me from the intolerable menace of lurking slavery.

It was my regiment that represented this world apart, a world denied to the slaves and even the buckras of this island. It was my home. It did not matter that no one entered the regiment by choice. It did not matter that once inside this . . . cocoon I would have to assume immediate unquestioning obedience. None of that mattered. In truth, being in the midst of disciplined, obedient men thrilled me!

My time in the regiment had become a wonderful age-long day of power, authority, honor, self-respect, great fellowship, adventure, proven manhood. Once in the regiment

I had no desire to look beyond it. My life since coming to the West Indies had been spent entirely in its service. Its welfare was my welfare, its reputation was my reputation. In putting the interests of the regiment ever above my own, I became honorable and esteemed by others.

Chapter 5

Jack's Story

They came over to where I was sitting alone in a corner of the prison yard. Suddenly I was in the middle of my comrades: Hussar, Lively, Cuffy, Genus, Manby, Pedro. They all gave me a friendly nod and smile.

"Y'know, it's yo' turn, Jack." It was Manby. "Each of we agree to tell de story of we life, where we come from and what it was like back home deh, across de big water. It's yo' turn. What 'bout it, Jack?" Manby's black eyes fixed on me with a keen insistence.

I did not answer immediately. "I doan' feel much like talkin', mon."

Manby appeared not to have heard me because he asked me again. "But it's yo' turn to tell we 'bout yo' life and family back deh, Jack."

A shock went through me at that word—that tremendous word—*family*! I was not prepared for that word. I had resolved to forget them, it was easier that way. But they kept on intruding into my thoughts. And here was Manby reminding me that I once had a family.

But had I not promised to tell them about my life in the long ago? Did we not all agree to tell our stories while there was still breath in us? "Arright, arright, I tell if yuh want. It's only a story. Sit y'self down." I tried to keep my voice calm, but I tortured myself in remembering.

The name my parents gave me was Madu. My birthplace was Madagali among the proud Margi people of the Mardara Mountains of northeast Nigeria. Madagali is in the heartland of Margi country and the Mandara Mountains are the legendary home of my people. There—among the mountains, the compact villages, the terraced farming slopes, the farms on the valley floors—the greater part of my life was passed. Many clans in this area called themselves Margi. However, Margi men of memory and old village headmen recognized only four main clans. The Margi Babal, which means the "Margi of the plain," includes the villages of Musa, Dille, Huyum and Lassa, where my blessed mother was born. The second is the Margi Dzirngu, the "Margi near the mountains." This is my clan and the name is given to Margis in the areas of Duhu, Maiva, Wannu, Gulak and, of course, Madagali, the village of my birth. The third is the "Margi of the west" or Margi Putar. To judge from their strange language, I believe they form a separate tribe rather than a clan withinside the Margi group. Lastly there is the Margi ti Ntam, the "Margi who mourn with a pot." They are so named because of the ancient practice of using a drum made from a pot in their mourning ritual. They are sometimes called the South Margi. Womdiu, Wuba and Baza are among the villages found in this region. The lands occupied by Margi clans are vast. Yet a Margi from a distant village would be warmly received in a new village and shown great respect for his customs.

I was born during the early guinea corn harvest to Elana, a Margi girl from the plains, near Lassa. We were five children: two boys and three girls. I was the first son and the first child. My blessed mother was the peaceful center for the revolving tumult of five young lives. My mother lived for her children. She was our constant source of love, warmth, food and comfort, and gave us a great feeling of security. My mother also had a strong sense of generosity. Giving us her food during hard times was nothing to her.

I still remember her suckling my young brother, her body smeared with ochre, as was the custom. But the outstanding impression she left on my memory was her earthy vitality. This force was expressed in many ways: in her gestures, in looking smart, when she sang, as she walked, when she spoke, and certainly when she danced, which she was always prepared to do, even when ill. With her hips pushed out, knees and arms bent, her straight-back torso pridefully held, and both feet planted fully on the ground, she would move sensuously in a crouching position close to the earth. Her body yielded and moved and bent and swayed so readily you could say that she danced as if she had no bones. The ancient custom of carrying loads on her head was mirrored in her flexible body positions in dance.

Her dance was a kind of passage which connected life with art. During these times she was obeying a vitality within the music while in deep talk with her body. I can easily recall her during these moments. Dancing lifted her up above the world, it freed her from her pain. And as she danced her eyes glowed with delight. I was entranced by her motions, not knowing that she was magically finding her youth in dance.

My mother's greatest wish was to see me, her eldest child, marry. "Ah, when I look upon the face of Madu's wife, then shall I know peace in this world!" Many times I heard my mother make known her strong Margi feelings for family continuity with these words.

A man named Mjigimtu was my father. I was told that he was already an adult when he asked for permission to marry my mother. He was a kindly and modest man who never had any desire to gather more cattle than was needed to feed his family. He was quiet and thoughtful and enjoyed listening to others speak, after which he would ask discerning questions. I remember the days when he returned home from tending the cattle and we would rush to him, beseeching him to tell us what wondrous new and strange things he had observed that day. He would answer briefly and then cheerfully allow each of us to talk about what we had discovered, which, as he well knew, was the intent of our questions. To make us laugh, he would often poke us lightly below the ribs with his strong fingers. In helping us to reach adulthood and to understand our place in Margi society and the world, he taught us in his usual silent, easy way, by his inner calm, deeds and love of the everyday life of his family.

My father was also a man of memory in our Margi village. He was a great storyteller. His skill in recounting the histories of our people was well known throughout the Mandara Hills. He would usually tell his stories at night, in the period after planting. Women, children and men gathered to listen to this tale telling. His stories of strength and power, of childhood, of why guinea corn is important, of how the poor become rich and powerful, and why one should never laugh at the ugly and the poor, brought excitement to life's dull round. These were times of amusement and learning, with elders and children together in situations of pleasant intimacy and harmony.

But my father was much more than a taleteller. His vast knowledge of the past helped greatly to maintain order and continuity in our village, from one generation of our people to the next. He was the link between the two. I remember him training me as a boy to become the next man of memory of our village. My father would often make me recite our royal and ancestral histories. As part of my training I was also expected to learn the important events that took place during the lifetime of his own elders. I can still hear my father questioning me about the importance of Margi place phrases and praise phrases in the lives of our rulers. To be a man of memory is a great honor, and my father could have ascended into high government office. But he resisted this great temptation and chose instead to live out his days as close to his family as life's demands would permit. How very deeply I loved and admired my father. (I wonder if he ever knew how much I did.)

He was a lover of his people and fought bravely against the Muslim Fulani. He was particularly proud of the Margi's skill in creating fertile soil on the rocky hillsides. With great ingenuity and labor they built elaborate farming and grazing terraces that girdled the rocky slopes of the Mandara Hills. Some of the terrace walls reached a height of only a few inches. But others were taller than the tallest man and extended for many, many miles. One would have to walk without rest for at least two revolutions of the moon to see them all.

We lived on little. But it was enough. The ground yielded a small surplus. We felt at one with the soil, with nature, and we celebrated the planting of the seed, a seemingly dead thing, that would rise with life and nourish us. My father would say to me, always looking hard into my eyes, "Nagu Margi! Nagu Margi!" (You are a Margi! You are a Margi!)

His father, too, took great pride in Margi courage and resourcefulness and celebrated this in my father's facial marks. When my father was a little boy, my grandfather paid a special artist a fee to cut the tribal badge of the Margi into his son's face: three long vertical cuts on both sides of his face, from the temple down across the cheekbone to the chin; four vertical nicks in the middle of the forehead; a long stroke extending from the middle of the forehead down along the ridge of the nose to the tip; and vertical nicks under each eye. After the cuts were made and the blood wiped away, bamboo and charcoal powder was rubbed in. Then ground nut oil was smeared over the cuts. When I was a small boy, my father took me to the same artist, now an old man. With the same sharp double-edged blade, set in a round wooden handle, he delicately cut the Margi badge into my face.

The spilling of blood is not an uncommon sight among Margis. It occupies an important place in our rituals and practices. But I must confess that I dreaded my appointment with that shriveled old man so bent with age. My father pointed him out to me one day before my visit; that was a mistake. His face and head were framed with grey hair. He was very thin and his skin hung loosely over his small frame as though it did not fit. It collected in ugly folds across his belly and even his knees. His penetrating gaze was at once tired and wise. When he looked at you he looked into your heart. Each time I saw him thereafter I would avoid that piercing look as I would the presence of an unfriendly spirit in the fields at dusk. Would his hand be steady? And what of me? Would I endure the sight of my own blood, or would his assistant have to place his hands over my eyes? I had to be brave.

But what joy when I beheld my new face in the polished mirror. My tribal identity was there for all to see and admire and it would remain enshrined in my flesh forever. *I be-longed!* I remember quiet moments gazing at my reflection in the still water of a nearby stream, the eager anticipation of walking through the village market with my father, oblig-ing all who wished to look at me. *I belonged!*

My ancestral home was a circular house. A round house signifies safety and security to us Margis. We had, in fact, three ancestral houses forming a family compound. They were grouped about a large open area where corn was milled on the hard, packed earth in dry weather. One served as a sleeping house, the second for milling small amounts of corn, the third as a kitchen. Each was built of sun-baked mud walls as hard as stone. They had to be stone-hard, for the first heavy rains would melt a lesser-built house back again into mud. Over time the scorching sunlight had faded out the deep brown of the mud walls to a sandy color. The sun and the rain were kept out by a well-tended thatch of bamboo or guinea-corn stalks in the shape of a cone.

As I think back I recall the constant scent of cooked food. The powerful smell of tasty meat-smoke, boiled yams, ground guinea corn seasoned with hibiscus leaves, and steaming beer left to cool drifted through the houses. When meat was served it was eaten quickly, for it was a luxury. No one really cared for hot yams and porridge when there was meat to eat. After we children had eaten we were called upon to chase away the mangy dogs made hungry by the tanta-lizing odors. We ran them down and out of the compound. We returned as quickly as we could from this chore to watch enviously as the adults finished the meat.

Platforms were the main items of furniture in my home. Except for the ground, they were the only things to sit on. They were built of hardened mud and were about the size of a low English cot, of the type seen in the officers' bar-racks. We had platforms for sleeping. The hand-turned grain mill rested on another platform. But the most important one adjoined the sleeping house and faced an open area. My grandfather was in the habit of sitting there each evening as the declining sun reddened our village from the west. He was a man of middle height, thin and coal-black like all Margis. He had a wide mouth which showed uneven yellow teeth when he smiled or laughed. But it was his eyes I remember most. He had large expressive eyes like black adinkra cloth in richness. They transformed his face from one mood to another. They were hypnotic, and when he fastened them on you, you at once stiffened where you sat and held your breath for a long silent moment.

Occasionally, while sitting in the courtyard, he would call the children of the village to him so that he might tell us stories of long-ago kings and battles. These were great moments, for his tales held me spellbound. One day when asked to explain his talent for storytelling, he replied, "You must listen to the music that lies within the simplest words. To speak of life you must study the music of the birds, hear the fall of the dew, listen to the leaves of the trees. The trouble with we Margis," he added, "is that we are too busy with our farms and cattle to hear the songs that lie within our daily language." He would raise his arm, his palm toward the sky. "How bad that we do not let life's grand moments inspire us, like the flight of brilliantly colored birds, the coming each day of the promised red sun, the mirages of heat, the dark which makes a man and a fool equal. I could go on, but it would take many revolutions of the moon for me to cite a scant portion of the incidents of life that assist one in turning simple sounds into poetry. Remember that simple things draw forth many emotions." At that moment I felt awash in a deep sense of comfort that I lived with my grandfather. I always felt that my little universe of parents, grandfather, brothers and sisters, cousins and other relatives was unshakable.

When the Madagali evening began closing in, and the courtyard was empty, I would sit cross-legged on the platform and stare out at grandfather's view. I would imagine myself telling captivating stories of my childhood and pieces of family history to little children. I thought of grandfather. By his wonderful stories, wisdom, dignity and independence, he gained moral authority over all who knew him. He is dead now, of course. He died before my great misfortune. His passing left a wide, sad hole in my family.

My favorite story was the tale of the faithful child. Madu Mamza was the favorite grandson of King Madu Palnar Mambala. One day, when King Madu was watching the women of his village dance, he became very thirsty. He asked Umwaru, another grandson, to fetch some water. Umwaru refused. Madu Palnar Mambala then asked a servant, but he too refused. Finally the king asked Madu Mamza to draw the water. He agreed and carried with him the royal double bell. On his way to the river he saw a beehive. He filled one bell with water and the other with honey and brought them to his great-grandfather, who was pleased.

"It is well known," my grandfather went on, "that Madu Palnar Mambala was a generous man, and in that spirit of unselfishness he proclaimed then and there that Madu Mamza would be the one to succeed him after his death. It is also well known that no child is born without blood. So when the old Madu finally died, several of his brothers declared that they would succeed him and instantly they went to war, one against the other. To protect the little boy from the wrath of his jealous kinsmen, young Madu was sent to the most remote area of the Mandara Hills. One brother was killed when a snake bit him. Another was attacked and eaten by a leopard. Two other brothers were eventually killed in battle by Madu Mamza, now grown, at a site that bears the name 'The Plain of Battle Where Madu Mamza Became King.' Madu Mamza established his court at Madagali Village in the region of the Margis Near the Mountain, and this later became his sacred village."

From that time on, all the kings of the Margi Dzirnu resided at Madagali. "Has it never struck you as strange," my grandfather concluded, pointing his long, bony finger at me, "that your name is also Madu?"

Could it be? For a long moment I was nailed to the spot where I sat cross-legged in imitation of my grandfather. Could it be that the kings of Margi Dzirnu and I were joined by blood as grandfather seemed to suggest? The thought continued to thrill me, and I can still remember the physical sense of excitement that raced through my body. Madagali was indeed the royal village as well as my own. Were we not also joined by having the same first name? Could all this be mere coincidence? Out of the corner of my eye I saw that all the other children were suddenly staring at me. I was embarrassed by all this attention but I enjoyed it. Of course, the kings of the Margi Dzirnu were not kinsmen. My father assured me of that. But it was a long time before I let go the idea. Still, that day when grandfather playfully pointed at me and hinted that I might be related to the kings of Margi Dzirnu has never ceased to hold me spellbound. To this day that event is caught in my memory like a fly in amber.

Grandfather was a memory man. He was an historical specialist. As such he could recall in great detail the origins of the Margi Dzirnu and the deeds of our kings in the long ago. But his taletelling was not limited to the royal family. He could also tell earthy stories of human desire, as I discovered.

It happened during the hot hours one afternoon. The sleeping house was sealed tight against the sun, and the adults, including grandfather, were sitting indoors enjoying the cool air. I lay awake in the adjoining room and listened to grandfather talking. The story he told me was one that he called "The Watchful Husband."

Once there was a husband so jealous of his pretty wife that he followed her everywhere she went. Even if she had to relieve herself, he went with her and watched. One day, after this vigilance had gone on for some time, she challenged her husband and said, "Since you do not trust me and like to watch everything I do, I will get a lover and have sex with him while you watch and you will not know it!" First, he said this was impossible; then he angrily threatened her if she did it. However, she persisted in her promise. She eventually found a lover and one day told him to come at once to her house and hide under the pile of chaff near the threshing platform. This he did, covering himself completely in the husks of grain except for his penis, which he left exposed as she had instructed. As the sun began to set and full darkness came on, the woman said to her husband that she needed to urinate. Ever watchful, the husband followed her outside to the chaff heap where she squatted down upon her lover's penis. After a few moments her husband said impatiently, "Drop your water, woman and get up." But she paid no notice of him as she was enjoying herself immensely. She then cried out, "Oh! Oh! Come on! Finish me off!" Her husband replied angrily, "Who are you talking to?" She replied breathlessly, "Do you see anybody?" He said, "Drop your water and get up. You are certainly taking too much time about it!" But, again, she paid no attention to him. Instead, she kept exclaiming, "Do it! Finish me off! Do it!" Her husband, now angry, demanded, "Are you talking to the spirits? Enough of this, get up, get up!" But she kept on enjoying herself.

Finally, when exhausted, she got up, but while she was arranging her loin coverings her lover let out a long deep sigh of contentment from under the chaff. Her husband heard it and cried out, "Oh, no! No! You have tricked me. Oh, no!" The woman merely smiled at him and said, "Yes! Of course I have. Did I not tell you I would?" Whereupon the poor husband resigned himself to his unhappy fate as a cuckold, while his pretty wife and her lover continued their lusty sexual escapades.

Howls of laughter greeted the end of grandfather's story.

"They were all foolish," my grandfather added abruptly, bringing the laughter to a sudden end. "In life there can be no gain without payment. Long accustomed to jealousy and suspicion, the husband was consumed by them. As for the wife and her lover, their punishment would come later, for it was both cruel and unwise to taunt someone so weak and inconstant as the pitiful husband."

A heavy, long silence followed grandfather's words.

I was momentarily stunned, struck dumb by the story. I had not expected grandfather to speak like that. Until that afternoon all of his stories (at least those I had heard) were about famous men who gave rise to the line of Margi Dzirnu kings. Their lives were devoted to building the Margi nation, and so they had little or no time for women and sex and such things. At least that was the picture grandfather conveyed in his stories. From that moment on I saw my grandfather very differently. His wrinkled skin and old bones were but a shell inside of which danced a youthful, vigorous spirit. The passion with which he told the story showed that he was not past the age for such emotions.

The story also excited me. It produced strange but welcome feelings. Since they bore no likeness to any other, I cannot describe them, save that they were sweet and were centered in my loins. The rush of those feelings caused me to stir. The noise caught my father's attention and he entered the sleeping room to see if any of us children were awake. I stayed silent, pretending to be asleep.

Grandfather called out to my father, "Do you think the children overheard me?" The tone in which he spoke told me that he had told a very wicked story. "No, I do not believe so," father replied, "and if they did they would not understand. They are just children."

My father was wrong, of course. I was about twelve at the time, and I understood perfectly what grandfather was talking about. I had seen boys and girls in the village exploring their sexual feelings. It was not uncommon to see persuasive boys and willing girls engage in physical expressions of emotions, caressing each other, even masturbating. At times my friends and I would expose those involved in this kind of excitement by reminding them of the old saying, "Masturbation shares a room with fornication." Although we did not fully understand what we were saying, we instinctively knew that what they were doing was forbidden. So I put grandfather's story to the back of my mind and went to sleep. I slept very well that night. But the thought was there inside me like that fly stuck in amber.

My grandfather's story was a sort of rite of passage for me. No, it did not mark my change from boy to man, or even from boy to youth. But something of great power and meaning was awakened in me: an awareness of hidden, unimaginable joys yet to come. That thought was my constant companion. The story also entailed a change in how I saw my grandfather and my elders. They were young spirits wrapped in old skin. From that moment on I had no difficulty in seeing their youth, which shone brightly just beyond their wrinkled skin and aged eyes. Oh, yes, they were too old to work in the fields and spent their days weaving mats, telling stories and taking their ease in the sun. But the sap of life and desire still coursed through their minds, no matter age.

The men were silent after I had finished telling the story of my boyhood. I knew perfectly well that after the first words were out of my mouth my regimental comrades had all drifted into their own remembrances of family and home. It was painful to watch them looking off into space, the thoughts of each absorbed in something sad. But how richly human their faces were, a richness concealed during these past few days by the threat of death. I felt a sudden impulse of tenderness towards each.

They all came back to life when they realized that I had stopped talking. They got up and, without saying a word, each moved off to a corner of the prison yard where, alone, they continued to dwell in the privacy of their remembrances. Out of the corner of my eye I saw Manby break off sobbing. Hussar, his face in his hands, sat staring at the ground. Lively suddenly sprang up and walked away. The others just sat in their own personal gloom. It was always like that when each of my comrades told his story of family and home.

Chapter 6

Petro's Chant

The business of the court-martial had, so far, gone well. Souvarine Petro had exposed the wrongdoing of the judge advocate. It was a stunning device. The judge advocate was embarrassed and forced to respect us as men and provide us with the list of witnesses as the law required. But the sight of Souvarine Petro presenting our case made me choke. He remained a self-seeker lusting after power. I was forced to look in cold terms at our decision to put our lives in his hands. He was very clever with instant retorts. He also had a fine way with English words and he never failed to demonstrate this whenever he spoke. There was more. He was learned, although I wondered, often, where he had received his learning and what end it served; learning always has a purpose.

Our decision gave us a certain amount of peace and comfort because in no way were we able to defend ourselves at a general court-martial. We knew nothing of military law and its tangled nature. What we knew was limited to those things the *Articles of War* prohibited us from doing. It was a chilling experience to stand there in court, on trial for our very lives, and yet be so completely unaware as to what we could do or say. None of us had done guard duty at a court-martial before, and the solemn ritual and language of the proceeding were utterly alien to us, even frightening. So it was well that Souvarine Petro had taken charge of our defense. Only he could match the court's fine words with his own. Only Souvarine Petro could see through the words and into their hearts for their true meaning.

Souvarine Petro would have to be at his best; among the witnesses that the judge advocate intended to examine was the vengeful slave, Hamlet. His mark and name appeared at the bottom of the judge advocate's list. This embittered field negro held every black soldier to be his mortal enemy. Unlike us, he must live and die in the grip of slavery. Eternal bondage, repression of every kind, and painful dependence were his destiny, from birth to death. He was forever scarred by slavery. His hatred of me was without bounds because I was a soldier and because I had wrested Jubba Lily from him. We could thus count on this miserable and worthless little field negro to do mischief to our cause. Souvarine Petro must find a way to defang him, and quickly.

Still, Souvarine Petro troubled me. Had he thought beyond his mutinous speeches? Would he think beyond the words of the judge advocate and his witnesses? His interests were not the same as ours. He appeared to speak over our heads. He seemed to be fighting a different battle.

I caught a good glimpse of this absorption one evening some time ago while on my way to deliver a message to Captain Cameron, who was dining at the great house of one of the planters of the island. My route took me to the thick woods. The murmur of the falling water, the whistling of wind through the high trees, and the constant singing of the birds among the branches made the dark green woods a romantic meeting place. The woods also harbored secret, solitary places and on my journey that evening, I heard the throbbing beat of music and the deep, rich sounds of many human voices singing and chanting from a dark glen. I was eager to see what lay just beyond. I warily approached the spot, and there, after creeping from tree to tree, my sight fell upon a remarkable scene.

A large number of negroes knelt in a wide circle in the middle of which were four poles supporting a simple thatched roof. An old woman, standing under the roof, sifted cornmeal or flour onto the ground in the form of a cross before disappearing into the shadows. The whole scene was lighted by large fires which cast a thousand darting shadows. Suddenly Souvarine Petro appeared in the circle. He had discarded all of his regimentals, which lay in a heap off to the side. In place of his red grenadier's tunic, he was dressed in a French officer's uniform, the kind I had seen worn by a high-ranking officer whom we captured at St. Martin in 1801. Souverine Petro wore a long dark-blue coat with a high red collar. The coat was richly decorated all along the edges with gold lace that sparkled in the light thrown off by the many fires. His tight white pantaloons were stuffed inside shiny black boots which were also edged along the tops in fancy gold material. And wound around his slender waist was an enormous black and red sash. His small head was bare except for a blood-red scarf which circled it at the temples. A long, straight, fancy sword dangled at his side and completed his unusual dress. At his feet was a motionless white cock.

He appeared dazed, unable to stand on his feet, his limp body upheld on each side by several of the slaves. His outstretched arms were thrown loosely over the shoulders of his supporters, and tears streamed down his cheeks. On both his hands were splashes of a substance that looked like blood. His drooping head and sagging body reminded me of something I had seen in the English sacred house in Portsmouth: the cross with the figure of the man Jesus nailed upon it.

A number of black women dressed in white sprang magically from the quivering shadows and began to dance to the somber sounds of drums and tambourines. They chanted and whirled in an atmosphere of bodily release. Their bodies moved in a wave-like motion around the poles. The candlelight barely reached them, but I could see the dreamy expressions on their sweaty faces. Their shoulders and hips were as active as their feet. Several of the women broke away momentarily from the others and danced in what reminded me of the Margi pose: the left hand on the hip and the right hand held outward. Their bodies swayed and the insistent drumbeat controlled the grinding motions of their hips. The exuberant movements of their bobbing breasts and grinding hips had begun to engulf me when, without warning, they all melted away, as if on command, into the waiting shadows.

All except one. She was young and pretty and she continued to dance in slow sensuous movements around the four poles. She was naked except for a white cloth that barely covered her hips and the region where her thighs met. Her full breasts, long legs and flat stomach were beautiful as if formed in a dream. I was close enough to see the perspiration glistening like dew around her erect nipples. Her nakedness tantalized and I tried unsuccessfully to make my eyes leave her.

The negroes squatted before her and repeated various oaths as she, with extended arms, pretended to accept them. All the while the drums throbbed and her body swayed, arched and stretched in a snake-like motion. Several of the group rose and placed offerings of food and drink in her path when suddenly she threw her head back and her body became rigid as if it had turned to stone. She stood there, looking straight up into the night sky, a detached expression on her face, her mouth drawn back and open as if in great pain, the bulging veins at the bursting point in her slender neck. She spoke without ever moving her mouth. The sound was strange and cracked forth like sparks from a dry log. This voice was answered by the negroes whose shouts roared like thunder. The exchange went on until an old man wearing blood red pants squirted liquid over her body from his mouth. As I watched, the young priestess, breathing heavily, collapsed to the ground beyond her conscious self.

The drums stopped and Souvarine Petro suddenly stood erect and cried aloud that he wore the uniform of the Legion of Equality, that the colors of his sash were the colors of the new nation of Haiti, that he had been inspired by the Supreme God Spirit and that orders were transmitted to him from heaven by the white cock, still motionless at his feet. He cried forth again that the enemy was dying everywhere like fallen leaves, that the enemy's guns were only bamboo, that his own power could deflect the enemy's bullets, that those who followed him would be victorious, that they should kill all the enemy when the time came, that the signal to kill would be given soon. Then, in an instant, all became unearthly silent and Souvarine Petro chanted:

The family has gathered

Tell them we are here, eh!

The family has gathered

Tell them we are here, eh!

There is no more guinin

The family has gathered

Tell them we are here.

He continued to chant those words over and over until they seeped into my brain, my being.

Suddenly, I grunted and without warning found myself chanting the same strange words. Each one left my mouth like a cannon shot.

The family has gathered

Tell them we are here, eh!

The family has gathered

Tell them we are here, eh!

There is no more guinin

The family has gathered

Tell them we are here.

I could not resist the chant; it had taken command of me. Against my will, I continued to repeat it until my tongue went dry. My head felt light and my body became as weightless as a bird's feather. I was about to lift off into the air when a gust of cool breeze slapped across my face, and I woke as if from a deep sleep. And I awoke with a memory.

I recalled overhearing a Haitian soldier of my regiment speak the words of the chant to a group of his countrymen. He never once told what they meant but his voice was fierce. He spoke proudly of Guinin as the place where the souls of his ancestors resided. He spoke of Vodou and its great power and said that death would one day consume the white man's world.

I knew the chant was a call to arms, but against whom? And why is Guinin no more?

Family? What family? Who was gathering? The Haitians? Would the Haitians in our regiment rise one night in rebellion, cut our throats, and desert to their brothers and sisters?

Enough! Enough! Before me stood a road leading to death and destruction. I had no wish to see anymore! I ran away as fast as I could, confused with what I had just seen and Souvarine Petro's shocking part in it. He had a secret that I had almost learned. My comrades and I were in the grip of a frightful man. Woe to us!

Chapter 7

Jack's Story Continued

"**I**s you 'sleep, Jack?" It was Manby. His soft, pleasing voice floated over to my cell window, which was next to his. "Is you 'sleep, Jack?" I could imagine Manby as he spoke, his broad, flat face pressed tightly against the bars. I dragged myself over to my window and looked out. All I could see was Manby's big fists gripping the bars.

"Tell de rest o' yo' story, Jack," he pleaded.

I told him that I had no stomach to talk more about my past. I reminded him that evening was rapidly coming on and we should get our rest, for we would have need of it when we faced the judge advocate again. But then sadness flooded me. I had not realized until that moment just how much I longed to tell someone about me. I reached through the barred window, grasped Manby's hand, and said I would do as he had asked. And as the sun dropped behind Devil's Mountain, leaving the guardhouse in a darkening shadow, I continued my story.

When I was a youth, it was decided by my parents that I should enter the ranks of fathers. I was soon betrothed to a Margi girl. Like my mother, she was from the plains, west of the Mandara Mountains but near the area of Musa. She was very thin, as are all Margi girls. Her chest bore but faint traces of the breasts that would one day distinguish her body as a woman. Attached to the front of her iron girdle was a pretty apron made of strings of colorful beads. A single porcupine quill pierced the middle of her lower lip. She wore a simple necklace of small blue-and-white beads. Several iron and brass bracelets were wound tightly around her upper and lower arms. During the period of seclusion which marked the beginning of our betrothal, ochre was smeared over her body by a maiden friend each day, morning and evening. As was customary, I made annual presents of cotton grass, corn and string to her mother during the next three years. But I would never see her suckling our child.

It was at this time, when life held much promise, that death began to stalk me. One day, during a period of widespread famine, I stole some guinea corn from the village granary. I had to. My family was slowly wasting away before my eyes. Despite their pain my mother and father maintained outward calm, even sweetness, to steady us children. This could not go on. I could bear their suffering no more.

I was so anxious, so nervous when I stole the grain. My heart was pounding louder than the growl in my empty stomach. But once the deed was done I felt an immense sense of joy. My family would live, we would talk and listen to stories together; everything would be better.

This happinesss was short-lived. My crime was soon discovered and I was brought before the king. Because I had offended the gods and my ancestors, I was punished by *mafakur*, slavery. As a *mafa* I became an outsider, without identity and normality. All links to my family and ancestors were severed. But I was not expelled from my Margi community—that would be less humiliating. No, I remained in it, yet separated from it. As a marginal being, neither free nor true alien, I was at once a piece of the social order as well as a threat to it. I was despised yet tolerated, an institutionalized outsider, a necessary evil. I would live and die in this manner, always on the boundary, in the hem of society. The challenge of my existence became to find purpose and identity in what was for me a kind of limbo.

Because of my crime I belonged to the king. I knew that without him I had no separate existence. And so my basic need to exist, however flimsy that existence might be, drove me to establish myself as an essential member of the king's community. In that way I would have some status, some place. It was the only way to give meaning to my life under these circumstances. What is a life without meaning—even in limbo?

The king assigned me the hard task of maintaining the dry-stone terraces belonging to the royal village. At this I worked unceasingly, and quickly became quite expert. I soon rebuilt the crumbling terrace walls. On gentler slopes, I buttressed the lines of fascines holding back the earth with boulders and small mounds of earth. I performed much of the land-clearing with a billhook, a knife as long as my arm, sharpened along its length and on the inside of the sharp curve at its end. It was a tool that I soon despised since it was the enduring badge of my dishonor as a *mafa*.

Cattle, goats and sheep grazed these terraces. Their grazing was limited, so for part of the year they had to be confined to huts, where they were watered, fed and bedded down with weeds and grass. I collected their manure and carried it to the terraces, where I carefully scattered it around the plants of guinea corn, beans and bulrush millet. Human waste was also used to fertilize the soil and this, too, I gathered from the houses in the royal village and carried long distances to the terraces. My terraces were celebrated in Margi villages far and near for their construction, size, neatness and productivity. I took great pride in them. But still there was no end to my punishment and humiliation. My good works changed nothing. I was still a lowly *mafa*. I learned that there is no honor, no true reward in slavery. I was the victim of a curse!

One day the circumstances of my life changed dramatically. It happened during the time when the corn is taken to bins. I was about eighteen years old, and felt the strong power that comes with youth. I was returning from the village of Tur alone, on foot, when I was surprised and kidnapped by a party of Fulani slave raiders. They beat me and bound me with rope. There were already forty or fifty other captives in the coffle. All were males except for a lone Higi woman and her baby, whom she carried strapped to her back. I could easily identify each tribe by the distinctive patterns of their body markings. I recognized Buras, Pabirs, Katabs, Pitis and Ngamos.

One strange man fascinated me. His face and shoulders bore no tattoos. However, his teeth were filed to sharp points, like a leopard's foreteeth. I had never before seen anyone decorated in this manner. When he opened his mouth he was fearsome to behold. What was his tribe? And why would the Fulanis take this man? Surely no one would have him dwell in their midst; he might rise up at night, seize them and tear at their flesh with those sharp knives in his mouth. Perhaps the Fulanis had captured him when his mouth was closed. Still, at every opportunity I crept close to him and stared in utter astonishment each time he opened his mouth to eat or speak. I was to learn later that he was an Ivbiosakan from the northeast of the Benin region.

We were all linked together at the neck with a leather thong, a few feet apart, like a line of tethered goats. We ate, slept, rested and relieved ourselves on the ground a few feet apart. We were made to carry heavy loads, even the Higi woman, who bore her burden in terrible silence but with womanly calm. Some carried large elephant tusks. My load consisted of heavy sacks of corn. It was fitting that I should struggle under the weight of corn. I concluded that my burden had been chosen by the corn spirit whom I had offended by my theft at the granary. It was his clever way of revenge. The coffle traveled all the way from Margiland, southward along the great Benue River to where it meets the mighty Niger at Lokoja. From there we journeyed across the kingdom of Benin, to the port of Lagos near the great salt sea. We had traveled a great and difficult distance, lasting several moons.

It was there, at Lagos, that I was sold to a British captain. His long light hair, red complexion, strange language and violent manners filled me with unimaginable terror. He wore hair on his face and along the bottom of his chin. How uncouth and disagreeable this custom appeared to me. My body was crudely examined by his accomplices to determine if I was physically fit, apparently for hard labor. I was, of course; strength still blazed out of my body despite the hardships of the trek from Margiland.

The captain's canoe stood motionless offshore like a hovering phantom. What a huge and strange craft it was! It was longer and wider than any canoe I had seen before. I guessed that it was large enough to easily carry everyone who lived in my village, which was about two hundred and fifty people! It was stoutly built of wood and dark brown in color. I looked about for paddles but could see none. "How does it move?" I wondered. "There must be a hidden thing to push this great canoe forward in the water." Just then my eyes fell on three long poles that leaped straight up into the sky from the center of the canoe. They were tall as the tallest trees. And hanging from each were heavy-looking white cloths and a maze of ropes that resembled a spider's web. Here was a mighty thing of wood, cloth and rope, the sight of which filled me with astonishment.

I quickly discovered that this long canoe was a place of death crammed with many evil spirits. Offerings of corn have been known to appease the appetites of some evil spirits. But not these. They were bent on murder. Many of the human cargoes stuffed withinside the bowels of the long canoe died pitifully during the long water passage from their homelands to a new world filled with old evils. Their tortured bodies were casually thrown overboard by the crew, discarded like any other refuse. There was no ceremony. No one mourned their passing. No one would venerate them. Without graves no one would seek their assistance. No one would smash up their calabashes and pots at the crossroads in their memory. They would not be included in the annual feasts of all souls. No one would build altars of cylinders and cubes in their honor. And there were many of these unfortunates. For I later learned that my long canoe of death was but one of many thousands!

As a *mafa* I had been deprived of society, the one thing I wanted most in life. To die as a non-being in a squalid slave ship was unthinkable. And so, ceaselessly and intuitively I avoided death. I was blessed with the strength that comes with youth. But there was much more than raw energy that kept me alive. I forgot the past and the future and concentrated instead only on surviving the journey. Each death in the long canoe quickened my vital aliveness; the more grisly the death, the more determined I was to live. Each night I made the same journey in my mind: triumphant return to my home in a rich gown of green and gold, reestablishment among my kin, the king kneeling to my higher force. These images helped me survive the loneliness, terror, death and despair of my own middle passage.

If I was determined to avoid death it was not without a great struggle. My constant worry was that of falling asleep never to wake again. I feared that if I fell asleep my soul would wander away outside my body on a mission where it would meet with misfortune and never return. In this way sleep resembles death; it is the little death. Each night I attempted different ways of defeating sleep. On the first night of my water passage, I was constantly alert to my own existence, my own thoughts, my own sensations, and my surroundings. Every creak and moan caught my notice. There were no soft sounds; every noise was sharp-jagged and forbidding. I avoided sleep. But sleep is a mortal necessity, and from then on it defeated me night after night.

But it was not enough just to live. In the choking, sickening stench of the hold of the long canoe, I also had to keep myself from going mad. Judging from the screams and moans arising from the different sections of the hold, untold numbers of stolen Africans had already lost their senses. The bowels of the canoe breathed with their noises. At first I was drawn to them. By lying quiet and listening intently I quickly learned to tell the different sounds of madness. There was the abusing madness, the violent madness, the laughing madness, the babbling madness. There was also the madness of complete silence, when a person appeared listless and refused to speak. Except for breathing sounds, no other noises came from them.

Constantly listening to these sounds filled me with terror and very nearly caused my sense to leave me. They were like angry waves dashing themselves against me. Each wave broke over me but, like the great salt sea, wore away an ever so little piece of me. If allowed to continue, the rushing waves would one day roll unchecked over me and I would go mad. I had to keep myself focused on something that would block out the cries of grief, particularly at night when the evil of the hold—the moans, curses, intense heat, suffocating stench, the strange high-pitched laughter, the wails— closed round me and surrounded my body like a warm, sticky wind.

To block out the clamor of the hold, I tested myself out loud on the distinctive facial marks worn by the men of various tribal groups I had seen as a youth. "What are the decorations of the great Oyo nation?" I would ask myself. "Four horizontal cuts on either side of the mouth," I would reply. I would continue: "What badge did Hausas wear? Six horizontal cuts from the outside corner of the eyes to the mouth. And what of the Pabir? Six short vertical lines under each eye and six long vertical lines from the corner of each eye down to the jawbone. How are the Higi distinguished? Five . . . no four, yes, four short vertical lines under the eyes between the nose and the ear. What have the terrible Fulanis adopted as their emblem? The same marks of the great Oyo nation, but the cuts are of a . . . lighter stroke, not as deep. Recall the ancient decoration of the Bolewa? Six . . . no seven long lines down each cheek, seven more on each side of the forehead, two short cuts across each cheek to the nostril, and a main cut down the forehead to the tip of the nose. What tribes have similar marks? The Borgawa and the Abewa. Who are the most skillful decorators? The Kaje."

When I could no longer answer questions about the men of certain tribes, I tried to recall the decorations of the

women. "How are Pabir identified? By the distinctive manner of dressing their hair over a raised pad with a braided
lock of hair hanging down on either side of the head. What
other tribe bears a close resemblance to the Pabirs? The
women of the Bolewa. Describe the body designs of the
Baronga. Four triangles drawn under the breasts in the form
of a square in which the navel occupies the exact middle."
    Each night I played this game with myself until sleep
finally claimed me. At times, however, the voices of the hold
broke through. When that happened the waves of madness
again beat themselves against the coast of my mind. The
wash of each wave wore away at me. In the end I succeeded
in silencing them, and the feared abandonment of my sense
never happened.

    It began as just another desperate day. With the first
peep of dawn we were led out from the stinking hold to
exercise before we were given our unchanging meal of
boiled rice with a liquid covering of boiled salted fish and
water. The weather had become oppressively hot, so much
so that the ship's crew had spread awnings of sail-cloth over
the upper deck to prevent the pitch from boiling out of the
seams between the wooden planks. The vast sea stretched
away to the distant horizon in the same wide circle. I remember an unusual, faint scent that thickened the air. I also
recall that the color of the water had changed from deep
blue to a blue-green. The surface of the water was smooth,
and the big canoe cut its way through effortlessly, with
hardly any of the rocking and pitching motion that always
sickened my belly. Still the canoe leaned to one side, which
I found peculiar. I was often afraid that she would turn over
and go down beneath the water's surface. This prospect
terrified me since we were almost always kept in chains
below deck with the hatches bolted shut. If the canoe went

down, I thought, I would die trapped like a rat in a burning field, the water for my grave, this foul canoe my coffin. Death by drowning, what a horrible way to die, slowly, with plenty of time to struggle. During these moments of apprehension I looked into the faces of the crew. They seemed unconcerned as they went about their work, and I was somewhat comforted.

We were squatting in silence under the awning, fettered together like goats, when suddenly a voice above us cried, "Land discovered! Land ahead!" The crew stopped dead in their places and stood quite still. All sounds ceased except for the creaking of the ropes in the rigging and the smack and rush of the bow waves, which now seemed louder than usual. Then a second cry pierced the air: "Barbados! Barbados ahead!"

The crew, who only moments ago seemed unable to stir or exert themselves, suddenly darted around like frightened monkeys. A great shout went up from their throats, startling us. Their dispirited mood gave way to coarse laughter and excited conversation. Many began to sing in spirited unison as they eagerly went about their tasks. The canoe had been transformed by those simple cries, but we were ignorant of their meaning. As we watched, a section of the crew made for the deckhouse, a small shelter on the upper deck, and disappeared inside. In a few moments they tumbled out, stern-faced, armed with muskets and cutlasses. Jabbing at us with the points of these weapons, they herded us back down withinside the hated bowels of the canoe, back among the dead and dying and the wrenching stench of the overflowing necessary tubs. The hatches were slammed shut and we could hear the metallic click of the locks being fastened. Once again we were entombed, our fate at the mercy of strange, rough men and a rude sea.

It had begun as just another desperate day, except for those strange cries from above that clearly affected the behavior of the crew. We sat and waited for the next rattle of the hatches that would announce the arrival of our food. These harsh sounds were our only way of telling time in a world where our sense of time had been cut short, in a world where nothing could be taken for granted, in a world that forced the young to live as old men—awake at odd hours, asleep at odd hours. The simple rattle of the hatches gave stability to our lives, yet it was also a painful reminder of our internment, our misery.

Several hours passed. Nothing. Then my nostrils again picked up the distinct scent of a sort of perfume that gave substance to the air. It seemed to grow stronger by the moment. Suddenly we heard great roaring noises quickly followed by several loud crashes, as if large and heavy objects had fallen into the sea both before and behind the canoe. In a few minutes the craft slid to a full stop and straightened up with a soft jerk. In the faint light of the canoe's hold I noticed a lone figure rise up from the mass of huddled bodies on the deck floor and warily creep up to one of the small round openings cut into the canoe's side. We often peered through these holes to look at the watery waste of the sea in the hope of sighting land and to suck in fresh air to revive our worn bodies and spirits. No sooner had he thrust his face into the tiny opening when he screamed: "Vi dangu! Vi dangu! Vi dangu!" He was a Kilba man and as the language of the Kilba people resembles ours so nearly I knew at once what he had cried aloud: "Many houses! Many houses! Many houses!" I immediately leaped up from my living place on the damp deck floor and raced swiftly toward him, stumbling over bodies in the semi-darkness as I ran. When I reached the spot where he stood I brushed him aside and looked out.

Each object that met my eye was new to me; everything I saw filled me with wonder. The sight that greeted me was a blaze of different colors that hurt my eyes at first as I attempted to adjust to this sudden onslaught of bright hues: gold for the sun, white for the sand, blue for the sky, green for the lush, leafy vegetation, and red for the different flowers that interrupted the low green landscape. How deeply satisfying it was to see the land, and the land in color. Color is vital; it confirms the changes in time through nature, it gives form to time, it is the clothing of time. We Africans are always hungry for color and every color strong. Even African white is strong; it is stark and intense. The most simple African compound and village is a blaze of alive color. The constant grayness of the great salt sea and matching sky, and the dark and dreary inside of my prison on the slaver, starved my soul of the energy and vital aliveness that comes with color. How splendid it was to eat with my eyes once again and to nourish my spirit with the sight of rich, vital color, color made even brighter by the bold, golden sun.

"Where have I come to?" I thought, amazed at what I beheld before me. The water under the bright sun wore a beautiful yellowish-green hue. It was clear and deep, so clear that you could easily see the bottom and the plants that grew there in abundance. The canoe had come to rest close to shore in a wide bay crammed tightly with many other canoes of different designs and sizes. Most, like the one in which I was entombed, were a dull brown color, not unlike the Mandara Hills when the bush is fired and the repair of the houses begun. But others were great in height and had bulging wooden sides painted in several horizontal bands of colors: black, brownish yellow, lemon yellow, blood-red, deep and pale blue, and orange. Extending from the forward part of each canoe, great or small, was a colorful carved figure. One canoe's decoration was a large woman with shiny white skin and abundant breasts, whose nipples were the color of bright red berries. These figures appeared to be venerated by the crews, who could be seen cleaning and painting them.

Beyond the bay I saw large houses built of brick and stone, in levels, one on top of the other, and every feature different from those in my native land. The largest of these were clustered on the edge of the waterfront. The face of each was topped with a crown of steps and all were roofed in thin, bright red stones. Behind these, at some distance, were other strange-looking structures. They were wide and squat and built of large stones. Attached to each was a large wheel and tied to this were white cloths that caught the wind and went round and round in a circle. "How strange this unnamable thing is," I thought. "It is the result of the marriage of a house with a long canoe. What purpose does it serve?"

But what astonished me most was the sight of black people in plenty. I observed a number of men and women with face and body markings and from these I concluded that Africans of all languages lived here. And they were everywhere, even in small canoes rowed mostly by women. Carrying baskets of brightly colored fruit, milk, bread and vegetables which they intended to sell or barter, they swarmed around the larger canoes. A few of the men on land were obviously warriors, dressed alike in smart red jackets, white pants and black hats that reflected the rays of the unrelentingly bright sun. (For some reason these colors—red, white, black—stuck in my mind.) Flat-bottomed canoes loaded with silent black captives headed for the shore, rowed by other blacks. How did they all get here? Were they all slaves? Could I still be in the land of black people?

While I was caught in this astonishment, one of the small canoes came alongside, just beneath my window, rowed by a large black woman. Delicious fruits were part of her little cargo. She held up several bottles in her hand cried out many times, "No pay, no pop, massa!" Just then one of the crew was being lowered over the side to go ashore. From the smart fit and gold decorations on his uniform I concluded that he was an important person. As he descended, the same woman hollered after him, "Ah! Massa, Johnny Newcome, go back to shippy, too hot for 'im here, kill 'im." (When I described this landfall to him some time later, Sergeant Major Bostonian told me that the harbor was Bridgetown and that the low green land was an island, Barbados, in the West Indies.)

I resisted each and every attempt by the other stolen Africans to push me away from the opening in the canoe's side. In my determination to stand my ground, I gripped the rough metal edges of the window so hard I cut my hands. No matter. I kept my gaze fixed on the glimmering sight and sucked into my soul the superiority of color and form produced on this strange shore by the rich vegetation, by the many man-made creations of all kinds and by a warm African sun. Here I remained until it was almost full dark. As night rapidly closed in, I could still make out the town and the swaying palm trees in the fading violet light. Finally I surrendered my vigil to the unyielding pull of sleep. As I sank to the deck, one bloodied hand retained its hold onto the window, and to a wondrous view which restored hope to my life.

Was it all a horrible dream? Was some evil spirit playing tricks with me? I awoke the next day to discover that the bright vista of alive color and black people in plenty was nowhere to be seen. It had vanished! What greeted me from my tiny window onto the outside world was the sea. Once again I was seized with fear, the same wrenching dread I had known when the ordeal of my captivity began and time had ceased for me. I knew though, that fear was not useless. To survive one must be alert to danger's signals. One must know fear; it is a large part of reality. But fear is not enough for survival. Life would quickly whither away and die if nourished by fear only. Hope, too, plays a role in sustaining life. Without hope, without the chance to look forward with confidence to some fulfillment, life would have no meaning. The blue-green water and the faint yet persistent sweet odor of tropical decay that hung in the air gave me hope that land was just beyond that far horizon, and that this desperate passage would finally come to an end. Land was certainly near. It had to be!

I was thus prepared for what happened next.

At daybreak, only a few days after departing Barbados, as the canoe beat with difficulty against the strong wind, the same voice I had heard day before shrieked "Land! Land! Scots Head, Dominica!" This time I beat the little Kilba man to the round opening. What new wonders met my eyes. Straight ahead, just off the side of the canoe, an island appeared, pale purple and hardly visible at first against the low clouds. Then, as the canoe drew nearer, the land slowly changed colors as if by magical thought—pale purple to blue, then green with a lingering pale blue overtone, finally brilliant, dazzling green. As the canoe came abreast of the island, the land seemed to leap straight up out of the blue-green water. It was a land of towering green mountains, the peaks of which disappeared into low lingering clouds. The mountains formed a high ridge composed of a jumble of many cross ridges and valleys running in a confusion of directions. In many places the high ridge tumbled away in sheer drops to the waiting sea below. The whole was rugged and vigorously lush.

As the canoe crept lazily along the lee side, the wind having now dropped off almost completely, the island at first seemed welcoming, like a garden of lovely greenness with brilliant flowers and colorful hovering birds in plenty everywhere. But on closer observation the island was everywhere wet as though it had just risen from the bottom of the sea. The sheer cliffs rising from the shore were forbidding, while the towering highlands, half-hidden in a blanket of clouds, gave the island a mysterious aspect.

As the canoe continued to drift along, close to the shoreline, a village came into view, at first a pale line then a slender row of colorful assorted houses, some in stories, all at the very water's edge. The village was held fast to the shore by a barrier of sharp ridges which ran downward from the highlands like massive green arms. One of these ridges dominated the village. It was unlike the others. Its spiny top seemed to have been cut away, leaving a flat brown crest which contrasted sharply with the surrounding jagged green ridges.

There I observed a number of long, massive houses, also in stories. They appeared to be constructed alike and were set apart at regular intervals. All were painted a dusty light brown, the color of the sand at Lagos. A long pole stood in the center of these curious dwellings from which fluttered a cloth bearing some sort of magical design in three colors: red, white and blue. I could see only a few small canoes pitching and tossing in the open sea before the village. There was no harbor here, no opening in the land or projecting points restricting the progress of the sea as at Bridgetown, only a slender ledge of land that sloped steeply downward into the dazzling, blue-green water.

I must remark that the manner in which that frail piece of earth dropped so suddenly into the sea caused me to ponder the depth of the water under the canoe. Did the sea have a bottom? This frightened me. It was too vast. It was powerful, even when calm. It had a spirit I did not understand. Unlike the land, it could not be managed to do our bidding. I would never be comfortable with the sea.

The canoe slowly and silently glided past the village. No sooner had it done so when there was a grating noise at the hatches and they were thrown open. A welcomed rush of sweet, light air flowed down into the canoe's hold. The crew were soon in our midst, herding us like cattle on deck with coarse sounds and hard blows. As I made my way up the narrow steps and through the opening into day, I reeled violently backwards as if struck by an invisible fist. The full force of the unrestricted marvel of the island was astonishing. For a long moment I gripped the raised walls surrounding the hatch to steady myself. I slowly lifted myself out onto the deck, only to be enveloped by the awesome physical presence of the island. I was at once astonished and fearful. The island towered over the canoe, which now seemed so tiny and its human cargoes so pitiful. How insignificant I felt. The white newcomers to this island had named it Dominica. The ancient inhabitants, the Caribs, who I would come to know and admire, had a name more fitting: "WAI'TUKUBULI"— "tall is her body." As we were led to positions in the waist of the canoe, our eyes remained fixed on this bold and beautiful land.

When the crew was finally able to wrest our attention away from the splendor of the scenery sliding past, we noticed three large wooden tubs in the forward part of the ship's waist. Each was filled with the same thick, black liquid. The crew made crude gestures for us to stand and when we did they darted quickly among us, ripping the remnants of any clothing from our bodies. These were hurled over the sides as fast as they were torn loose.

A deep sense of loss instantly swelled up within each of us as we solemnly watched our tattered clothing float away in the track of the slaver. They were not mere bits of colored rags. Each bore some distinctive tribal color or design. The spirits of disease fled before *that* red cloth once carried proudly by *that* Yoruba man; the star over a crescent moon in *that* adinkra cloth worn by *that* Ashanti youth was a sign of faithfulness; the pair of interlaced curves woven into *that* panel cloth belonging to *that* Ejagham woman was the sign of love; the stool, double crescent moon, the large eye, and the rays of the sun in *that* rough country cloth was the Ashanti sign of the totality of the universe; the deep blue of *that* indigo-dyed cloth was *that* wearer's own personal midnight; *that* undecorated bokolanfini cloth announced to the world that the wearer was a poor Bambara man. Except for our flesh, our pieces of clothing were our last physical link with our homelands. And now they were gone forever.

In a few moments we were all stripped completely naked. Then, in threes, we were led to the tubs. The ordeal of the passage had taken its toll on us, the living. We were weak from the poor food we had to eat, our constant depression and our frequent inability to control our bowels, which added to the indescribable filth and suffering below deck. This ordeal showed in our bodies. Our skin had become ashen in color and *cra-cras* covered our bodies from face to feet. Our lamentable condition did not go unnoticed by the crew, who took measures to mask rather than cure our afflictions. They, of course, were encouraged by interest much different from our own. Our bodies were thus smeared over several times by the crew, from face to feet, with the black liquid in the tubs, a smelly substance I later learned was a mixture of gunpowder, oil and lime juice.

Every part of our bodies was dressed over, even the tops of our toes and the backs of our fingers.

Once this potion had been smeared on it appeared to rid our bodies of the *cra-cras*. It also gave our skin a smooth, black, polished appearance, rendering it fine and sleek. In this way we were made to look fit. After our bodies had been dressed in this fashion, we were made to stand about, naked, so that the liquid which enveloped us might dry. We were then handed a length of osnaburg, a heavy, coarse, cotton material. It was our first clothing, our first possession, in this new world. But it was a simple fabric. No African symbols distinguished it and gave it special powers. It lacked patterns of familiar blazing colors. In fact, it was a lifeless, grayish white, the sign of ashes, degradation and shame.

The hastiness with which we were stripped of our old clothing, smeared with some unknown liquid, and then dressed in coarse-grained white cloth shocked and confused me. Why this sudden concern for our flesh? Until this moment our bodies had meant little to them. They fed us just enough to maintain the breath-link between spirit and body. Coolly they watched as our bodies festered. Was this a trick of some kind? At first it seemed that these cruel creatures had suddenly become caring. Had they been moved to do what they did from a stirring feeling of mercy? Did some untapped gentle passion long asleep suddenly come to life and calm and sweeten their evil tempers? From the scowls on their faces they did not enjoy their contact with us. And the rough way they handled us spoke of a continued hardness in their hearts. No, their actions were inspired by some mean situation, not passion. I was certain of it. But what? What dark reason moved these pitiful white men? Few things in life are straightforward and simple, this unexpected interest in the outward appearance of our bodies being one. Then I had a thought. All of this reminded me of a Margi neighbor who, in the hope of selling a sick cow, dressed its withered skin with a paste of water, milk and the whitened discs of guinea corn stalks.

Rejoice! Miracles still happen! Sometime later that same day, as we captives sat on the deck, the slaver reached its final destination. After all our many perils upon a fickle sea, we were to stand once more on solid earth. No matter what dangers awaited me on yonder island, the thought of standing on the heavy soil filled me with great joy. Land was a wondrous place completely lacking in a single gross part. I cannot recall what o'clock it was, but the day I do clearly remember, for it was later stamped into my military record. It was 29 January 1799! I believe it was a *Hlumaws* (Friday) although I can not be sure. But January, being the first month of the European year, corresponds to *Slientang* the first month of the Margi year and the beginning of the wet season when the guinea corn is planted.

Portsmouth (for such, I later learned, was this place's name) was an even smaller village than the one we first encountered soon after sighting this island. It consisted of one lane running closely along the shore, with houses, a few in stories, peeping through a cover of leafy palms on both sides. As with the first village it, too, was restricted to a slender edge of land along the shore.

"But what manner of life exists here," I wondered, "squeezed tightly between the great sea on one side and the relentless presence of the bold land on the other?"

If the sea rose in fury it would dash the village and all life to pieces against the waiting mountains. This was life on the anxious edge. Who would wish to live in that manner? Here I was reminded of my own life as a *mafa* in my homeland. Although no single action in the landscape forced itself upon me—indeed, all was calm and peaceful—I felt a rushing sense of dread. I felt a need to act, but against what? The sea? The mountains? The crew? Was this an omen of some kind? Despite my uneasy anticipation, I looked forward to leaving this floating prison and living once again on land.

As the canoe headed straight for the shore, the crew became a whirlwind of activity. There was much shouting and much apparent confusion. But all of the crew worked as if one, as if some higher invisible spirit organized them to achieve the same desired end. My gaze fell on one man who was leaning over the side of the canoe with a long, twisted rope in his hand. At the end of the rope was affixed a weight of some kind. The rope was clearly marked at regular intervals with strips of colored cloth which served as some sort of sign. He let go the rope into the water by tossing it forward in the direction the ship was moving. "No bottom found!" he cried aloud upon reclaiming the rope from the water and studying it.

Closer the big canoe came to the shore, closer. My heart began to race as I considered the possibility of the canoe striking the shore. The anxious looks on the faces of the crew, the first time I had observed this condition in their features during the entire passage, confirmed my fears that disaster was about to overtake us. The man with the rope again let go and then hauled it back in, examining the strips of cloth and the bottom of the weight as he did. I watched him nervously as he repeated these motions, each one followed by a slightly different cry and each cry more excited than the earlier one. "Seventy-four fathoms—loose rocks!" "Forty fathoms—loose rocks!" "Twenty-five fathoms— loose rocks!" Then—"Fifteen fathoms—sandy bottom!"

"Let go anchors!" someone replied immediately. I heard the now familiar roaring sounds coming from withinside the canoe. There followed reports of successive crashes of heavy objects hitting the water at the front of the canoe and behind it. While this was taking place, crewmen darted high above the deck in the rigging, rolling up the large, heavy cloth sails that were used to trap the wind and thereby move the canoe forward in the water. In a few minutes the big canoe slid to a stop. I could feel it tugging against the ropes in an effort to break free and continue on its course to the shore. Soon the spirit of the canoe gave up this plan and resigned itself to a stationary rolling motion in the blue-green water.

We had come to rest in a big bay, a beautiful and noble bay, with the village of Portsmouth off to the right. On the rim of the bay, on the left, was a dramatic scene. Reaching far out into the deep water from the shore was an astonishing point of land. Upon my first observation, it appeared to stand free of the island. On closer inspection it was joined at its neck to the island by a low, flat area which was the nesting place of different colorful birds in plenty. Just past the flat area, the land rose suddenly into the sky to form two steep, high hills, an inner hill and an outer hill. Later I learned they were referred to as the Cabrits, the Cabrits hills. The Outer one was the larger and taller, being some six hundred feet in height. Viewed from the canoe, it had a round crest and a steep slope that plunged defiantly, almost straight down into the sea. The inner hill, which was some four hundred feet in height, was in the shape of a pyramid and sat on a narrow base. Between the two hills ran a narrow valley in a straight line from sea to sea. The surface of the floor of the valley was everywhere clear and clean. The slopes of both were thickly covered with trees and small bushes.

Beyond this leafy cover were many thickly made square houses, all built in stories of dark gray stone. Although of a different color, these dwellings instantly reminded me of those I had noticed earlier, perched high above the town on a hill with a flat brown top. A number of the houses were gathered closely together at the mouth of the valley where it overlooked the bay. They were in many sizes and shapes. Surrounding all was a high, thick wall that proceeded by sharp turns, much like the design made in the dirt by a snake in its travels. Windows had been cut into the sides of the wall through which ugly black cannons poked their forbidding mouths in my direction. And planted in the middle of all of this was a tall pole from which flapped a cloth with what appeared to be the same magical signs I observed earlier in this eventful day.

Completely dominating everything within sight was an awe-inspiring sentinal of a mountain. Its peak cloud-wrapped, it looked down its deep-green slopes to the town and bay below. I sensed its great active power and held it to be the home of strong spirits. When I learned that this wild, hovering rock before me was called Devil's Mountain I was not at all surprised.

Just behind the village of Portsmouth the constant ridges loomed abruptly and raced skyward, disappearing eventually into the sluggish cloud cover. I noticed several rivers and small streams beating down from the highlands on both sides of the village. One of these was wider than the others and entered the bay south of the little settlement. At the point where these slender flows of water met the bay, the water turned from pale blue to a dirty brown, a color which once again made me think of the bare Mandara Hills after harvest.

Many objects were not new to me at this time, but I was still filled with great wonder as my eyes took in every view. There were not so many big canoes here as at Bridgetown. And they were scattered across the wide bay. The very big canoes, however, those with cannons thrusting out of their sides, were all fixed in place in one section, all in a straight line. These great canoes seemed to occupy a place of honor in the center of the bay directly before the village. With their large cloth sails rolled up, the tall, bare, wooden arms from which the sails were hung gave the appearance of a forest of leafless trees growing upon the sea. Here, as at Bridgetown, the crews of the several canoes could be observed crawling over every part of them like busy ants in a frenzy of cleaning and painting. Every object met the same fate: the various large and small wooden machines on the deck, the decks themselves, the barrels, the ropes, and the masts. Even the cannons and round shot were smeared with fresh coats of black paint, in the manner of our bodies. The outer part of the canoes was not forgotten. I could see men busily painting while dangling over the sides on ropes like so many nimble spiders.

As I observed this activity, my eyes clapped on a thin line of black men marching behind a white man on a horse. They seemed to be coming from the direction of the two high hills on a narrow point of land. They moved with authority along the shore, heading towards the village. They were dressed alike in white pants, blood-red jackets, and large black hats.

White-Red-Black! This trinity of colors again struck a chord of memory in my mind.

Yes . . . I remember! The mystery of the three rivers: the rivers of whiteness, redness and blackness. They are the primary colors of life that are linked together. They are rivers of power flowing unceasingly from the great High God throughout the whole physical world, and they are given visible form in the white-red-black trinity. Proof of these powers is scattered throughout nature in objects of these colors. The white-red-black stripes down the back of the *nkala* mongoose sprang suddenly to my mind, as did the white-red-black horizontal bands on the banner of the Ndembu people and the white, red and black mud pillars—symbols of the personal cults of the Mbum chiefs. Then the words of my father followed:

"The only truth about the world is the three colors which are linked with primary values and substances. White: life, health, begetting, power, purity, semen, activity; red: blood, blood of all women, blood of mothers, blood of all animals, flesh, murder, illness, maleness, goodness, power, activity; and black: fear, evil, disease, darkness, secrecy, sexual desire, death, peace. These things are common to all mankind."

Behold! These three colors appeared together in the dress of these men of evident power. Whatever land this was, it was a land where these colors were honored. So my long passage over the dreary waste of the great salt sea had not taken me to a foreign world. No, I must be in some corner of the world into which I had been born.

Each black man carried a sign of his power, a long dark-brown stick. All seemed to be of middle height and thin, except one. He was a tall, large man. Unlike the others he carried a towering staff. It had a fearsome, shiny spearhead which the sun licked, causing me to blink and turn away. He carried this mighty spear as if his calculated desire was to impress those looking on. Even at that distance I could see that he hoped to stun. And he succeeded. It was clear to me that all of these men belonged to some special order or group.

The riding white man was certainly a ruler who exerted great power. But he acquired little or nothing of his force from the beast that he rode. This was clear by the unusual manner in which he sat atop the animal. All Africans who possess horses ride them in a special way. They show in their style of sitting that they can never be dismounted because their authority has been divinely ordained. Thus, they sit as one with the beast, tilted back and looking at no mortals but into the godly heavens in a glory of power. This white man merely sat on the horse as one would lay a calabash on an uneven stone. He was not part of the beast, he derived nothing from it. He sat awkwardly in his saddle, slumped forward in a sickly fashion. "Any evil spirit could topple him from the beast," I thought. As I looked upon this strange sight, this awkward blend of man and animal, I knew inwardly that his power had not been divinely called forth and therefore would not last.

As the group advanced upon the village, I perceived black people, and even white people, stopping in their busy movements and making way for this solemn procession of important persons. These men heightened my wonder. "Who are they?" I wondered. "Are they on their way to perform some ritual? What gods do they worship? How could one join their order?"

The smack of small canoes against our sides rudely ended my daydream of glorious membership. The babble of voices rising from these canoes also seemed to serve as a signal to the crew, who sprang suddenly among us and quickly shoved us into a long unbroken line all round the open decks of the ship. There we stood in silent ignorance, a human chain of blacks of every African nation. What manner of desires and needs drives these strange men to net so many different black men and women? No sooner had we been set in line and made to face outward toward the water when a swarm of white men of every description came up like an eruption from the water below and spilled through openings in the canoe's rails. In their haste to reach us, they knocked into each other and several tripped and fell heavily onto the wooden decks amid cries and harsh words.

I stood there, nailed to the spot, wondering why all this was happening. Why were all these crazed white men fighting to get on board this stinking, miserable canoe?

It seemed possible that these men would crash into me in their savage haste. I braced myself and held my breath when suddenly the surging crowd of noisy white men came to an abrupt halt. A man hidden by the crowd raised his red-sleeved arm high above the heads of the mob. His pink hand grasped what looked like a large bag of coins. The mob read in that sign an important message, for it was quickly smothered in a respectful silence.

Still holding the bag, the unseen man slowly moved his hand over the heads of the crowd until it pointed in my direction. That gesture caught the attention of the captain of the canoe, who quickly pushed his way through the crowd and seized the bag from the extended hand.

Clutching the bag, the captain emerged from the crowd. He shouted at the mob of white men which once again found its boisterous voice. Some of the men were angry and argued with the captain until eventually they all moved off, leaving me momentarily alone and wondering what had just happened.

Three men in scarlet coats now stepped up to me, out of the red glare of the sun. There is no way I can make known my astonishment when I beheld them. They were the same persons of obvious power I had observed earlier advancing on the village from the direction of the two high hills. Standing right before me was the white man who had been riding at the head of the line. On each side of him, but a step behind, were two large black men whose faces I quickly searched, without success, for some sign of their nation and language.

All were dressed in clothes of hot and cool colors. I remember how smart they looked. Such was the grandness of their dress that I believed them to be showing off. The blood-red jacket was opposed by pure white pants. On their heads they wore tall, round, very shiny black hats which were dazzling in the intensely bright sunlight. To these were fastened a white ribbon and a white-over-red feather. The white man had bound his waist with a rich, deep-red cloth, the ends of which came to rest at his side. From face to feet their dress was encrusted with metal ornaments, each with curious magical signs. Some ornaments seemed to be made of iron, others of bright gold.

The bright splendor of their costume gave them great advantage. It could not fail to excite the eye of every female beholder since it increased the manly features of the wearer. It would invade and subdue an enemy. It oozed with authority. Then, too, the general appearance of these black men was wholesome. Their skin had a healthy hue and no sharp bones protruded through their fine clothing. "Pray, they came for me," I whispered to myself. The white man gave a command and the black men turned as if of one body and spirit. They placed themselves on either side of me and we walked for a short distance along the waist of the canoe. Our tiny party went past groups of wrangling white men, who only moments ago had swept onto the decks of the canoe. In twos and threes other captives were being led away much in the manner I was. We reached an opening in the rail where we descended with some difficulty to a small canoe by means of a wood and rope ladder. The black rowers took no special notice of me and my escort as they moved the little canoe ahead to the waiting shore.

I jumped quickly from the boat as it nudged the shore and threw the clear water over my whole body to wash away the recent past. We splashed ashore except for the white man who rode through the surf on the back of one of the black boatmen. I worked my feet deep into the earth and could feel its soothing warmth work its way up into my body, renewing the fire that sustains life. *"At last! On land! On land!"*

We again formed into line, the white man, once more on his beast, leading the way. The course of our walk was toward the two high hills. Again my eyes took in many interesting things which flew at me with a rush and left me confused. There were black people in plenty as before. They came from all nations, but the language of a few resembled mine so nearly. They were to be seen everywhere and doing every task. A number were women who carried their children across the hip in the African way. I noticed one white woman carrying her child in this manner. She looked to be very poor. Were these black people captives? They did not appear to be since they moved freely about. A few of the black men even carried long knives much like those carried by the crew of the canoe. Many of the houses we passed were in stories. A few had walkways along the top with beautiful, decorated fences of wood. A sloping roof protected people who sat there from the hot sun.

The most striking thing that occurred to my notice was a group of people neither black nor white but of a yellowish-brown color. Who were they and what was their origin? From the manner and costly preparation of their clothing I did not believe they were captives. The women dressed their feet and bodies in the custom of white women. They fitted their feet into shoes with metal buckles and they wore many skirts, one atop the other, which gave them the appearance of having wide, meaty hips. Wound about their heads were many small cloths of different bright colors which they tied into a long turban. These, I recalled, were worn by women in Yorubaland when I passed through that place on my hard passage to Lagos. Some of them affixed a little red, black or yellow hat with a brim to these headdresses by means of a long pin. The hat was so very small it appeared as if it were made for the head of a child. Their whole appearance created a fancy, bright picture. They took no notice of me.

The village was now behind us, and our tiny band made its way along the shore in almost silence. The only noise was the steady crunch of the big black shoes the men wore and the sharp, regular stamp of the beast.

My imagination suddenly saw all the members of my family: my mother, my father, my sisters, my brother, and all the other members of our clan. I observed them in our peaceful fields of Margiland on the far side of the great water. I attempted to hail them in this remembrance, to see their faces and to let them know I lived still. But they did not stop in their tasks and look up. They went on without end and took no notice of me. A degree of horror over-spread me, and my remembrance came to an end with that discouraging picture.

Up ahead a group of black men stood in a clearing. Our band approached them easily. A few were dressed in the manner of the men in my party and they, too, looked smart and healthy. At their sides were fearsome weapons of the type carried by the crew of the canoe. They leaned on these as they talked among themselves. A little way off was a scene into which I was thrust bodily. It almost exceeded description for its gloom. Some twenty or thirty tall black men stood in two rows in complete silence. No one spoke. They looked to their front. They hardly moved any part of their bodies. The constant bites of the mosquitoes that swarmed about their sweaty bodies made no impression on them. They were ghostlike, these captives. Set in the face of each was a grave expression. Tied around the neck of each was a large piece of coarse white paper with strange writing on it. I was led to the front rank and shoved next to the end man.

Upon noticing me, one of the armed men approached. He looked carefully upon my face and left, returning in a few moments with another uniformed man. I recognized by the single line down the center of his forehead that he was a Kilba. I could understand his language!

"*Ga za ka da mina ka?*" (Are you ill?)

I lied. "*Au!*" (No!)

"*Naya Margi*" (You are a Margi.)

"*I,*" (Yes) I said proudly.

"*Ima kinga?*" (Where is your house?)

"Madagali," I answered with equal pride.

"*Wa hlim nga?*" (What is your name?)

For a moment I had to think what it was. Since my capture I had become nameless. I lifted my head fully. "Madu, *bzar ga* Mjigimtu *qa* Gadzama." (Madu, Mjigimtu's son, of the Gadzama clan.) The man looked ashamed and quickly cast his eyes down to the ground, away from mine. For a long moment nothing was said. He then pointed to a nearby gourd on the ground and said gently, "*Biti ada aku taku.*" (There is water in the gourd.)

I was curious as well as eager to learn who he was. I gathered my courage and spoke up. "*Hlirm daga yu zarzar ra?*" (What do you do every day?) "*Iya kwa-*" (I am a-) "I am a British soldier!" he continued, after a pause, almost in a rapture, and withdrew.

He returned with the riding white man and other soldiers. They proceeded to examine me attentively. They inspected me for my height. They peered into my mouth. One soldier counted the marks on my face by touching each with a little stick. I was made to jump up and down on one leg and throw out my arms in every direction. What they discovered from this attention to my body was relayed to a soldier who put it into a large book. When this was done he recorded the day of this inspection: "29 January 1799."

The white man studied the large book carefully and I observed him making signs on a piece of white paper. The Kilba soldier then stepped up to me and attached the paper to my neck with a string. "*Hlimnga* CONGO JACK!" (Your name is Congo Jack.) He repeated it. "*Hlimnga* CONGO JACK!" I was so taken aback and confused by this pronouncement that the meaning and sadness of the moment was to have its effect a short time later.

There was little left of the day. As the sky had begun to lose its light, the land, water and heavens became cloaked in a blue-gray haze. Our party made its way towards the high hills on the point of land. We followed the shore closely. The low, flat ground which joins the two hills to the island was altogether a foul, deep swamp whose emanations were conveyed to us by the wind as we passed it. The ground began to rise slowly as we reached the base of the inner hill. It also fell away sharply to our left so that we could look down without obstruction into the peaceful bay. Here, along this narrow track, we began to encounter small groups of black soldiers. Ahead loomed a massive, dark gray house with high, thick walls. It bristled with cannons and overflowed with soldiers. My destination was no longer a mystery.

It was now very dark as we made our way, with some difficulty, past the many strange gray houses and lolling soldiers. We continued to a point behind the houses where we came to a narrow, winding, steep path that took us to the top of the outer hill. When we gained the crest, our silent party was greeted by the rising moon, full and of a clear, bright copper color. It illuminated the sky and stained the dark empty sea with a shimmering golden path. The soldiers led us to a long stone house which we entered. It was poorly lit with candles, but in the moving light I could clearly see sleeping cribs on a wide wooden shelf running along the bare stone walls. Long wooden tables surrounded by stools filled the middle space. Black soldiers occupied one end of the room. They spoke in strange tongues and many smoked short white pipes. We were placed at the opposite end, two, even four captives in a stall covered with old straw. Here I quickly took my first sleep on land in a new world.

Very early in the morning, I awoke to much noise, hurry and pain. Soldiers swarmed among the stalls shouting and cuffing us about the head and shoulders in an effort to bring us quickly out of our sleep. I believed myself to be in the bowels of the filthy slaver and there set upon by the demon crew. Once I had recovered my senses, I, along with other recruits, was drawn up in a line before the cribs. We were all puzzled. Almost immediately we were made to strip off our clothes which were gathered from us and later set afire behind the house. We were then presented with new clothes.

How best can I tell you the effect my uniform had on me? Long white pants that gave my legs strength . . . thick wool jacket of a fierce red that made my chest swell . . . broad, black, crossed leather straps to contain my swelling chest . . . tall shining black shako with its white and red plume and decorations . . . was I still Madu, or was I Congo Jack?

After an inspection to discover that we had dressed ourselves correctly, we were led by several soldiers down the steep, winding trail up which we had labored the night before. Upon reaching the base of the outer hill we moved along a very narrow path which followed the course of the valley. In a short time we arrived at a wide open area, the four sides of which seemed to be of equal length. The surface of the ground was free of stones and unnaturally flat and smooth. Here the soldiers separated us into groups by language and the whole of us were made to form into a single line. Two men were placed next to me to form our group. One was a Higi man; the other was a Chibbak of my age.

The Kilba soldier, whose language was related to ours, took up a position in front of us.

As we stood in ignorant silence, the soldiers darted in and out among us. Their object was to impart to us the carriage and air of soldiers. They made us hold ourselves perfectly upright, facing to the front, shoulders kept back, the belly pulled in, the breast advanced, the arms hanging stiffly close to the body, the fingers extended, the toes out to form an angle.

During the activity and exertions of this preparation, I noticed out of the corner of my eye a great many lizards. They came in all sizes and were beautiful in color, partly bright green with a trace of gold and light purplish blue. I was amused to see them darting among the rocks that formed a rough border all round the open flat ground. The living scenery swarmed with them. Up and down the trunks of the nearby trees they raced without pause.

"ATTENTION!" a large black soldier yelled. I winced. The command was heard again and again as it echoed down the valley to the sea. The soldiers instantly ran to their places, some before the line, the others to the rear of us. The Kilba soldier fell in a few paces in front of me. He stood erect, rigid, and moved not a muscle. No noise was heard save the constant drone of mosquitoes in search of blood meals.

In a few minutes a solitary figure riding a horse came into my sight from the corner of my eye. Rider and beast moved slowly across my line of vision until they were directly in line with me but at a distance that made it impossible to make out the features of the rider. He then turned and seemed to head straight for me. He approached to within a few paces when the horse suddenly came to a rest. He was a member of this clan. He was a tall, slender white man with a sickly yellowish hue. He was dressed in the manner of the soldiers, except for a deep red cloth wound about his waist and a long straight knife on his hip.

Here was yet another mounted white ruler. He undoubtedly possessed a fearsome vital force since the soldiers became silent and stood without motion in his presence. As I looked upon him atop the horse, I thought of a courageous warrior. I thought of power and speed. I also thought of war. In a sudden it all came together. There could be no doubt now. I was in the company of warriors. I was to be a warrior. Bravery, obedience, loyalty and discipline would be expected of me. But I would be esteemed. Warriors are always esteemed!

He had come for the purpose of addressing us. His voice was unlike that of the soldiers. His was calm, gentle but firm, and barely heard above a loud whisper, or so it seemed. His address was broken into a number of short declarations. After each expression the soldiers would translate its meaning to the recruits in their charge.

"Soldiers! Fortune has favored you.

"You have been selected to serve as British soldiers in His Majesty's Eighth West India Regiment.

"British soldiers have covered themselves with honorable distinction.

"It is by the courage of the noble British soldier that commerce can extend its benefits to all in these islands.

"It is by the bravery of the noble British soldier that justice can be equally distributed.

"The pernicious doctrine of liberty, equality and fraternity of revolutionary France will forever by destroyed by the courage of men like yourselves.

"As British soldiers you will have the honor of protecting our negroes from the evil influences of the Haitian Revolution.

"Calm and security will once again be restored to these islands.

"Soldiers! You have already begun your passage into the regiment.

"The honor of a new name has already been conferred upon you.

"Today you will continue that passage by observing those negroes fortune has not seen fit to bless.

"Observe carefully! Take in every sight!

"Soldiers of the Eighth West India Regiment! I have the honor of addressing some events connected with the history of the corps.

"The regiment was first raised in 1795 but disbanded in 1796.

"The regiment was re-raised in 1798 at a most stirring time in the war against tyrannical France.

"The men were provided by the Loyal Dominica Rangers, a corps of faithful blacks drawn from this island.

"You will have the honor of serving alongside these men.

"I hope the time is not far ahead when you shall be called upon to face honorable danger.

"Soldiers of the Eighth West India Regiment! I feel assured that all of that time you will do honor to the uniform you wear and to your new king."

The address was over. Rider and horse turned about and returned the way they had come. In a few moments they were out of sight.

I will not pretend that I understood everything that was said. In truth there was much that confused me. "What was liberty and equality," I asked myself. "What was the Haitian Revolution?" "France?" "Negroes?" "Who was this king with emissaries who all rode horses?"

The soldiers returned to life, and our party was soon made to march back along the main track between the hills in the direction of the fort. There, ahead, was a large gray house in two stories. It was imposing, made entirely of large blocks of stone. Two black soldiers guarded the entrance. A single horse, the same one that carried the white soldier who had addressed us a short time earlier, was tied to a wooden stake before the house. At a branch in the track where I noticed black people baking bread, we turned and proceeded downward around the base of the inner hill, past the Cabrit swamp and along the road to the town.

The column turned north and headed into the interior of the island. We proceeded up a broad river valley and I noticed how the land had been turned into fields and how these had been marked for planting. On the far side of the river, from whence we had just come, I sighted something I was not prepared for. On the steep slopes of the hills that tumbled down to the river, the land had been leveled into what appeared to be drystone terraces. In height and design they resembled closely those I had constructed and maintained in my homeland. They extended around every spur. On the earth between these terraces were row upon row of small trees, the branches of which were being picked for some unknown fruit by small groups of black people. This view was like entering a special dream, one that brought immense sensual memories of my lost homeland: the thin dusty hill soil; the scent of fresh cut grass; the gritty feel of seed corn; the muffled stamping of my mother's feet on the hardened earth; the distinctive body odor of my father; the sharp stench of animal dung. It was difficult to leave this dream but earthly matters demanded my return to the everyday world.

Still, the land held fast my attention.

The soil was clearly rich and fertile, and I had the strong sense that crops grew quickly. Here I felt close to the elemental forces of nature. The cultivation also had all the signs of long-term human occupation. Yet there was something very new about this land. Those parts that had not been farmed made me believe that the creation of the land had not been long ago and that no human foot had ever before stepped here. The land simply oozed with the vigor that comes only with youth. "Could this be how my homeland looked when it was born?" I wondered.

The beauty of the land was not confined to its deep green freshness. Noble were the vast woods which covered the island down to the water's edge. I noticed on the dark humid floor of the forest many seedlings beginning their long journey skyward. But the forest was also thick with trees that grew to great heights and overtopped everything, interrupting the flow of warm air from the sun. And in rising into the heavy fogs they trapped moisture which fell constantly from their leaves to the land below. The damp and chill which I felt in this valley was no doubt occasioned by these woods.

We had been making this journey in a constant light rain. The lightness of the falling water gave it the appearance of a rain shadow. As we made our way higher into the valley, our party was subjected to heavy downpours which occasioned us to seek shelter. We finally gained cover in a dark cove formed by the coming together of the upper branches of several enormous trees. No sooner had we placed ourselves into the protective interior of this leafy cave when there arrived on the road we had just abandoned a traveling group of whites and blacks. They came down from the highlands at great speed. The white men and women were all riding horses; running alongside each and holding on to its tail was a black man. Each slave was weighed down with a large wooden box which he carried on his head. Some blacks even carried a glass with liquid in one of their hands.

The slaves held onto the horses' tails to keep pace with the riding whites, who took no notice of their uncommon efforts. The whites seemed determined to reach their destination and thus escape the heavy rain. They thundered past and down into the valley, with the black men somehow keeping up. I followed the course of this odd caravan until it had disappeared from my view around a turn in the road, the blacks still keeping pace. This way of traveling was a frequent sight all over the West Indies. I later learned that the blacks kept pace for the purpose of giving drink to the whites on the road and to provide them with fresh clothes when they reached their destination.

The heavy rain gave way to a rain shadow, and our party continued on its way in silence.

In the course of this day we passed by a number of large estates. On each was a great plenty of society, nearly all being black people. While passing these farms I noticed many interesting things. My attention was first arrested by the manner in which the houses of the black people were made. They were built in the African style. The houses all seemed to be made of mud walls with peaked roofs thatched almost to the ground with what looked like dried grass. The houses were shaded from the heat of the sun by neat rows of coconut trees. Upon closer inspection I noticed that all of the dwellings were built separately and in straight rows. None were connected in the Margi style, with flat-roofed enclosures of dried grass matting. I was curious to learn if these houses contained areas for storing grain, which is the custom in all Margi houses. Since I was some distance from them I was not able to observe their interiors.

My eyes swept each village for signs of human life. What I discovered was the same for all. I saw little children and a few old people, for the young and the strong were all toiling in the nearby fields. On one estate, men and women were all together, in a single long row, like a file of soldiers. They were all naked, men and women, save for a small piece of white cloth wound about the loins, brought up between the legs from behind and secured before. They all wielded hoes, which they moved as one, first throwing them high above their bare heads into the air. CRASH! The hard report of the hoes striking the ground together suddenly ended all conversation in our party.

As they labored in this manner, I could hear the women singing some sad songs which were answered by the men. I believe they sang in this manner in order to soften their hard labor. What I noticed next confirmed this view. At their backs stood several black and brown men. Each wielded a long black whip. They were ugly and frightening to behold even at this distance. A hiss and snap! A black man had applied the lash across the back of one of the *mafa*, the reason for which I was unable to discover. My body shuddered. Another hissing, snapping sound. Another lash bit deeply into the naked flesh which brought forth piercing cries and lamentations. Again my body shuddered. Despite these instances of inhuman punishment, the singing never ceased. In fact, the singers seemed to respond to each hiss and snap of the whip with songs that were louder and more defiant. I stood staked to the ground, stone-like, a witness to this horror.

The column moved on past those wretched people whom I was determined to forget. I sighed deeply. But before I had gone more than a few paces I saw her. She was standing alone among the slave gang, dirty, with a bit of cloth around her waist, but I quickly saw her beauty. I could see nothing else. At first I could not believe my eyes. She glanced only once in my direction, sending a ripple of delight and excitement through me. On we marched and she was gone as quickly as she appeared. My mind was instantly filled with thoughts of her. Where did she live? Does she have another man? What has she endured as a *mafa*? Was she born on this island or stolen like me? What was her name? I easily imagined every detail of her body. What nameless pleasures and depths did it hide? What an age it seemed since I last felt the promise of such warm sensations. I longed to see her again. The words of a Margi song darted into my thoughts and I sang it again and again to myself as we marched along the road. It made my skin tingle.

She stood there in the first spring moonlight
She stood there on a night of soft mists
She glances at you then she averts her eyes
That look can cause a rush of feeling
That look can cause a rush of feeling

Her beauty drives out the darkness
Her every move is like a dance
All agree she perfumess the air
She is everlasting - real - eternal
She is everlasting - real- eternal

You send a message with the clouds
That your love is strong and true
You pray the time of union is fast approaching
You are struck by the arrows of love
You are struck by the arrows of love

But when she disappears from view
And night seems like an endless fever
You will think your life is over
With only joyless days to come
With only joyless days to come

But still she lingers in your thoughts
You can feel her slender arms around your neck
Her radiance drives out the darkness
With the joy that's on its way
With the joy that's on its way

The column continued its march. Everything along our route was new to me, of course. The island was a lush garden with a deep, sweet scent of primitive beginnings. But I could not get that nameless girl out of my thoughts. The awful yet pleasing solitariness of the vast woods only encouraged me to think about her.

We went through a long stretch of trees with enormous girths. Their spreading boughs extended far around and could easily protect hundreds of people from the heaviest rains and scorching sunbeams. Here and there were quiet pools where we halted and drank our bellies full. Each turn in the road brought a scene more majestic than the one before. Single trees dressed out in several different leaves. Wild vines, as thick as ropes, fastened to the branches of trees. Birds singing and chirping. It was a beautiful land.

The day was still young when we walked up a narrow valley. A sharp turn at its head brought the column to a crest on which stood a large house. Very near this place we came upon a melancholy scene. A group of slaves, men and women, were employed in lifting enormous stones to build a fence alongside the road we traveled. Their industry was encouraged by the cruel hiss and snap of the whip. In the middle of the road, no more than a few arm lengths from me, a huge, brown slave driver flogged unmercifully the motionless, shrunken form of an old black woman. With each snap of the lash across her naked back and legs rivulets of blood burst forth from her skin, which bore the raised marks of past beatings. The burly driver cursed and lashed her repeatedly to get her to stand. Hiss! Snap! Hiss! Snap! He was fully committed to this disgusting duty. His naked feet gripped the ground for balance. He appeared to summon all the power of hell in his movements. He flung the trunk of his body back and then quickly forward much like the whip he brought behind and then flung forward, laying on each stripe with great determination. Hiss! Snap! Hiss! Snap! Not a single murmur came forth from the pitifully slight, crumpled black form in the road. It was unbearable that she uttered not a sound. If only she could let escape some of the great misery she had to feel.

I don't know what her offense was. Was it her inability to move those giant rocks? It must be that! But how could this old woman, weakened by age and abuse, perform this labor? What manner of madness would insist on the impossible? What infernal system would cause one human to become blind to the humanity of another? Was she not more than a beast laboring in the field? Was she not someone's daughter, perhaps someone's mother? Disgust, rage, horror, frustration all welled up in my breast. I wanted to dash the whip from his hand. I wanted to kill him slowly and brutally. I grieved for this person I did not know. Yet, I did nothing. I stared at her misery and did nothing. I was sick at heart. But I did nothing. I had been tested and failed. Why? I must confess—I might have lost the precious membership in my new tribe had I acted. There! The ugly secret is revealed!

"FORWARD!" yelled one of the sergeants. "MARCH!" I welcomed this command to action. I no longer had to face my own cowardice. I looked back. The driver had given up his futile quest. The body of the old woman was alone in the road, motionless and unattended.

Later in the day, on our return to the Cabrits, we approached the place of the flogging. As the column passed the spot my glance fell on the woman still lying in the road.

Her body no longer bled. There was the stillness of death about her. Where pools of her blood had once formed, only dark stains could be seen in the ground. She was as worthless as the bits of my clothing that had been torn from me on the slaver and thrown casually into the sea. She was but dirt.

I now realized what I had escaped by being taken into the army. The warrior does indeed seal his devotion to his trade with his life. If he avoids death, he must face wounds, perhaps life as a cripple or a beggar. These are facts and facts are stubborn things. But the soldier also has the chance to win honor for himself and to be honorable in the eyes of others. With honor comes a certain measure of power, even for a black soldier. I had already observed this link when the white people stepped aside for those black warriors—now my comrades—in Portsmouth on the day of my journey's end across the great salt sea. Yes, it is true that a white man on a horse led the way that day. But the thirst for the ruin of the black soldiers was not primary or even secondary among the watching white people that day. Why? The black soldiers had adopted great pride as warriors which they never ceased to demonstrate. I observed this in the smartness of their dress, in their air and carriage as soldiers, in the confident manner in which they spoke—even in the presence of whites— and in the way they wielded their fearsome weapons. All this bespoke of their authority. They were a force to be reckoned with, however much they went unsaluted and were despised as black men. The white people accepted the authority of the black soldier, however grudgingly. They knew instinctively of the terrifying time-honored way of angry warriors: rampage and looting. They understood the power of the black soldier to help or hurt them. The connection between honor and power is unbroken. It is direct.

There was no honor to be gained outside the world of my regiment, only dishonor and agony. And without honor there can be no power. The farms were mere places of misery, cold violence and, eventually, physical death. Is this not so? Were they not each laden with ill-fated male and female blacks who were regarded as mere beasts insensible to pain and fatigue? Look, there, in the road! Look hard at the body of the old, decrepit black woman. Consider the constant tyranny of her life. Dare gaze at her back. One continuous sore, new wounds upon old scars. Stare at her frail body. Bowed down with misery and hard labor. She has finally found her only repose as a slave—death, a violent and dishonorable physical death. Truly there was nothing banal or escapable about the evil of slavery. This experience seared me!

At last my story had run to its end. I believed Manby was happy because I felt that my story had been a good thing for him. And that was enough for me. But these remembrances had exhausted me. I flung myself down on my cot. I needed the peace that I found in the welcomed smells of a West Indian night, cool, damp, earthy aromas from the tilled fields mixed with the pungent smoke from a thousand secret breadfruit fires. As a salty sea breeze blew away the scent of cooking and glowing coals, I began to drift into sleep.

Chapter 8

Dialogue of Love

Jack:

It is the male who attracts the female, not the other way around. Even if he remains quiet, he cannot be ignored, the female will become excited. The male does not have to wiggle to give her the idea. This is an ancient truth.

Her name was Jubba Lily. She was standing quite still when I first observed her. She did not take notice of me as I stared at her when our column passed on its way through the high woods. I was very careful not to let her notice that I was looking. She stood there with her troop of male and female slaves. They were all naked, male and female, down to a simple girdle. I couldn't take my eyes off her. She assaulted my senses just standing there and made me feel hot under my uniform. She was the most sensual creature I had ever seen. No one who saw her could fail to forget her, nay, could fail to notice her. My eyes traced the curves and hollows of her body. She was young, at least the age of twenty. She had a pretty face with large challenging eyes and a full mouth made for kisses. I imagined that if she smiled it would be a strange, beguiling smile. She was lean with a stomach as flat as a skin stretched taut over a drumhead. Her legs were long and supple. But there the leanness ended. Below her wide, smooth, black shoulders were the arrogant breasts that came only with youth, high, round, full globes that rose to peaks well in front of the rest of her body. Further down her hips flared provocatively from a small waist. I imagined those insistent hips rolling with a grinding majestic rhythm when she strolled. It had been so long since I wanted anything. But as soon as I saw her I wanted her with a fervor that nearly approached madness. To want is to be alive and she made me want. Despite all this there appeared to be a hardness about her, no deep womanly weakness and softness. Although she was only a field slave, there was an air of power about her. I found this somewhat troubling. Nonetheless, I lay awake many a night imagining the joy to come and relishing the fact that it would come to pass for I had the power to make it happen. In an instant of seeing her I intended to make myself known to her at the first opportunity.

Jubba Lily:

How like a man to regard a calm and unmoving female as being a passive thing. How childlike he was to believe that a female could not be enterprising and still, all at the same time. When will men discover that it is the female who attracts and chooses. I was practiced at these arts. I had to be in order to survive a lowly life as a common field negro. Not possessed of a light-colored skin which might increase my value and get me into the great house and a trade, I was condemned till I died to toil away my life in these fields like a beast. So my natural ability to know things was as sharp and strong as my body, which was everything to me, a kind of fleshy tool it was. Of course I took notice of him that day, but I did not let him know it. I saw him stare at me with eyes hot and hungry. I acted as if I did not see him. I was dirty and naked. I was not ready. I would choose the moment of our meeting and that would be when I was fit and in my fancy dress.

It was in Portsmouth when we first met, although Jack did not know it. It was on a market day and I had gone there to sell provisions as was my custom. It was in June when I and several other negro women were discussing the coming of the hurricane time. "June, too soon; July, stand by; August, come it must; September, remember; October, all over," we used to sing together when things went slow. And there he came, strutting too bad in his fancy, tight uniform, almost listing from side to side like a boat in a high wind and feeling so well in his effort to attract us women. I took cover and observed. I was still not ready to make my appearance.

Jack:

I embraced every opportunity to pass the estates where she toiled in the high hopes of seeing her. Each time I passed I became stiff and awkward, whether I saw her or not. I did not know her, yet I loved her, or so I thought. It was a real love such as I would die for, or so I thought. But how could I feel this way? No matter, I was swept along by a strong physical feeling deep withinside of me.

Jubba Lily:

He was tall, just under the six foot mark. His face was decorated with tribal lines. His dark eyes and the shape of his full mouth were marked by a forceful expression. Smiles danced easily and often across his open face. Yet his eyes spoke of unhappy places withinside him. Jack saw a coldness in me and would insist that the order to love was as intense withinside all people as the command to hate. This made an impression upon me. I did want to love him and know his heart and his secret thoughts. To this task I did set my heart—eventually. But most of all I wanted to breathe the sweet air of free life. I wanted this above all else before I died and became an ancestor. Jack alone could give me that.

Jack:

I would splash in my sleep while dreaming of her. Too long my passions had been trapped withinside of me, freed only in dreams.

Jubba Lily:

No doubt he turned his pillow over so that I might have the same dream of him.

Jack:

Merry noises! Drumming sounds! Music! Raised voices! Tap-tap, tap-tap went the hand drums and stick drums. The sharp chatter of the calabash rattle filled the air. A crowd of brightly dressed negroes singing and dancing to the strong beat of the drums. Two dancers withinside a ring of noisy spectators went through their paces on the wide stone platform used for drying coffee. I made my way through the crowd and there I saw her. Jubba Lily! She was one of the two dancers. She was clad in a bright jacket and many printed petticoats like the dress of white people, and the head-tie and gay cotton colors of Africa. She danced in supreme excellence in the manner of my blessed mother. Head bent slightly forward, elbows erect and pointing from the side, solemn face, crouching, she moved her whole person without lifting her feet from the ground. Our eyes finally met and for a long moment we exchanged a deep and earnest gaze.

Jubba Lily:

He strode towards me in his strong and smart-looking uniform. I allowed our eyes to meet and by my manner encouraged his approach.

Jack:

Our eyes met. She looked into mine without flinching.

I placed myself between her and her negro partner. She responded and we danced together. When we had grown tired, we footed it.

"I am Madu, son of Mjigimtu, but here, in de West Indies, I am called Private Congo Jack."

"How dee! Me is Jubba Lily."

"I sees yuh often here 'bout, Jubba Lily."

"Dat so?"

"True!"

"How long so, Private Jack?"

"Long enough, too long enough. Yuh be often in me dreams."

"Me in yuh dreams wid consequence, Private Jack?"

"Wid consequence, Jubba Lily, wid consequence."

"Dat so?"

"True, Jubba Lily."

"How is it yuh here now, Private Jack?"

"I wish to see yuh, to know yuh well, Jubba Lily."

"Dat so? Yuh tell lie!"

"Certainly not, by de help of de great High God it be true, Jubba Lily."

"As de king's soldier, Private Jack, yuh must got woman plenty everywhere. Dat so?"

"Not so. I got no connection wid different woman 'bout. But I could find a place in my heart for yuh, Jubba Lily."

"Ah com. Dem say here 'bout dat if yuh play wid girl widout serious meaning, yuh would be beaten up too bad some dark night."

"All I say be true, Jubba Lily."

"Yuh have serious meaning for Jubba Lily."

"True, Jubba Lily."

"Yuh don't make mock of me cause I simple negro who toil in de fields?"

"Certainly not, Jubba Lily."

"Dat leaves me well. Dat leaves me very well."

"I no like anybody like yuh. Ax any soldier at de Cabrits, dem tell yuh same. Do yuh feel some ting in yuh heart for me, Jubba Lily?"

"Me need time to tink 'bout dat as me no know yuh, yuh know."

"But what 'bout negro man yuh dance wid? 'Im looked crossed when we footed it."

"Hamlet? No mind he. 'Im only simple field negro."

"Come, Jubba Lily, le' we go to love matters, le' we love."

"No, le' we wait longer, it will serve to heighten our pleasure."

"No, Jubba Lily, come, le' we go."

"Arright, then le' we go if yuh have a mind to."

"Le' we go to yonder cane piece."

"No! Dat no place for we to make love. Dat is where only sorrow grow, watered wid de blood of poor field negro. No! Le' we go to the river bank where, in de moon's whiteness, our minds will lif' free of our bodies and where I may wash me self and believe me self free."

Jack:

She uttered a soft cry but not one caused by hurt. At long last I found expression for my passion. I was happy.

Jubba Lily:

He was gentle and gave me true joy. He did not boast. He was not rough like all the others.

Jack:

Each time I saw her was like entering a dream.

Jubba Lily:

My life as a field negro as a whole was mostly one of sorrow. There have been moments of rough pleasure. This connection with Jack was one which I intended to stretch.

Jack:

It is true, the command to love is deep. Slavery had not destroyed it!

Jubba Lily:

That may be true, but the command to be free is as deep, if not deeper.

Jack:

That negro Hamlet still worries me. I could plainly see from the hurt in his looks that he and Jubba Lily had a deep and long connection. I do not believe I have seen the last of him.

Jubba Lily:

Hamlet would not step 'side, quiet like, when I told him I had plans to connect with Jack. He threatened to make it warm for Jack and he went to a stinger who helped him try to get back my love.

Jack:

One day someone left food in the barracks for me to eat. Cuffy, who is always hungry, ate it and nearly died.

Jubba Lily:

I made Jack wear a skin guard around his neck. It was a little sack of hairs, feather, sulphur and dried ants. It would protect him from all kinds of harm. I made him take it off only when we made love so that its powers would not be spoilt.

Jack:

That negro Hamlet was spreading rumors about Portsmouth and on the ships in the harbor that we African soldiers would be sold as slaves as soon as the war against the French was over. He claimed that our fatigues in the swamps alongside the Inner Cabrit was only a trick to see if we could do negro work. This made us all uneasy.

Jubba Lily:

Hamlet was vexed. He had a blood lust. He was determined to catch Jack's shadow and impale it.

Jack:

There is an exciting rumor about that the army will purchase African women and attach a number of them to every black regiment. Each woman will be at liberty to choose a husband from among the most well-behaved of the soldiers. I asked Captain Cameron to look into the possibility of the regiment purchasing Jubba Lily from her owner. I am much attached to her and in this way we can form a permanent connection and have normal domestic happiness, such as I remember in the home of my father and mother. It is also rumored that the plan makes provision for the children of soldiers and their women.

Jubba Lily:

The owners of the estates are behind this plan, some say, as a way of keeping the black soldiers from raiding the estates in search of female mates. No matter, it provides a sure way for Jack and me to be joined. I would become the property of government and thus escape the field and slavery. Then, too, becoming a soldier's wife is the only way I would think of having pickanee, who would also be the property of government. Pickanee born of slave become slaves. It is the law here that slave parents pass on slavery to their pickanee. How that is so I never understood. One day I asked my owner where does slavery exist in my body. He had no answer. But I did. Slavery is not in my body. It is in the minds of the slavers. This business of slavery proved to me that one can believe anything one puts their mind to. Is not the human mind an amazing thing? It can be made to believe in things that aren't.

You know, Jack, that marriage is practiced by buckras only. The field negroes accept this as law. They have come to believe that it is silly for woman to be under one man. They will say that I think I am as good as a buckra. They will mock me for sure. Still . . . I will not object if you think it is a good idea. Perhaps it will be worth it for me too. It will put an end to rape and a multitude of buckra men dropping their seed in me at will. It is you I love. But it is freedom that I love more.

Chapter 9

The Trial: Attack and Parry

At the beginning of this second day's proceeding, the judge advocate cleared the room of all of those people cited to appear as evidences so as not to permit them to be present during the examination of any of the previous witnesses: "All who are named as evidences, and who may chance to be present here, are to retire at once and not to enter the court till such a time as they are officially summoned to be sworn." As I was to learn later on during these proceedings, this was done to protect the purity of the evidence by discouraging witnesses from testifying wrongly. "Are not the laws of the English doubtless very wise and good?" I thought.

On this day Hamlet was present in court. He looked pitiful wearing his coarse and worn osnaburg work clothes. He looks and moves the field negro, I thought, dull, defeated, sluggish. He was in the room well before his appointed time to give evidence, as his mark appeared at the bottom of the list of witnesses of the judge advocate. No doubt he was in a hurry to testify against us and thereby put a nail in our coffin. He was filled with vicious hatred for us, particularly me. In truth he looked disappointed when one of the guards escorted him out of court.

When the heavy door had closed behind Hamlet, a hush fell in the long room. I could feel the moment of some drama was here. My eyes swept down the room towards the court. They, to a man, had turned their eyes to the judge advocate.

The judge advocate, who had been sitting, rose slowly from behind his table and drew himself up to present his opening speech to the court. There was no trace in his bearing of the embarrassment he had suffered two days ago. He showed complete confidence in his own grasp of the situation. In fact he made a point of calling attention to himself. Smiling boldly (yet falsely, I thought), he deliberately cleared his throat, exchanged long looks with members of the court, and pulled and tugged at his tunic until he was finally satisfied that all was in order. Then he spoke politely with great precision:

"Lieutenant Colonel Owen Watson and officers of the court-martial, although you are met here together upon a most important occasion, the subject is much too painful for unnecessary details, and the sad events are too recent and too deeply impressed upon the memory and the sentiments of every man and woman in this command to require that I should take up much of your valuable time by reciting a full description of the shocking and unparalleled event in opening these charges. I must, however, remark that the cruelties exhibited during the recent mutiny were enough to rouse a dead man to rage. Nay, they were enough to make even devils weep. May we hence not have to learn again to what a pitch of depravity the human mind may go if allowed to fill up the measure of its iniquity. This is an awful commentary, gentlemen, but if all the evils that lurk in the hearts of men like these were permitted to break out again, in an event like this, what a field of blood would our dominions exhibit!

"It is needless to tell you that the several prisoners at the bar are that party of soldiers belonging to His Majesty's Eighth West India Regiment, a negro corps, who from the 9th to the 11th instant were induced from some cause or other to mutiny at this post. Let us assume for the moment that their cause was just. Can any person justify killing in the name of justice? I say nay! The laws governing the actions of His Majesty's forces, gentlemen, lay a restraint on the passions of the troops, that no soldier shall be the avenger of his own cause even though that cause may be just. If a soldier might at any moment execute his own revenge, there would be an instant end to law in the army and society.

"The charges are indeed solemn and important, no less than whether His Majesty's army will remain loyal and do its duty in accordance with the sundry rules and regulations which govern the actions of the British army. The charges are grounded on the most melancholy event that has yet taken place in the British dominions in the West Indies. The diminution of our military fame must be felt at all times as a great national calamity, but at no period so severely as this long crisis with tyrannical France and revolutionary Haiti, when our military character has become more essential than ever before, not merely for our glory and honor, but for the existence and independence of His Majesty's West Indian possessions.

"It is, however, a great consolation that whatever may have been the stain which our military renown has received, the conduct of the European troops in regaining possession of this vital post added to our glory, for no troops and no officers displayed more zeal, more courage, more devotion to the common cause of that most triumphant engagement.

"But I must return to the serious nature of the indictment. Permit me to make a very brief and cursory survey of the authority in law that speaks to the crime of mutiny. We find in the *Articles of War* rules laid down by the greatest English judges, who have been the brightest produced by mankind. These same *Articles of War*, as you gentlemen know, which are read aloud once in every two months before His Majesty's troops, are clear on this heading. Mutiny is the greatest offense of which a soldier is capable because it strikes directly and immediately at the foundation of all military subordination, and by necessary consequence, at the destruction of the state itself. It is by the martial law punishable, when it is committed in its greatest extent, with death.

"As the main danger from this crime stems from its being joined or shared in by numbers, any inactivity or silence will be justly held to be an approbation and acquiescence in the criminal design and will be declared to be punishable in the same degree with the actual crime. Thus, by Section two, Article four of the *Articles of War*, it is enacted that 'any officer, non-commissioned officer, or soldier, who being present at any mutiny or sedition shall not use his utmost endeavor to suppress the same, or coming to the knowledge of any mutiny, or intended mutiny, shall not without delay give information thereof to his commanding officer, shall suffer death, or such other punishment as by a general court-martial shall be awarded.'

"I have thus been lengthy, not for the information of this honorable court, but to satisfy you, gentlemen, of that law which extends to each of us, as well as to the prisoners, for it knows no distinction of persons. It is a doctrine which has been laid down for the safeguard of us all. And, nay, it is not a rigid notion of a dry system. Rather it is founded in the wisdom of ages.

"In support of the charges against the prisoners at the bar, it is incumbent upon the crown to ascertain that they, the prisoners, were among that party of the Eighth West India Regiment who committed the facts mentioned in the charges: the fact of the killings, and the circumstances attending and aggravating that fact.

"I will now, gentlemen, call the witnesses for the crown in support of this indictment, without, therefore, trespassing any longer on your patience."

My heart crumbled as I listened to this cruel message, which was inflamed by an ignorant zeal. How could he be saying those things about me, *me,* a loyal soldier of the British King? If words are grand clues to discover the temper and designs of the speaker, then this man was determined to believe what he spoke and he wanted others to believe as he did with the same passion. I felt so dishonored. I felt caught by fate. For some time I sat in shame with my head bowed and eyes shut. Suddenly someone stepped inside the room and the guards sprang to life and snapped to rigid attention.

Major Clotworthy, the adjutant of the Eighth West India Regiment, entered the court. This officer was at the Cabrits on the night of the mutiny. He made straight for the witness chair without looking in our direction.

"Major Clotworthy, do you swear upon the holy *Evangelists* to declare the truth, the whole truth, and nothing but the truth insofar as shall be asked of you upon the trial?"

"I do."

The simple witness chair had been placed halfway down the long room, across from us but facing the court. How far away and lonely it looked standing there. He sat down and kept his eyes turned away from us as though we were invisible.

The judge advocate opened his examination:

"Major Clotworthy, were you at the Cabrits on the evening of 9 April of the current year?"

"Yes."

"Major Clotworthy, kindly tell the court what transpired on that night."

"On the evening of 9 April, about eight o'clock, I was at the officers' quarters in Fort Shirley talking with Sergeant Major Broughton of the Eighth West India Regiment when the orderly sergeant came in to learn the parole. After receiving the parole from Sergeant Major Broughton, the orderly sergeant left to warn the various guards and picquets.

"No sooner had he left the building when several musket shots were fired at us through the window shutter. Suspecting it was an attack by French troops, we ran unarmed along the upper gallery of the officers' quarters to the end of it. As we descended the steps we were fired at from below, at which point I was rather led to think that a mutiny had broken out.

"A corporal in the Sixty-eighth Regiment was mortally wounded by this fire and toppled over the railing. At the same time Sergeant Major Broughton fell dead with a shot through his heart. I then decided to escape through the back gate of the fort, but here I suddenly encountered a mutineer who flew at me, thus preventing my escape from that quarter.

"Having been stopped in this effort, I proceeded to regain the room from which I had sallied. As I did, the mutineer discharged his flintlock, the ball narrowly missing me. I managed to reach the room and whilst there I perceived a trap door in the ceiling. I forced the door with the aid of a sergeant's halbert and with the further assistance of a table, which I quickly mounted, I made my way through the opening to the roof.

"When I got on the roof I entertained the hope of being able to throw myself over the wall of the fort. This hope was quickly dashed since the distance from where I was standing to the boundary wall was greater than I had anticipated, with the result that I crept back to the center of the roof. Here I remained quite still and watched for an opportunity of jumping down to the ground. I succeeded in doing this after a short period and finally got free of the fort by passing myself through one of the embrasures.

"I then made my way towards my quarters in the center battery atop the Inner Cabrit. As I ran along the narrow path leading to it, my way was blocked by a group of mutineers who were in the act of butchering the commissary, Mr. Lang. On discovering this melancholy sight, I retraced my steps with a view of seeking assistance atop the Outer Cabrits where an officers' barracks was located.

"In ascending this hill I was fired upon by mutineers but continued my course till I reached the top safely where I found Major Gordon of the Eighth West India, with the officers of the regiment who had escaped, and about 120 men of the Eighth who had refused to join the mutiny. No sooner had I arrived atop the hill and joined ranks with Major Gordon and his party, than the mutineers in the batteries atop the Inner Cabrit opened a hot fire upon us, in consequence of which a party of volunteers, of which I was a member, proposed to take the powerful Douglas Battery at the north end of the valley and turn its guns on the mutineers atop the inner hill.

"We marched off silently, about twenty strong, and got to within twenty yards of the battery when we were met with a tremendous fire by a group of mutineers concealed in the scrub in the vicinity of the battery. Many of the storming party were struck down. Those of us who survived this ambuscade instantly made off to the rocks along the shore beneath the battery where we concealed ourselves. We soon siezed an opportunity to depart this area and followed the north shore of the Cabrits, turning south through the Cabrits swamp under the very guns atop the inner hill. By daybreak we had reached the access road into the garrison and made quickly for Portsmouth, along the outskirts of which our tiny force met the advanced party of Governor Johnstone's relief column."

The judge advocate moved out from behind the table and approached the officer.

"How nigh you was the mutineer who discharged his musket at you?"

"I would say not more than twenty paces."

"To which part of the regiment was the mutineer posted?"

"He was a battalion company man."

"How come you to know this?"

"In the light passing through the open windows in the officers quarters, I could plainly see that the woolen tuft worn on his shako was in the battalion colors, that is white over red."

"You have stated in an earlier question that you encountered a group of mutineers who were then in the act of murdering Commissary Lang. How many were they?"

"I cannot be exact, but I believe them to be about six or seven in number."

"To which part of the regiment did these mutineers belong?"

"I believe them to be all battalion company soldiers."

"How do you know this?"

"It was a very bright night which permitted me to observe the mutineers. They wore the white over red shako tuft and the large white shoulder tuft of battalion company men."

"To which companies are the prisoners posted?"

"All are battalion company men."

"You have also stated that the black troops in Major Gordon's party were soldiers who had remained loyal. Where were these men housed on the night of the mutiny?"

"Unless they were on duty of some kind, they were quartered in the soldiers' barracks atop the Outer Cabrit. All the soldiers' barracks at this post are to be found atop the Outer Cabrit."

"To which part of the regiment were these men posted?"

"I later learned that eighty among them were flankers belonging to the Light Infantry Company. The rest were all private soldiers, except for two corporals, from Seventh Company."

"To the very best of your knowledge and recollection, did you encounter, at any time during the mutiny, any *other* soldiers of the Eighth West India Regiment who had not joined the mutiny?"

"No, I did not."

The judge advocate seemed satisfied with this testimony and retook his chair. "The prisoners may examine the witness—if they wish!"

I sat there for what seemed like a long time, thinking. I thought about what Major Clotworthy had said. The things he described, did he truly see them? Each of his words clung to me like a leech sucking out my honor, my life's blood. I burned with the shame of our mutiny. Damn those men who debased the regiment.

My thoughts then drifted to Captain Mapp. I eyed this fussy little piss-of-a-man whose tongue I wish I could silence. I thought about the clever way he led Major Clotworthy with his precise questions. I thought about the mocking tone in his last words, followed by that faint grin on his mouth, until the voice of the president broke into my thoughts.

"The court taking notice that the prisoners may have weighed the possibility of conducting their own defense, and concerned that they may want in ability to do justice to their case, feels compelled to make the following remarks. It has been founded in established usage in courts-martial that professional lawyers and counsels are not permitted to interfere directly in their proceedings. Nor is this class of men permitted by pleading of any kind or argument to endeavor to influence either their intermediate opinions or final judgment.

"This I consider a most important and wise regulation, for lawyers are in general utterly ignorant of military law and practice as members of these courts-martial are of civil jurisprudence and the many, many forms of the ordinary court. If this class of professional were to participate in court-martial proceedings, the results from the inevitable clash of such contradictory and warring judgments would be nothing less than inextricable embarrassment and ill-founded and illegal decisions.

"This, I might add, is why the judge advocate not only prosecutes in the name of the sovereign, but assists the prisoner in the conduct of his defense. In discharging this latter function, the judge advocate is motivated solely by justice and humanity, for it frequently happens in the trials of ordinary soldiers who, wanting all the advantages an education provides, must certainly stand in great need of advice in such trying circumstances as are enough to overwhelm the keenest intellect and embarrass or even suspend the powers of the most cultivated understanding.

"But although it is thus very wisely provided that professional lawyers are prevented from interfering in these proceedings, it is at the same time not unusual for a prisoner to request the court to permit him the aid of legal counsel to assist him in his defense, either in the proper conduct of his vindicatory proof, by recommending suitable questions to the evidences, or in drawing up in written form a connected statement of his defense.

"This type of benefit the court will never refuse to a prisoner because in those unhappy circumstances the prisoner may either want ability to do justice to his own cause, or he might well be deserted by that state of mind which is absolutely necessary to both command and bring into use those abilities as he may actually possess. Of course, the prisoner's counsel must properly understand his duty and see at all times that he not tease, embarrass or confound the court, but instead conciliate the favor of the court by prudently directing and regulating the conduct of his client. Do the prisoners wish legal counsel?"

"No!" shouted Souvarine Petro. "There is no need of that. We have the talent. And we intend to conduct our own defense. My comrades have agreed that I will speak for them. And we are ready."

"We don't want your dead blood," I heard him say softly to himself as he strode confidently towards the startled witness.

"To which companies are the defendants posted in the regiment?" Petro asked.

"Although it is not evident from their prisoners' dress, they are all private soldiers in 4th Company," Major Clotworthy replied.

"How do you know this?"

"As regimental adjutant, I am familiar with the periodic muster records of the corps. I also know the prisoners on sight."

"In your testimony you refer time and again to the so-called mutineers whom you encountered as only battalion company soldiers. Why were you not more precise as to the specific company postings of these men?"

"It was not possible to tell from their uniform and equipment which companies they belong to."

"Describe the uniform and equipment worn by these men at the time you saw them."

"If my memory serves me correctly, they had turned out in their trousers, jackets and shakos. They wore ammunition pouches and, of course, they were armed with flintlocks charged with bayonets."

"What else did they wear?"

"Nothing else, to the best of my recollection."

"What, then, was missing in their appearance that made it impossible for you to identify their company posting?"

"The water canteen."

"Why is that so?"

"The light blue water bottle is the only piece of regimental equipment bearing company identification."

"Explain what you mean."

"In addition to a broad white arrow and regimental number, the company identification number of the owner of the canteen is painted on the flat surface of the bottle in large white lettering."

"Did the absence of the canteen make it impossible for you to specifically identify the company or companies to which these men belonged?"

"As I testified before, yes, it did."

"State the effective strength of the Eighth West India Regiment on or about the time of the so-called mutiny."

"The April monthly return shows the regiment with a rank and file strength of 850 men."

"How many were battalion company men?"

"The same return lists 690 battalion privates and corporals."

"Would you not agree with me, Major, that knowing the company posting of the so-called mutineers is of material importance to this case, otherwise the net thrown by the judge advocate ensnares those who took action and those who did not on the night of 9 April?"

"Yes. I would agree with that observation."

"You have further testified that you had several confrontations with the so-called mutineers. Did you see the faces of any of those who fired their flintlocks at you?"

"Yes, I did."

"Do you believe you could identify them if they were brought before you now?"

"It was evening, but I believe I could."

"Look upon the prisoners. Do you recognize any of these men?"

"Yes, I do."

"Inform the court if any of the soldiers who fired upon you are among the defendants."

The officer turned his head slowly in our direction and stared at us for a long moment. My body suddenly became tense as his gaze reached my face. A deep sigh escaped me as he went down the line looking hard at the others.

"No, I do not recognize any of these prisoners as mutineers."

"Are you familiar, Major, with all parts of the Cabrits?"

"I do have a fairly extensive first-hand knowledge of the post, having served here for several years."

"Would it be possible for a body of men, fearing for their lives, to secrete themselves in some hidden fold of the land and thereby avoid detection?"

"Yes, it would be possible."

The judge advocate sat staring in our direction. His face had a surprised look upon it. "The witness will withdraw," he barked, his face now colored like scarlet.

We had not been undone by that evidence. Souvarine Petro's presence of mind never seemed to forsake him. He had successfully blunted the efforts of the judge advocate with those good questions. But damn that officer, that snake at our breasts. There was much more to the story than he reported. The mutiny was preceded by frightening events at the Cabrits.

Chapter 10

The Palaver

It was the evening of 7 April, two nights before the mutiny, and the sun had just dropped from view into the darkening sea. A small party of the Sixty-eighth, a white regiment, had entered Fort Shirley on some unknown business. Their coming here was so sudden and surprising that we were not sure if we were awake or in a dream. Buckra soldiers had long since quitted the Cabrits on account of the yellow jack which doomed them to certain death. Except for a few buckra sergeants in our regiment and our officers, and some several others posted here on special duty, no other white soldiers were quartered at the Cabrits.

The news spread from barrack to barrack like a raging fire.

I had heard a sharp cry outside my barrack window as I was resting in my crib, fondling my delicious thoughts of Jubba Lily. Manby rushed in with anxiety painted on his looks. "*Backside!* Dem very improper fe to be here," he cried. "Dis is black man's fort. Dem likely to behave in no very nice manner."

"What yuh see 'bout dat vex yuh so?" I asked.

"Me jus' goin' down de bottom to Fort Shirley, wen me see plenty buckra soldiers dem of de Sixty-eighth Foot. Dem here fe to escort we black soldiers as slaves to de estates. Negroes, dem talk too. Dem say dat black soldiers finished, dem mus' get ready fe work in de fields like poor negroes. Buckra soldiers a trouble. Me see me death clearly now. We all dead done. What we fe do?"

"Never mind," I replied. "Here, mon, drink some rum, der is no trut' in what yuh say. It can't be so. It jus' can't be so."

But I knew it was. Their coming forced upon my mind the recollection that nearly all buckra soldiers were gone from the Cabrits by the time I had arrived three years before. Old timers in the regiment remembered that deaths were so frequent among the poor buckra soldiers that the commandant ordered an end to processions and ritual at military funerals, and directed that the coffins containing the mortal remains of the dead be carried to the cemetery in the valley without drums or band and without even a party to fire over them.

The old veterans told the story of the poor Fourth Battalion of the Sixtieth Regiment. Of the 360 buckras sent here, all were quickly taken ill with fever, 300 of whom became ancestors! The speed with which these unhappy white men perished made it necessary that thirty negroes were constantly employed in digging graves in the Cabrits valley. Three, four, five, six dead buckras, their bodies stripped naked of all clothes, were tumbled in a heap into the same yawning pit. The earth from the pit was then piled upon their naked bodies. No markers identified the place of their long homes. The dead carts were constantly employed in this sad service, from the first peep of the dayspring to sunset. And scarcely was one cart empty, though some held as many as twenty dead buckras, but another was full.

Each buckra, according to the black veterans of the regiment, went to his death in the same pitiful manner, blood bursting from every pore; eyes like red-eyed demons, covered with blood as bright as any scarlet tunic; blood vomiting; raving madness; flies gathering at the corner of the open mouth and on half-closed eyelids; death's rattle. Away went the creaking dead carts. The old black warriors were struck dumb by this calamity. Surely some evil spirit was angry. But which one? And why? There were no known causes for this spirit attack. The only sounds that broke the loud silence were the coughs of dying white men and the buzzing of a few mosquitoes.

It is said that these deaths caused the commandant to order the change in the King's regulations regarding funerals because the constant recurrence of that imposing ceremony greatly depressed the spirit of the living, bringing them close to the dread effects of panic. I am led to think that the order had something to do with the location of the commandant's house, which was in the valley directly across from the cemetery.

If buckra soldiers died like falling leaves, we African soldiers were hardy and seldom fell victim to evil spirits. If one of my comrades did take ill, we resolved to keep him out of the garrison hospital as long as it was possible. The hospital was to us but a dead house where sick buckras went to die. In fact, the Cabrits was without a true garrison hospital. The stone foundation of a regular hospital that was to have been built was still to be observed in the valley. In its place we had several miserable shingle buildings or huts atop both hills where soldiers with fever were treated.

So, instead of taking our ill comrades to the hospital, we brought them to Pedro, a Yungur-speaking African who was the shaman of the Eighth West India. Pedro would quickly name the ancestor or disease spirit that caused the sickness. If a sickness was caused by an ancestor, then Pedro fashioned a small statue of the ancestor and appeased it. If Pedro declared the disease to be some spirit, then a pottery sign of the disease was made and it, too, was appeased. Sometimes I saw Pedro circle the head of a sick comrade with soft clay and then call upon the disease spirit to leave our comrade and enter the clay. "Kimara, leave dis man," he would intone in a strong, deep voice. "Leave and I will make for you a pot for your home and put it in a place where de rain will never touch you." The clay circle was then made into a shape like that of the disease spirit. Soon after Pedro made the likeness, our comrades became well and returned to their regimental duties.

Pedro's powers were very strong. It was for that reason that we African soldiers were not assailed by disease spirits, despite the fact that we lived withinside the often foul-smelling air that arose from the Cabrits swamp. This air drifted over and through all the buildings where we lived. The white shamans believed that since nothing could cleanse the swamp air of its disease spirits, duty at the Cabrits must be the sole lot of the Eighth West India Regiment.

Consequently, the sudden arrival of buckra soldiers to the Cabrits on 7 April—under the cover of darkness—was viewed by my comrades as a trick of some kind. They believed that their evil mission was to escort them to a life of slavery on the estates. Many of the soldiers in my own barracks came to believe this idea, and with very good reason.

Only a fortnight before, on 25 March at daybreak, my company was paraded before our barracks without arms. We had been ordered the day before to appear on parade in fatigue dress. I was observing the fact that the top of Devil's Mountain was clear of clouds when Sergeant Major Bostonian, the duty sergeant, ordered us to attention upon the approach of Lieutenant Rogers.

"Number Four Company is hereby ordered to clear the ground and cut drains in the Cabrits swamp," announced the young officer in a high voice. "You will march to the engineer huts in the valley where you will be provided with tools to undertake this fatigue. For this fatigue, each of you will receive the extra pay of nine pence sterling daily. Take charge, Sergeant-Major!"

"Yes, sah!"

Tools to undertake this fatigue. We had no way of knowing that this simple command would be of great consequence for us all.

"NON-COMMISSIONED OFFICERS, TAKE POST IN FRONT OF YO UNITS!" roared Sergeant Major Bostonian, his long silver-tipped cane tucked proudly under his left arm. "COMPANY, LEFT TURN! QUICK MARCH!"

Immediately upon being drawn up in line before the workshops and huts of the engineers, we were each handed a billhook! A cursed billhook! A low, mournful groan burst forth from the throats of a hundred men, and the once smart and straight formation reeled as if struck by an invisible enemy. A billhook! A negro's tool! I could not believe my eyes. It was with great difficulty that I made myself touch this thing and take an uneasy possession of it. I winced from holding it and kept it some distance from my body as though it stank and was covered with glowing coals. From left to right I could see that my comrades reacted with the same shock and disgust. When ordered by the sergeant-major to shoulder this *thing*, we resembled a gang of miserable field negroes.

Our column then proceeded to the entrance of the Cabrits and passed over the drawbridge in a heavy silence. The duty picket looked upon us in astonishment as we marched past like ghosts with our faces fixed on the ground in shame. As we entered the Cabrits swamp we met with a party of slaves on their way to Fort Shirley. They were all day-negroes, common slave laborers hired out each day to the ordnance and engineer departments by their owners. These poor devils were the most tasked of all the negroes on the island. They quickly made way to let the column pass through. As we marched between this gauntlet of human wrecks, each greeted us with a smug, hateful grin.

The cursed billhook reminded me of those bitter, lonely, dried-up years I spent as a *mafa*. The special horror of that tool seemed as though it would never wear off. I shook with anger and resentment.

Our labor matched the common round of toil fixed for estate negroes. We worked from the first of dayspring to sunset with brief periods of rest permitted at breakfast and dinner. To this misery was added the full heat of the sun, which burned into the backs of our necks. We endured all this without the extra pay promised us. Only an extra ration of rum was sometimes provided to ease our constant thirst. We marched to and from this miserable negro work for a fortnight in a deep and mounting anger.

Until now my three years in the regiment had been ordered, predictable, even comfortable. Each day had begun and closed in the same familiar manner. The sharp sounding of the lone bugle call at five o'clock in the morning shattered the calm and a thousand dreams. It called us to the first military formation of the day, the morning drill with arms. There were the breakfast and dinner messes at which we jerked the tasteless army beef and traded away our other salted provisions for cassava, sweet potatoes, yams and delicious ripe plantain. We washed this down with coconut water which Hussar swore gave him his lustful energy. There were also the daily inspection parades, the usual dull fatigues, guards to mount, orderly duties, and, of course, duty at the military funerals of white men.

Then, too, the credit of the regiment had to be cried down, whereby innkeepers and rum-shop keepers in Portsmouth were warned by the beat of the drum not to trust the soldiers for any cost above their day's pay, for the commandant would not pay it. This was by far the best duty since those who accompanied the drummer got to fill their bellies with the hot, burning rum. In the afternoon one could always expect more drill, designed to cultivate in each of us the dog-like virtues of courage, obedience and fidelity and to prepare us to die at the command of a sergeant. There must be roll-calling once or even twice a day. When these duties were completed, the various wings of the regiment quartered at the Cabrits were united at the afternoon parade atop the Outer Cabrit and there dismissed. As we made our way to our barracks we could hear the drummers beat off the officers' dinner down below. And each day came to an end, as the day before, at dusk, with a lonely signal sounded on a drum or bugle by a soldier of the regiment on the main parade down, down, far away, in the narrow, darkening valley.

Now that comforting routine had suddenly changed, blown away by a violent, relentless wind, like the savage blast of a white squall racing down the slopes of Dominica's mountains into the sea. Now the tidy world of our regiment had quickly become a landscape of uncertainty and fear. The usually dull and mindless fatigues had been replaced by a loathsome ordeal of toil which sapped our physical and spiritual endurance. Living itself seemed to speed up. We seemed to be rushing headlong to our ruin. Had we been betrayed?

Only Souvarine Petro seemed unmoved. Even then he had that faraway look. "The path has already been chosen," was his reply when I asked him to make some sense of the changes falling about our heads. "Buckras' day will soon be dead here 'bout."

To do nothing meant only frustration. Thus we flew to Pedro upon our return each evening from the toil in the Cabrits swamp. Pedro had been charged with special powers. He knew well how to deal with superior and unpredictable spirits. He alone could determine the cause of this misfortune. By his words, objects and gestures he would also try to influence these events that had overtaken us and the regiment. After several days of looking into this matter, Pedro was ready to reveal what he had come to learn. We all gathered into Number One Barrack at dusk to hear him speak. He swept us all into silence with a hard look.

"Yuh tink is ill will of spirits cause misfortune," he said as he sat on the edge of his crib polishing the metal mirror in his hands. The tone of his voice was always respectful but persuasive. "No, sah! Is big buckra man cause it."

"What kinda buckra man 'im?" cried Manby, pushing his big body closer to Pedro.

Pedro then ordered the barrack to be darkened. He placed the iron mirror between two lighted candles and told me to gaze into it until the face of the man appeared. Shapeless lights and shadows flitted across the polished iron slab without a fixed or regular course. This continued for many long moments. Then suddenly they seemed to take shape into a particular form.

"Backside!" cried Manby. "We all dead done. Is we colonel!"

At first this revelation defied understanding. How could this be? Why did Colonel Johnstone humiliate us so and wish us dead, we who served him so loyally and won lasting fame for the regiment against the French at St. Martin in 1801? Fear quickly filled the minds of all of us. And in another instant a great shout went up from the throats of those of us in the regiment who were born on the far side of the great salt sea. Each man uttered but a single word in his own African language. *"Aloka!" "Wahala!" "Diambu!" "Milonqa!" "Bwalu!"* Each word echoed up and down the long room before finally escaping out through the open windows into the black Caribbean night.

Each word had the same meaning. It was the cry for an open debate, a great gathering, a discussion, a *palaver!* The palaver is the traditional African way of settling a conflict, through discussion. It is truly the only way of treating an outrage, through the all-powerful influence of words. Two tribes stumble into conflict; they hold a palaver; they enter into it and become part of the process; they restore peace. This is how the great palaver works. Yet the shadow of menace was all about and the men's blood was up.

Would the palaver be an orderly discussion in which only one member of the regiment spoke at a time? More important, would it lead to a decision as to what we should do about the daily slave work we were forced to undergo, one agreed to by all as African custom required? Before we scattered into the night we decided to hold a palaver but only when the various wings of the regiment were reunited at the Cabrits, an event scheduled for the end of April. It was only fair to wait, since every soldier in the regiment had the right to express his opinion at the meeting.

But all our plans for orderly debate were blown away by the arrival of the buckra soldiers during the night of 7 April. Faced with the presence of these troops, the majority of the men loudly and angrily called for a meeting the following night, the eighth day of April, at Number Three barrack.

When the time came, our heavy gray greatcoats were nailed over the barrack window to prevent the escape of light and sound that might warn our officers of the palaver. The doors were closed and bolted and lookouts were posted. The long stone room was thick with soldiers. They sat in the cribs and along the floor up and down the long room. My African-born comrades sat in small knots according to their language. In each group was a soldier who was conversant in the particular African language as well as English and who intended to serve his countrymen as interpreter.

Some of my comrades wore their dull white drill jackets, others the red coat. The creoles among us puffed and pulled nervously on their long white clay pipes, a horrible, filthy habit that appalled me. In the dim and almost airless room I could barely distinguish the faces of my comrades. The room was thick with great expectation and everyone sat stiffly, tense, as in anticipation of some important event. A lone table stood midway down the long silence-filled room. Most of us knew the rules of procedure at a palaver, but we were hesitant at first to stand up to speak. Only some coughing and the movement of soldiers' heavy shoes across the rough wood flooring broke the lingering stillness.

"Who is we?" A deep voice. "Me wunna know. Is we freeman-soldiers or is we slaves?"

We were all startled for a brief moment. The words, loud and strong, came from the back of the crowded barrack. I could not tell what man spoke them, but they were in everyone's heart. It was the question of the moment.

Silence, again, Then a shout!

"AFRICANS! MEN! BROTHERS! THERE ARE CHAINS TO BE BROKEN—YOURS!"

It was Souvarine Petro! He swept out from one of the dark corners of the room where he had been hiding in the dimness. The soldiers fell back in awe, making a way for him as he strode confidently and dramatically out from the shadows. This demon-man was a true actor. He approached the table and casually leaped upon it. In his left hand he held a piece of paper with printed writing on it.

"LISTEN THIS!" he snapped, his reddened, glowering eyes fixed on something known only to him, his head thrust forward in an attack position. "You live in a world withinside a world. The outer world, the world of the buckras, controls you and your world. Your world, in here, in these barracks, in the regiment, exists only for the good of white people. Now the buckras no longer need you and they are about to send you into living, social death—slavery! You must come quickly to terms with this reality before it is too late. You must rise above this circumstance. There are chains to be broken, my brothers—yours! It is time to act!"

He stopped talking and looked slowly around the room. I knew what he was up to. His cunning was so ready. He had paused to allow his stinging words to eat their way into the thick skulls of us soldiers.

The same heavy silence once again took possession of the barrack, only now no one cleared his throat or shuffled his feet. No one stirred.

"What yuh mean *act*?" a second voice rang out. They had taken the bait. It was the signal he had waited for. His cunning was so ready. There was satisfaction in his looks. He leaped onto his reply as a hungry leopard would pounce upon a fat, unsuspecting goat.

"LISTEN THIS!" he commanded. "Domination continues only so long as those who are dominated give their consent. You, my brothers, are as much a slave as the yonder field negro, the same field negro you have been taught to despise. As a slave your existence depends on the existence of the buckra master, the army! You have no separate existence as freemen have. You must do what is ordered, no matter what it is. You have no choice. You believe yourself to be superior to the field negro. Yet now you work as he does. How then are you different? *How then are you different?* Your true identity lies not with your masters. Your true identity lies with your African brothers and sisters who toil each day in the fields. To be free you must refuse the role of the slave. Then, and only then, will you not be a slave. Then, and only then, will you be free.

"Follow the glorious lead of our African brothers and sisters in Haiti where buckras' day is dead. The mighty Toussaint, a free man, once refused an offer of protection from the British. Had Toussaint accepted he would have become a mere king withinside the British empire. But he rejected this plan, preferring instead to be his own authority, the master of his own destiny, the source of his own salvation. If the great Toussaint can decline the role of a puppet, albeit a king, so must you renounce your role as a slave. Refuse the roll of slave! Become your own authority!

"Yuh try to fool we wid' words yuh dug up only dem spirits knows where." It was the first soldier again. "Yuh mus' tink we dumb. Is too much at stake fuh we to trus' yuh an' yuh lively, hot-up words dat will only kill we off."

"Listen," replied Souvarine Petro rapturously, his raised arm pointing to some imaginary place in the nighttime heavens, "my words are like the rainbow in the sky, a vibrant band of colors that lead to freedom, honor and peace. My words are rainbow words, a shaft of truth thrown high into the sky by the great spirit, free of the white man's evil touch."

Souvarine Petro's words struck me like a whirlwind of fire. *Slave! Master! Identity! The army as buckra!* Each one burned its way into my thoughts. Was it because they possessed truth? An intense and uneasy quiet fell over the packed room. Then, in a sudden torrent of voices, my comrades pressed him. Souvarine Petro disposed of each attack with a clever reply.

"Souvarine Petro, yuh mad!" snapped a voice. "Yuh outah touch wid' us an' de regiment. We got plenty power, slave have none. Yuh advisin' we wrong. Yuh can't be 'pon we side. Yuh wrong! Yuh lie!"

"You have been taken in by your own fancy dress and firelock."

"Yuh tink we foolish den." The second voice again. "We no slave! We is special. *We is British soldiers!*"

"Does not your profession sicken you? You defend the evil heart of slavery! You are instruments of an evil that must die. But first you must die to the old self!"

"We is freemen, I tell yuh," said yet a fourth voice. "Don't I shoot Frenchmen at St. Martin? No slave dem do dat an live."

"Freemen? Freemen? Freemen name themselves. All else, slaves and goats, are named by their masters. Who, my brothers, named you?"

"How important is freedom den?" questioned the fourth voice once again.

"How important is air?"

"Souvarine Petro like he mad!" The third voice again, only angrier now. "Yuh mussy workin' fuh de French buckras. How yuh know we is slave? What proof yuh have?"

"Listen it good!" Souvarine Petro stood rock-like on the table. The flickering light caught him as it had that evening in the deep woods. It gave him a magical appearance. He slowly raised his hand, holding a paper,

"In December 1801, nine months after you proudly killed Frenchmen at St. Martin, the principal advisors of the

British king were asked to give their opinion on the legal position of African soldiers serving in the West India Regiments. That means they were asked whether or not you were slaves or freemen. This, my brothers, is what they wrote. Listen this!

" 'We are of the opinion that our African soldiers do not in consequence of their being employed by His Majesty in military service legally become soldiers, and we think they remain to all intents and purposes slaves, and that their condition as slaves is in no respect altered in consequence of their being engaged in military service, but they remain precisely subject to the same laws as they would have been subject to had they been the property of His Majesty and employed in agriculture or public works.

'It seems to us that they cannot cease to be subject to such of the colonial slave laws as immediately respect the police and internal government of the colony, and must be subject to every species of personal incapacity which attaches upon the slaves of any other proprietor.' "

The words pierced through me like a bayonet. I recoiled as if struck.

Souvarine Petro slowly and carefully lowered the paper from his face. Our eyes followed its downward course as they were meant to. A hush had fallen again. We were shaken, struck dumb by this revelation. It all seemed to be a deadly game. He had provoked us with his taunts of slavery and then produced that paper. He had known its contents for some time. He was merely waiting for the right opportunity to use it. Yet, there was a ring of truth in what he read. Although I fought inwardly against it, it sounded true, game or no.

"Now, my brothers, what have you to say to that?" he snorted, his eyes dancing, satisfaction once again all over his looks. "You have been deceived by your masters. Slavery is your reward for loyalty. Can there by any doubt what you are in the eyes of the buckras?" He taunted us again. "It is time to act now, before it too late. You will never have another chance. Forget this African notion of life is death is life. You are mortal. Death is final. Time is precious. My brothers, the time to act is now!"

A commotion at the far end of the room. "Look out there. I comin' thru!" It was Genus! I had difficulty believing my eyes. It was really Genus. He could read but he never spoke during all the time I knew him until this moment. This creole from Barbados preferred instead to sit alone atop the Inner Cabrit at dusk and gaze up at the dark mass of Devil's Mountain and pull and puff on his clay pipe. Now he seemed to have come alive as he broke forth from the dimness in a fury and stormed towards the table bearing Souvarine Petro. Now he had broken his silence. How strange.

"Look out there! I comin' thru," he said again, his voice soft and calm. He seized the paper from the hand of Souvarine Petro and his large, sad eyes skimmed quickly over it. " 'Im no advisin' we wrong. Dis creature does speak de trut'. Buckras tekin' over de regiment. We pull de triggers. But buckras still tellin' we wuh to work. Buckra still tellin' we wuh to die. We headin' fuh trouble fuh so!"

He suddenly stopped speaking as if something had turned off in his head. He bowed his head as if his spirit had been crushed, and he returned to the dark corner from whence he came. I never heard the soft and pleasant voice of Genus again in life.

"You see, my brothers. I speak the truth. I 'pon we side." Souvarine Petro had recovered his calmness and returned to the attack. "It is time to act! Now! Be slaves no more!"

"Dat law yuh read doan' enforce here in de West Indies." The third voice again, and still angry.

"What more proof do you need?" Souvarine Petro replied impatiently. "Is slave work not proof enough? You must come to terms with this fact. Breaking the chains of bondage will be painful, but the release will be sweet, my brothers. Close your eyes to truth and you will perish fuh so."

A mad rush of excited voices suddenly burst forth. The words tumbled out of their owners' mouths with such violent speed that Souvarine Petro was unable to break in. The words expressed many emotions: fear, anger, hate, sorrow.

"Souvarine Petro like he mad."

"Maybe 'im is, but 'im speak trut'."

"Chase he out, he outah touch wid' we. 'Im nutten but a wet fart."

"What to do? Where to go?"

"Me slave once. Me no go back deh!"

"Hush it! Le' we pull together. Tings will arright. Doan' let 'fraid destroy we."

"Suppose he right doh? I got this bad feel."

"Doan' make me laugh. Yuh makin' joke. Souvarine Petro 'im playin' a big shot."

"I doan' believe de regiment dem mash up. It nevah happen."

"Yuh can trus' nobody. We no wuk fe slave fe nutten."

" 'Im 'right! How yuh cyan't see dat?"

"Dat law 'im read doan' enforce here."

"How yuh can know dat?"

"Suppose Souvarine Petro right? Who can help we?"

"Souvarine Petro fe warn we. We mus' act!"

A pause.

"What 'im mean act? 'Im nevah say!"

"Souvarine Petro! What yuh mean act? Tell we now. Tell we quick."

Silence reigned for another brief moment. The palaver had reached its turning point. It was time to talk plain, to come to a decision, to agree upon a course of action.

Souvarine Petro never yielded his position atop the table. Of course not. This master of drama wanted all eyes and minds to be constantly on him. He held up his hands and accepted the offer to explain himself. A trace of a slight smile flashed across his looks as he did.

"Take power as in Haiti!" Again a vague response.

"Slavery must be done up. Freedom is sweet. Take power!" What was he avoiding?

Another pause. "Yuh talkin' mutiny." It was that third voice again. "Is mutiny yuh talkin', doan' it?"

"Mutiny is bitter, but the release from bondage will be sweet."

"We have laws dem dat we mus' follow as British soldiers."

"The man who is bound by a law to which he did not consent is a slave."

"If what yuh say is true, we can reach adjustment wid' we officers." It was the fourth voice again.

"There can be no compromise with evil."

So that is what this monster, this brute, is up to. *Chains to break. Freedom to make. Choices to have. Time to act. Haiti to follow.* All those high sounding words to get us dumb soldiers to mutiny. To destroy ourselves. To destroy the regiment. *To destroy our position!* His words were evil, murderous, poison, death. Give all this up? For what? For freedom? Whatever that is. For Haiti? Wherever that was. No!

That third voice again. "Mutiny? Yuh dreamin'. Yuh mad. It cyan't be done."

"*IT CAN!*" Souvarine Petro burst out. His eyes were now like blazing lights streaming out of his skull. Sweat enveloped his face. He seemed possessed by spirits. "Whatever you think you can do," he proclaimed wildly. "Yes, my brother, it is that simple. Whatever you can imagine you can make happen. Think something, anything, and it can be. This is power and it resides in each of you. This is power and it is limited only by your imagination. History confirms this, my brothers. History demonstrates that whatever you can imagine you can one day create. Long ago someone thought of using exploding powder to throw a stone at his enemy. That thought became real, did it not, my brothers? There's your proof, your musket, your flintlock. Because of that thought given life long ago, you now use your flintlock to fling a ball at your enemy. Consider the sky, my brothers. Only birds fly there now. Man cannot. But think it. Think of man flying high in the sky and one day we will. Not in our lifetime perhaps, but one day we will. Man flying in the sky will become just as common as your musket became.

"Everything begins as a thought and every thought can become real. There are no limits to what you can do. If you think mutiny, you can do mutiny. Think freedom and it will be. We are surrounded by evil beliefs that tell us how imperfect we are. My brothers, free yourselves from this tyranny. Free yourselves from this bondage.

"Power is within you! Your power is without limits! Your power is your imagination! Therefore, my brothers, whatever you can think can be. This is power! Seize it! Use it!"

A long silence enveloped the room.

"What else yuh talkin'?" Again that third voice. "Mutiny mus' have a purpose. Don't it? What else yuh lookin' fuh?"

"Your true identity lies with the other slaves, not with your . . ." Souvarine Petro's words had now become a violent speech.

But I cut him off. I realized that we had all been his fools. He was again avoiding something. He was not telling us the full truth behind his stirring words. I knew inwardly that he was deceiving us. So why let him continue to speak and confuse us further with his trickery. I knew I must stop him. I had to seize this moment and undo what this evil magician had done. The regiment—our ordered way of life—was at stake. I leaped upon the bare, rickety table, shoving him off as I did. He opened his mouth to speak, but I leadened his tongue into silence with a hard look.

Feelings. Blood rushed into my head. I believed myself about to explode. My heart pounded. *Anger*. Never had I felt such rage. *Words*. Sounds suddenly erupted from my mouth like cannon shots. I seemed not to be in control of them. It was as if someone else spoke them through me. *Heat*. My tight uniform made me sweat profusely in the close air of the packed barrack.

"Comrades of de glorious Eighth West India Regiment!" I began, to remind them of their proud achievements and the fame of our regiment, "de question before us is indeed one of life an death. When I was kidnapped on de African side of de great salt sea an' den came to serve in de regiment, I embraced dis opportunity as favorable. From how I see de lowly field negroes live here 'bout, I say, here in de regiment is a place dat look like good livin'. Dis is fuh true! Are yuh hearing me?"

They responded as I had hoped they would with loud and repeated shouts of "Yes!" Encouraged, I continued with ever-growing confidence.

"Breddah Africans! De regiment is de only place where free air blows in de West Indies for black men like we. Here are liberty as we shall ever know it. Doan' we shoot French buckras at St. Martin an' get reward? Doan' we corporals an sergeants give orders to English buckra soldiers and dem follow it, like it or not? Doan' we have chance to marry before we become ancestors? An' doan' we carry flintlock?

An' doan' we know how to use it? All dat is power an' is power dat gives life. My breddah Africans! Are yuh hearing me?"

Louder shouts of "Yas!"

"Breddahs and comrades of de regiment! De path of duty in de regiment is always de path of safety. Do nothing else. Never me no join mutiny. Dat is death fuh so. De regiment is life-giver. De regiment is we father. De regiment is we mother. De regiment is we present. De regiment is we only future. De regiment gives we power. De regiment gives we glory. De regiment gives we position. De regiment is like a lone mountain on de dry plain of slavery. Breddahs, der are no chains to break, only ties to make, in de regiment! Breddahs! Are yuh hearing me?"

Shouts. Loud and many and the same word—"Yas!"— over and over again.

"Breddahs! Yuh hear dem fancy words of breakin' chains, takin' freedom, killin' buckras. All dat is nothin' but a doctrine, and if yuh want to make war against we tribe, nourish dis doctrine of Souvarine Petro. Doctrines are evil spirits; once dey get inside yuh head dey betray yuh to yuhself. What are dey all? Doctrines are always unclear. But dem mean one ting fuh so—death! Outside de regiment is death, only death. Comrades! Are yuh hearing me?"

"Yas! Yas! Yas!"

"Breddahs! We will never see mother Africa again. Face dat simple fact. We will live an' die here, in dis land of stolen Africans. We mus' come to terms wid' dat. We mus' adjust to dat. We mus' seek a special place for we here. Like it or not, de West Indies is we new home." A pause. "De regiment is we tribe!"

With those last words there was a great stirring in the long room as my comrades leaped to their feet. And from their collective throats they now chanted:

"De regiment is we tribe!"

"De regiment is we tribe!"

"De regiment is we tribe!"

"De regiment is we tribe!"

It was over! My heart was still pounding in my chest. But I felt relief and even joy at stating my feelings as I had. There would be no mutiny. The regiment would not be harmed. I had expected some protest, but there was none. So I had silenced the troublemakers and won over those who were wavering. I jumped to the floor in triumph. I shook hands with many of my comrades. Hussar, Pedro and Manby I embraced. Souvarine Petro was nowhere to be seen. He had apparently scurried away like a frightened hyena when it became clear that his plans were defeated. Arguing the cause of mutiny made him a traitor to the regiment in my eyes.

The palaver was over. It was now very still in the barrack. My comrades had all dispersed, some to their cribs to sleep and dream, some to secret places where they smoked and talked of Africa, some to the Cabrits swamp and lusty encounters with slave women who gathered there each evening for that purpose. Before the palaver ended we agreed to send a group of comrades to Captain Cameron, a kindly and understanding buckra officer. They would voice our concerns to him in a most respectful and polite manner and seek assurances that the slave work in the Cabrits swamp was nothing more than a mistake and that in the future we would be employed only on normal fatigues for which we would be given the customary extra pay of nine pence each day. My comrades were instructed to learn if Colonel Johnstone approved our fatigue in the Cabrits swamp and if so, why. They were also to ask Captain Cameron about the mysterious paper Souvarine Petro had read from. I secretly hoped that it would not be established worthy of belief. I tried to convince myself that the paper was a trick of some sort. Yet Genus confirmed it, did he not?

No matter, it was done. All would be well.

Stil . . . I could not easily order Souvarine Petro's words out of my thoughts. They resisted every effort to expel them. *"There are chains to be broken . . . Domination continues only so long as those who are dominated give their consent . . . Become your own authority . . . Your true identity lies with your African brothers and sisters . . . You cannot think the impossible. Whatever you think you can do . . . Think something and it can be."* Would all truly be well?

Despite these doubts, I was thankful the palaver was over. And I was pleased . . . no, I was amazed at how well I had done. My speech was a victory. And if I trusted myself to speak once, I could trust myself to speak out on things again and again. It was a new feeling of power and I loved it.

Suddenly I felt very weary. But I did not want to sleep. No, sleep was impossible. I was possessed by a living force which the palaver had summoned but failed to exhaust. It was an odd sort of energy that flowed through my body, it was alive, throbbing, wiggling, tickling in my mind, my arms, my back, my . . . loins. I would never sleep in this condition, never. I had to fine some way to physically exhaust myself. I had to . . . spurt, yes spurt this aliveness out of me . . . into, into . . . Jubba Lily!

Yes, it was a time to rejoice in pleasure. Her womanparts capturing me, pulling forth my seed in squeezing, shuddering waves of sticky joy—that was just the thing I needed to waste myself. I would go to her at once. I would crawl in and lay quietly next to her as she sleeps. I would run my fingertips slowly over and around her large nipples, then down over her flat belly. She would soften and murmur strange cries. When my fingers reached where her legs join, her open, sticky woman-parts would greet them. With eyes closed she would offer up her mouth which I would lick and suck into mine. That would be my moment. With a soft cry, I would fling myself deep into her body. With eyes still closed, she would gasp out my name in jerks.

A sudden rush of pleasure filled me at these delicious thoughts.

Afterwards, lying quietly at her side, I would tell her about the palaver: how that snake Souvarine Petro tried to trick my comrades into mutiny, how I exposed all his talk of freedom for the stinking cow shit that it was, how I saved the regiment! Rebellion, I would try to explain to her, was the gravest thing men can do. It is a gamble too hazardous to take, a road too stormy to travel. Fortune never favors bold men; she favors cautious, sensible men like me, I would tell her. "Continue, continue!" she would order me. "Tell me more of your triumph!" She would be so proud of me. She would look upon me with wonderment that I had out-shone Souvarine Petro. Now she would have to believe all those things I told her about being a Margi memory man. This would convince her that all those things I told her about my incredible speech ways were true. How else could I have convinced my comrades that the safest way was the best way?

Jubba Lily:

There was no greeting. The air in my little hut was sharp from the heat and sweat of his rush to satisfy himself upon myself. I looked over at him in the candlelight. He was lying on his back. Sweat still popped out of his forehead, then collected in little streams that ran down his temples. He was so pleased with the way he had convinced his comrades to side with him at the palaver that his face glowed all over in peaceful contentment. His voice vibrated with excitement and his eyes danced as he exclaimed how his speech brought out the best in him and once again made him the great man the High God intended him to be. There was another reason for his comfortableness. He cried out that he was almost at his peak as a man. He had honor and power as a soldier which was greatly expanded now that he had rediscovered his voice and, along with that, confidence in himself. All that he lacked to reach his peak as a man was to have me as his wife, he said.

He smiled at me with a look of great satisfaction on his face. For a while he said nothing, but I could easily read what was on his mind. He was thinking, "In the past she found me desirable, now she will find me impossible to resist. She will rush to tell her friends about my great triumph, and before the coming day is done my name will be on the lips of every mafa on the island."

He continued to smile at me. I wanted to smile back, but it would not come. Nothing would come, not words of praise, not smiles of adoration. I did not want to hurt him, but I could not allow myself to become part of his victory.

At first I asked myself silently, "How could he? How could he abandon his luckless African brothers and sisters to evil slavery? How could he think only of himself?"

Then I felt a hot, hot anger tear through me. I knew I should not speak to him feeling the way I did. I should wait and let this hot anger cool. But the anger was too pure, too hot. I told him I was a slave but that I was not stupid. I told him that he did not understand power, and the power he had was not his own but the army's. True power is that which a person can give or confirm. He could do neither. I told him that he could not see himself for what he was, a slave just like the rest of us, living in life's hem just like the rest of us. I told him that there was a difference between being honored and being honorable. He may have been honored by his army masters but that did not make him honorable as a man. I told him that I loved him more than anyone in the world but not more than anything. I reminded him that I loved freedom more. I told him all these things.

His head snapped back. He looked at me with a stunned expression. He looked at me as if he saw me for the first time.

Jack:

Why did my actions and words anger her so much? Did she expect me to risk all, to embrace mutiny, to bare my chest and throw myself heroically upon waiting sharp-tooth bayonets? How arrogant of her to want me to commit suicide from the comfort of her mafa hut. How dare she! Why did she require my death? Was it to satisfy some failure, some weakness in her, something she never did that she should have? Could it be that at some point in her life she shunned the call to rise, kill and take her own freedom or help others take theirs? Did my death vindicate her of some cowardice? What a comfortable way for her to prove herself worthy—through my physical death. No! Why should I destroy myself just to make her feel better about herself? No violent injustice lay at the core of my personal existence as a British soldier. I am not a daring or resourceful man. I am not a hero and have no wish to be one. I am not made of iron. But I do love life, even a hard one, as she does.

I am an ordinary person who seeks some kind of accommodation with those powerful forces one does not like but cannot change straightaway peacefully. She should not despise me for that. Accommodation has its benefits. It keeps one from falling prey to the pressures of self-hatred and dehumanization, the twin fires of oppression. Is not that the way most humans have always resisted oppression? Yes, resisted oppression. My accommodation with slavery, in fact, enabled me to express some rights which set limits to my surrender. These rights also represented a clear denial of the evil system.

Forge an alliance with the field negroes? I dare not attempt to secure their freedom from bondage. That would be suicide. And what should have been our goal in such an effort? To create some sort of free African village life here in the West Indies, in the heart of slavery, in this torture garden? Sheer madness. The field negroes hated us. Consider Hamlet. Do men yearn to be free? I am not sure what "free" is. I do know that men yearn for comfort, safety and security. Maybe those things mean "free."

It was like a horrible dream. How did it happen? I was so eager to see her. And she seemed to be happy to see me. We made love hotly as we always did. Then, then she turned on me like a cornered animal. It was a side of her I never saw before and it frightened me. Who was she, really?

A sudden, heavy rain caught me in the open as I passed by the Cabrits swamp. The water cooled me off. But it soaked and nearly ruined my tunic. What a miserable night. First, she fought with me and then my tunic fell apart on my back. If I had remained in barracks this night my tunic would not have been damaged. The thought of having to wear something that no longer fit me snugly made me anxious. What will Sergeant Major Bostonian say when he sees me dressed so poorly? I can see him looking at me with a smirk on his hideous face.

Chapter 11

The Trial: Who Dare Visit Puxley?

Late in the morning of the second day's proceedings, the judge advocate informed the court that his next evidence, a Captain Puxley, was lying dangerously ill in the officers' hospital and was thus unable to testify in person as planned. Because of the importance of his testimony, the judge advocate wanted the court to instruct two officers to go at once to the hospital and there take down the evidence in writing from the mouth of the witness.

Who was Captain Puxley? Had I ever clapped my eyes on him before? Had I ever offended him? Was he that fat officer with the large, overhanging, purple nose whom I stopped late one night from entering the Cabrits because he was soaked in rum and could not remember the parole? As I recall, he cursed me with a flood of stinging words for making him wait outside the barrier until he remembered the password. He demanded to know how I as a bloody

African dare obstruct him, a white man, a commissioned officer in the King's army.

"You black raper, you brute, you gorilla, stand aside!" he screamed. He then tried to cut me down with a wild swing of his sword. I easily dodged his cut and he crashed to the ground in a sorry heap where he lay until the duty officer, attracted by the disturbance, arrived and spoke for him. I was only doing my duty. No one was permitted to enter the Cabrits unless they knew the password. He could have been a clever French spy posing as one of our many drunken officers who litter the Cabrits after tattoo.

A lone mosquito had come to rest on the back of my hand. It touched my skin in several places with its long, bayonet-like mouth, apparently seeking just the right spot to prick. In fascination I watched as it quickly braced its hair-thin legs and effortlessly thrust its mouth through my skin. It remained motionless as it sucked my blood. I imagined a pool of my blood rapidly filling up its . . .

Or was he that other officer? Was he that buckra in charge of the working party, the one who unfairly gave me three days of extra drill in full marching order simply because I had complained to the fatigue sergeant that I needed help in lifting and resetting the large stones of the main gate that had fallen down during the hurricane? I did not refuse to do the work, I merely said it was impossible for one man to lift those huge stone blocks. Was that him . . . ? Yes . . . ! His name was Puxley. I gasped. He was the officer with the sickly yellowish hue in his looks, which explained his presence in the hospital. Never were soldiers subject to a sterner discipline than that of this officer. Because he so hated service in the West Indies, he often visited his frustration on those troops so unlucky as to fall under his command. He abused us. He never pardoned. It is said that some soldiers were so afraid of his wrath that they refused to look him in the face for fear of bringing his anger to life. He was a bitter, yellowing, self-consuming thing who in truth hated himself more than he did others. Wise soldiers avoided him like an evil spirit.

Had this brute forgotten the hard look I gave him when he ordered me to do extra drill? Might he remember me? I feared him at once because of the terrible harm he could do to me and my comrades if he gave evidence. I wanted him to die before he could.

I looked down again at my hand. The mosquito was there, still motionless, still feeding on my blood. I noticed that when a mosquito feeds it can be removed only by force, such is its need for blood. It will remain motionless until its meal is finished, and all the while it is at great risk.

I watched as its gorged gut grew larger and larger. The sight sickened me. Rage flooded me. I brought my other hand down hard, crushing the thing on my skin. Blood squirted out from under my fingers. It was dead. Dead! I took childish and savage delight in squashing the life out of this life-sucking pest . . . Puxley!

The president of the court looked alarmed when the judge advocate requested that two officers take Puxley's testimony. I knew why. It was one thing to send a lowly *mafa* or even a black soldier into a hospital among the dead and dying. Should the spirit of illness catch them and kill them, no one would take notice of their passing. It was another matter to send buckra officers on such a dangerous mission. A buckra life was more important than a black one. That was the basic law of this land; it was the law that gave birth to all other laws.

Not long ago, a young, fresh buckra just arrived on the island foolishly paid a visit to another officer in the hospital, only to return to his quarters, lay down on his cot, and die within hours. Sending a buckra into the hospital when the fever raged was a sure way of killing him. No buckra wanted to visit the hospital, let alone talk to a man, even an officer, who might be dying and whose very breath, buckras believed, contained deadly vapors. But obtaining the testimony of an officer was a matter for officers.

I recalled the sickening scene that had greeted me when I was sent on my first fatigue to the officers' hospital as a medical orderly. I had been with the regiment for about three revolutions of the moon when I was given this horrible duty. The fever was raging. Buckras were dropping dead all around. There were so many dead it took days to bury a man.

I was one of two orderlies assigned to our regimental surgeon, an old, white-haired devil with the name of Codrington. "Surgeon Twitch" we called him because of the way his body shook at times. Just before entering the hospital, we halted and Surgeon Codrington took several long pulls on his water bottle, the effects of which made him wince and instantly steadied him. He then pushed open the tall, heavy, wooden doors.

Row upon row of cots stretched before us, each only a foot or two apart from the next. The cots were placed neatly and evenly in long lines like columns of soldiers. I stepped into the great room, to be greeted by a sickening stench and sight. The air was still and raw with the smell of shit and blood. It was so foul I nearly vomited. On each cot lay a figure so still that at first I thought each man was dead. I picked my way forward. Some were in full uniform. Others lay in their underclothing. Many were certainly dead. Some had turned blue and black. Of others their bodies had swollen to double their life size. One man had burst open across his gut. But all lay in their own filth, which had oozed through the bedding and collected in puddles on the wooden floor.

I had the miserable duty of looking for the living. To do this I had to carefully pick my way between the lines of stinking cots and their ghastly occupants. When I found a man with breath still in him, I raised him out of his muck, stripped him of his shit-and blood-encrusted clothes, and washed him as a mother would her naked baby.

At first I could not tell the living from the dead. All lay rigid like stone and deathly quiet. The flies did not help me as I thought they might. The dead and the living were their food and they covered both, thickly.

I kept pulling and tugging on dead men until Surgeon Codrington noticed my lack of progress and pointed at the puddle of filth in which one man lay.

"Look at their shit, Private!" His voice was sharp and he flung each word at me. "Look at their shit! The clue to life or death lies in their shit!"

He was right, of course, as I quickly discovered. The living lay in slime. That of the dead had stiffened and, where it had leaked onto the floor, crackled under my step.

The voice of the president ended this painful memory. He said he was not an unfeeling man, but the law of the army and circumstances compelled him to send two men into the officers' hospital. I watched the faces of the officers in the room with some excitement. On the looks of each was the same worried expression. As if to say, *may I not be the one. Spare me, spare me.*

Two young officers were selected. Each glowered for a moment, then saluted in assent.

"The court is hereby adjourned till 16 April at the hour of nine of the clock," intoned the president.

Chapter 12

The Battle of St. Martin

It is said that the medicine for fear is sleep. Though my mind was tired and required rest, fear of what was to come in my trial rendered sleep impossible. I did not have it in my power to force my mind to surrender its grip on reality. I expected fortune to strike a savage blow and snap the thread of my existence. So I lay awake on my hard prison cot and succeeded in losing myself in reliving my first military action.

It was in the month of March, 1801, in the so-called dry season. It began on the morning of the 21st day. The air was fresh and cool and the red sun had just begun its climb out of the blue sea. Reveille was beaten to announce the break of day and the morning inspection with arms. The companies, as usual, fell in on the several barrack parades atop the Outer Cabrit. Number Four company assembled near the single gun battery. After the roll call, Captain Cameron and Sergeant Major Bostonian made a very careful inspection of our dress, arms, and other regimentals. I recall no neglects in our appearance were observed that day, so no man was punished with extra drill.

The inspection completed, we formed in files and were marched off to the grand parade on the valley floor below where we were joined by the other companies. As each company entered the grand parade we were drawn up in line. Our officers moved to the center of each subdivision, and on the command "March," they each turned to see that their men wheeled up without breaking file. It was a beautiful sight as we warriors moved smartly without any shuffling. All the while our young drummer boys, who wore spectacular jackets of gray facing, numerous white chevrons up and down the sleeves, and the distinctive shoulder wings of the flank companies, beat the stirring "Point of War" on their painted wooden drums.

Once my company had formed line and we had dressed equally from either flank in close order, the earth and heavens quickly claimed my attention from this imposing sight of warriors gathering. The high blue sky was smudged with puffy white clouds, while the dark green bulk of Devil's Mountain loomed behind the Inner Cabrit. The beauty of the scene made me imagine that this West Indian island was as large as the world. No sooner had the regiment assembled on the main parade when suddenly the mounted figures of Brigadier General Maitland, Commandant Fuller, and our colonel, Governor Johnstone, appeared in our midst. The regiment, startled by their unexpected appearance, gave a smart general salute and was then ordered to form three sides of a square. (*Three sides of a square?*) This was the first time the regiment had been ordered to form this kind of formation. It made an uneasy impression upon me, but I knew not why.

As soon as my eyes clapped on these riders I thought—war! Unlike the other buckras I had seen riding upon the backs of horses, these three whites were the very image of mounted warriors. They were each pitched forward in a position of eager flight and movement. Each man sat in union with his beast, with the speed and power of the animal somehow within him. Did the thought of death quicken their being and make them one with the animal between their legs? War is, after all, the strong life; it is life at the point of death.

Giving his horse a signal, General Maitland, a tall, thin man, rode a little forward towards us. He then roared in a voice of power and energy that was at odds with his frail body. By his first words my suspense and curiosity, which had been heightened by the novelty of the scene, were relieved. It was war! We were to fight the French on the island of St. Martin! Everyone gave a tremendous shout of approval.

Even though I had no experience of war, I could observe myself in heroic battle on a strange shore, could imagine being honored by my comrades for my bravery, hailed as a victorious warrior and even crowned with laurels by my buckra officers. My body was raked by shivers of physical pleasure and sensual expectations. This sudden eagerness to enter upon a deadly contest was, I knew, deep-rooted inside me. I also believed I possessed an instinctive knowledge of war though I had never experienced battle. Not even the wondrous demands of the loins can be imagined until one has just entered the body of a woman. Not so with war. War is somehow knowable before one actually experiences it. And because battle is life enhanced by mortal danger, it becomes more exhilarating and irresistible than the joys of sex. The thought of dying a horrible death did not affect me.

I was yanked from these dreamlike thoughts when the regiment was ordered to be drawn up in line. With the prospects of glory before us, we performed this movement like never before, with snap and high spirits. We formed up in a long line, three deep from one end of the grand parade ground to the other. We made a very fine showing that day. Having been instructed to throw off the casual carriage of the peasant during our endless drills and to adopt the stiff self-possession of military posture, we were each the master of our own person. There we stood, in long, straight lines: inspired black warriors, tense with expectation and excitement like harnessed wild horses straining to bolt into action.

Our two sacred banners, the King's color and the regimental color, were placed in the front rank of the color party, between numbers Four and Five Companies. Every man in the regiment had been taught to realize that when the colors were paraded he was in the presence of honored symbols. In our oath of enlistments into the regiment, each of us swore never to abandon our colors. Posted in Four Company, I was but seven or eight paces distant from the color party. I was very proud to see our uncased colors held fast, each by a young buckra ensign. One old sergeant was posted between the colors. Three more fine veteran sergeants supported the banners in the rear rank of the color party. The King's color, the banner nearest me, fluttered in the soft breeze. This color was decorated with red and white power lines which crossed on a deep blue field. It was an imposing sight framed against the piercingly blue sky overhead. Every regiment was presented with this color. My eyes, however, lingered the longest on our special battalion flag. This was largely in the facing color—gray, with the name and number of the regiment painted onto a red shield encircled by a wreath of red roses and purple thistles with green spiky leaves. A small Union Jack was also fitted into the upper corner of the color next to the wooden staff. No warrior anywhere in the world served under such a glorious and special banner! In this service with the British, be it pleasure or be it pain, we were special.

The regiment was now ordered to form into columns in preparation for being dismissed. On command we wheeled to the right in sections, preceded by the colors and the band. Our officers quickly moved out of the ranks and onto the flanks. And away we all went as happy as young goats, but still the masters of our own persons as good soldiers always should be.

That afternoon orders came to clean out our muskets. Immediately we gathered for this purpose at the edge of the wide wooden shelf running along the walls of the barrack room. Everywhere down the long room the scene was the same: individual soldiers, soldiers in pairs, huddles of soldiers—all carefully cleaning their flintlock muskets as if for the very first time. Before each man, scattered on the floor, were the vital tools that kept his flintlock in good working order: picker and brush, worm and turnscrew. Still others sat intently cutting down pieces of flints to the desired sharpness, after which they inserted them carefully into the hammers of the cocks. Brief, sharp reports of flints striking the steel plates of the musket locks! A shower of sparks! Muted cries of satisfaction.

There was little clogging ash to clear away from the touchhole of my flintlock with the picker. On parade we were expected to deliver, by word of command, one shot every fifteen seconds. Our drill was constant and repeated over and over again. In this manner I learned the importance of iron discipline, quickness and the need to be precise. Constant drilling also preserved us from idleness, for there was precious little to do once these skills were sharpened. But, like the rest of my comrades, I seldom fired off my musket with ball cartridge. No one missed this part of the drill, for it meant escape from the fearful kick of the weapon. It also meant that we did not have to face the sheet of orange flame and bluish smoke that left powder on our mouths and completely fouled our faces and the working parts of our weapons. The work to clean our muskets was therefore not demanding; it gave us time to cast some extra balls and to talk about the coming battle.

"Where is dis St. Martin place?" I commanded of no one in particular, as I removed the chain bearing the picker and brush from the black leather strap holding the cartridge box and affixed it to the metal clip joining the musket strap to the trigger guard—a much handier place for it when the lock fouled.

"It is in dis part of de world," Manby replied, very pleased with himself, "only one day sail over on de north if de sea smooth dem. I can no' tell yuh everyting 'bout dat place." He gestured with his picker. "But it have plenty food trees; dem dense wid' star apple, breadfruit, banana, mango, plantain, jackfruit, ochre, cocoa, pear . . . " Manby's voice was now rising in familiar excitement.

Souvarine Petro, who was passing through our barrack on some unknown mission, cut him off. "Food trees may well grow to great perfection there," he sneered, "but St. Martin is first and foremost an island of stolen Africans, where black slaves are bent double to the ground with hard labor, like slaves here."

A hush fell, but only for a moment since we were all in the mood to talk.

"Mon!" cried Lively, a skin-and-bones boy whose face was pitted with the ugly, white, depressed scars of the pox. "Is since we get orders fe fight I don't eat. Me see de shadow of death circling over everywhere."

"Yuh don't ha' fe worry, bwai" whispered gentle Cuffy in a soft voice, "everyting arright, everyting will arright. Don't mek fear rule yuh. After we lick down de French, me mek some tasty coconut bread and souse fe yuh. But first me mus' get a pig head which is a mus' fe souse, y'know. Jus' yuh see what I prepare an' all arright."

"Food is fe eat, but can yuh eat what yuh cook?" Hussar taunted Cuffy, and laughter rolled down the long room like thunder.

"Keep yuh mout' shut!" Cuffy lashed back. "If one more hot word come a yuh mout', yuh gwine have fe eat dem down. What yuh could know 'bout food when all is woman's flesh yuh fe eat," he scolded Hussar. "All wise men know dat yuh can't tek all the pussy dem, so yuh mus' fe tek some and leave de rest fe yuh breddahs. Every mon an bwai mus' have 'im share. But Hussar, 'im cant, 'im want it all dem. 'Im preserve in pussy. Pussy rule 'im like 'fraid rule young Lively deh. To be ruled by some force is a *baad* ting dem. To be ruled by fear leaves yuh dead done. To be ruled by pussy is worse den dead. It won't kill yuh off. No, sah, dat would be mercy. To be drunk up in pussy, it mean fe live forever as a living wet fart, like Hussar deh!"

A howl of laughter greeted these words. Hussar sank down into his tunic where he belonged.

Still quivering with dread, young Lively felt driven to ask of the reputation of our foe, the French army. Fear or no, it was the right question. I wished to know all I could of them before I had them in the range of my musket and before they leveled their muskets at my breast. Once I overhead one of our officers remarking that no white army was prepared to meet the French on equal terms on the field of battle, least of all the British army! He spoke openly of major defeats of the King's soldiers, in Haiti and in the home of white people on the far northern side of the great salt sea. The effect of this frank observation by one of our own leaders greatly distressed me. In a short time we will fight the French. Are we being led to our destruction by officers who still may not believe in themselves and British arms? I felt ill at this.

"I have seen de enemy!" It was the unexpected voice of Sergeant Major Bostonian, the burly ruler of our regiment. Sergeant Major Bostonian. Seeing him for the first time had chilled me. He was a big, hook-nosed, sinister-looking man. His face was shriveled and torn with the pox, which frightened and disgusted me. And stuck in that mass of decayed skin were bloodshot eyes, closed up to slits. Behind his ugly face was a hard-working mind; he seemed to be always thinking, thinking. He was a man locked withinside himself. He allowed no one to see his every side for that would permit someone to know him. Of his many-sided nature he exposed only one part at a time. Nor did his terrible face give any clues as to who he was. It was always hard set with his eyes locked in a constant stare. He never smiled. A slight twitching at the corners of his eyes was the only mobility I ever witnessed on his face. I was enthralled by his character and would try to watch him unobserved to see if he ever weakened and showed a different, perhaps softer, side of his nature. But he never did; he never escaped from the domination of that style. And yet he stamped his mind on all of us.

He directed us secretly, guiding us first in that direction and then along another path. The outward forms of his control over us were formidable. He possessed unnatural self-control, a mask, perhaps, for some shameful flaw in his nature. He sought to make order of everything. And he succeeded. Wherever he went he had a small, brown, leather notebook tucked halfway into his tunic at his breast. After every meeting with us soldiers and officers, he could be seen writing something in that little book. This always set us thinking. His actions drew us into his web and the rest went like child's play for him.

"Where an' how? Tell me!" cried Manby. "Where, Sergeant Major, did yuh see de French dem?"

"It was in defeat wen I first beheld de French." The Sergeant Major paused a long moment and then sighed deeply, as though he was reliving a painful time. Upon hearing his voice we quickly dropped what we were doing and gathered about him. "I recollect," he continued, his voice strong and composed, "it was in de winter of 1794 an' 1795 in bitter Flanders." He studied the sky through the open window as though the words he spoke were written there. "At dat time I was de soldier-servant of an old British officer who had served in America, where 'im discovered me. De French wore white trousers an' a deep blue tunic, as I recollect. Upon deh heads dem placed a big black cocked hat which dem like to wear crosswise in battle. In de front of dis hat dem stick a bright red, white an' blue cockade, which dem were very proud of. Dem were spirited soldiers, as I recollect, an' dem came on in battle in a grand an' determined style.

"But before yuh saw dem, yuh heard dem a' comin'. First yuh hear de *rum dum, rum dum, rummadum dummadum, dum dum* of the drums. Den yuh hear de relentless, heavy tramp of thousands of men, de piercin' calls of de bugle, de bangin' an clatterin' of equipment, horses neighin', wagons an' limbers creakin'. Den, yuh sah dem—great masses of men packed tightly into columns, like muscovado in hogheads, gallopin' horses pullin' heavy cannons, masses of cavalry hoverin' in de rear an' on de flanks of dis mighty host. An' preceding all was a swarm of busy, dartin' skirmishers poppin' away at we wid muskets.

"As deh columns closed wid we in we long straight lines, dem quickly uncased dem colors, dem bands struck up lively tunes, an' every mon lifted his voice to de high heavens. Some shouted, others chanted, still others sang. In dis style deh came on an' drove us into one defeat after anoddah widout pause in de winter of 1794 an' 1795. What de French didn't destroy, cruel winter an' disease did." Sergeant Major Bostonian then reflected for a moment. "What I remember most of de French was de zeal wid' which dem fight an' die. Dem believe in a mighty cause, an' it be dis cause dat mek dem so victorious."

"An' what be dis cause dat mek de Frenchmon fight so, Sergeant Major?" someone asked.

"*Liberty*, Private soldier, *liberty*!"

"I hear of dis ting call' liberty, an dat is indeed a mighty force dem. Tell me someting, Sergeant Major, do de Frenchmon still fight fuh he liberty?"

"No longer! Deh give up dis cause long time now. Deh now fight fuh tings like authority, power, trade, empire, money, an' control of de world. Dat is what de British be wantin', dat is why de British be fightin' de French cause two bulls can't rule in de same pen."

"Is we cause liberty, Sergeant Major?"

"No, Private soldier, not now."

"What is we cause dem? What force lef' fuh we black soldiers? What cause lef' mightier dan liberty, Sergeant Major?"

A long silence.

"Survival! Yar own survival! Liberty is sweet, dat no mon can doubt. But life have a certain order to it. First yuh mus' demonstrate yar right to life, yar right to live, in uddah words, yar right to survive, what I calls survival! Once yuh have dat, den yuh move up to liberty. Yuh, my soldiers, are at de beginnin' of tings. Yuh mus' first demonstrate yar right to life as British soldiers, not as black men. Once dat is done, den yuh can move on to the battle fuh yuh liberty. To survive in a society, any society, yuh mus' become essenshal fuh its continuashun. If dat society fear yuh but need yuh, yuh will survive. But he who is not essenshal mus' dead. Yuh can die in two way. Yuh can die physically—deh shoot yuh—or yuh can die de lingerin' social death of a slave. 'Tis dat simple.

"De planters now sees de black soldier as a threat to de social order. Some of yuh here in dis room remember how de planter 'im fight bitterly to prevent de creashun of de West India Regiments in 1795. 'Im fear yuh will mek common cause wid' de slave an' kill 'im in he sleep. Victory over de French will mek 'im see yuh in a different light. 'Im may still see yuh as a threat, but 'im will also see yuh as a necessity for he own survival. Victory over de French will preserve fuh yuh an essenshal place in dis society. Yar cause, my breddahs, is a simple one, but no cause is more important. It is a question of survival, yar own survival. An' fightin fuh dis cause will mek yuh victorious. It is, my breddahs, a matter of life or death, an' as I sees it, yuh have no choice in de matter, unless it be death yuh wantin'."

Another long silence.

"Me sees what yuh mean, Sergeant Major," young Lively said thoughtfully. "Me see what yuh tellin'. But can me truly lick down de French dem?"

"Yes, mon, widout a single doubt!"

Sergeant Major Bostonian's reply was quick and firm. This was what I, too, desperately needed to hear after listening to the Sergeant Major's stirring story of the French, which I somehow knew to have the ring of truth about it. I suddenly felt good again and the excitement I experienced earlier in the day on the grand parade returned with a powerful rush.

"But yuh mus' remember ya drill," the Sergeant Major continued, pointing his cane out the window to the barrack parade ground. "It is important dat yuh move, shoot an' obey in de regulated way only! Keep yar muskets in good workin' order. An yuh mus nevah, no nevah, fall out to go to de aid of a wounded mon, cruel an' hard dat may be."

"What yuh have to say 'bout survival is true, sah," said a respectful voice from behind me. "Yas, sah, survival is important, Sergeant Major, but we beautiful regimental color, dem is widout a single battle honor. If yuh 'ave battle honors, yuh 'ave reputashan, yuh get respect from uddah soldiers, an' yuh feel proud wen yuh colors dem uncased in de presence of uddah regiments. But if yuh 'ave no honors, yuh fart. Bettah we hide we colors. Wen we lick down de French dem, Sergeant Major, will de generals dem paint St. Martin on we colors?"

The Sergeant Major was silent.

More silence. "Continue. Answer." I muttered. This was an important question, cause or no cause. Soldiers are made for such trifles; it is often all they ask for in return for facing death. Medals for bravery and the names of victorious battles commemorated on a flag in bright paint are soldiers' gold.

The room had swelled with uncomfortable silence. Then Souvarine Petro spoke. "Your true reward will be the experience you gain on the battlefield. Experience is knowledge and that knowledge will give you the means to take your own freedom."

What was he getting at, this man of words? I looked into his face. His eyes betrayed his cunning. There was no point to press him, to make him explain what he meant by those words. He fully intended them to be uncertain. They were formed so that they might stick themselves into our minds and get us to think constantly about their meaning.

"An' women in Flanders, Sergeant Major?" It was Hussar again. No laughter greeted his question. It was not the time for this kind of low soldiers' humor. Why didn't he watch his tongue?

"Women?" growled Sergeant Major Bostonian, who suddenly rediscovered his voice, "Why yuh could hav' yar pick of dem in bitter Flanders, as I recollect, dat is if yuh don't mind yar pussy diseased, dyin' and frozen dead stiff in heaps in a ditch."

Silence.

Dawn on 22 March came before six, but at two o'clock the dead silence of the Cabrits was suddenly changed to a scene of commotion and hurry. The early morning hours were taken up with preparation. I was sadly fatigued but my spirit was soon revived by the din and excitement that raged in our barrack kingdom. There was much lively conversation as we made ready our equipment according to the full marching order. I stuffed my knapsack to the breaking point with an extra shirt and an extra pair of shoes, a rolled blanket and eighty rounds of ball cartridge. One could never have too many bullets, so I carefully counted the number of cartridges in my pouch. Forty, good. I then rolled my caped greatcoat like a blanket and strapped it onto the top of my bursting knapsack.

Each man was issued rations for three days. They consisted of hard ship biscuit and unpleasant looking slabs of salted beef, which reminded me of my black leather cross belts. These rations had neither the look nor the smell of food. Nevertheless, I collected my portion and neatly stored it in my haversack. Next, I emptied the contents of my wooden canteen out the barrack window and filled it up to the neck and stopper with fresh cistern water. My eyes fell on my bayonet hanging in its white scabbard over my crib. I lost no time in removing it, and as I did I withdrew the blade and ran my fingers carefully and slowly over its long slicing edge. Time and again we were instructed at drill that the bayonet was the ultimate weapon of the British soldier, and that no enemy would stand their ground if we came at them with these terrible long knives locked on to the tips of our muskets. We were also told that the bayonet was to be particularly relied upon for night work. But could I bring myself to sink this stabbing weapon into the body of a man whose face was so close to mine that I could see and hear his terror and pain? I quickly pushed these thoughts away.

At last I was ready to harness my equipment to my body. It was a confusion of straps. Everything I owned in this world was on my back, hanging from one strap or another. The wooden frame of the knapsack right away dug painfully into me, and the several black straps which crisscrossed my chest squeezed me, making breathing difficult. As always, I resented the weight of my equipment, wondering how well I could load, fire, move, and stab under this burden. No matter, I would find a way.

Sergeant Major Bostonian, cane tucked inside his sash, moved in and out among us discovering and correcting problems in our uniform and marching order—rolling a loose spare knapsack strap after pushing it twice through the buckle runner; sniffing the contents of a canteen of a known hard drinker and draining it with manifest disgust out the window; straightening a bent picker; scolding a private soldier for having a dirty touchhole in his musket; tightening the straps holding a shared cooking pot to a knapsack; counting too few ball cartridges in the ammunition pouch of a slacker; folding and hooking the back fall of a man's shako.

"FALL IN! FALL IN! OUTSIDE! AT DE DOUBLE!"
The Sergeant Major was satisfied that we were ready. We spilled out of the barrack and onto the parade ground that was already filling up with soldiers from other companies. Number Four Company assembled in three ranks close order, muskets shouldered, files lightly touching. A final check and another order was sounded, upon which we wheeled smartly to the right and gained the path leading down the Outer Cabrit to the valley floor below. Despite the great weight of my equipment, I marched in high style. I was finally on my way to war. Into battle!

Like a long, red, muscular snake, the regiment wound its way down the steep hill to the southern end of the valley. All these armed men on the move; we seemed to possess an uncontrollable force. I felt as if I was being carried along by a powerful river whose surge could not be stemmed. I felt free to enjoy the coming adventure, this march to the unknown in a far away land of great warriors. I felt the exciting sense of release from the suffocating drills and inspections and routine that had shaped my life until this glorious moment.

We marched on in high spirits in the midst of a hushed West Indian dawn. Not a breath of wind; limp leaves on still trees; the deep blue water beyond flat with calm; clouds dead-stop in the sky; birds and insects in life's hem, between sleep and the hunt for food. Still, the absence of motion did not prevent the beautiful scenery of the earth and sky, distinct yet whole, from weaving a magical spell.

The trail led to the rear of Fort Shirley. As we approached the guard, commands were shouted back and forth. Our passage through was unlike any other. We were hailed as victorious warriors by sailors, soldiers, officers' wives, little buckra children, fort negroes and servants. They all stopped their labors to cheer us on our way. Even the lowly negro jobbers and buckras, men who once hoped for our destruction, lifted their caps high into the sky in our honor. These salutes caused me not to feel the slightest fear of death from any cause nor ponder the mechanics of the killing that was to come. My imagination saw only inviting forms of success. And, more than ever, I thought of the regiment as my home.

The sun wore its usual red morning color as we marched grandly through and beyond the main gate of Fort Shirley and down the sloping esplanade. Surprised sentries saluted us. Lolling prostitutes momentarily forgot the purpose of their rude mission to wave and stare at us in awe. Excited Cabrits dogs barked and raced up and down the long line of moving men. Even a grim burial party, on its way to fire off its muskets over the remains of a fresh dead in its long home, halted, turned towards us, and presented arms. Onward, past all this, the regiment flowed along the main trail before wheeling sharply to the right and then down the steep causeway and through the massive causeway wall and on to the wharf below.

It happened suddenly as the column reached the bottom of the cliff and as noble Prince Rupert's Bay and the town of Portsmouth sprang into view. My attention was caught by a sinister sight that chilled me through. Lying at anchor was what appeared to be *the death ship of my middle passage!* All the bitter memories of my ordeal across the great salt sea, which I thought I had buried so deeply, came roaring out. The ship loomed ahead evil and alive. A slimy, hollow-cold fear, the dread of impending death, took hold of me. Despite a sunburst overhead, I felt a darkness closing in on me at the sight of the ship I was about to board and enter.

My shades of gloom were slow to give way to a brighter picture. We were hailed by white sailors, their hair fashioned in a single tight braid, dressed in blue pants, blue jackets with bright gold buttons, and smart round hats, each with the name of the ship, H.M.S. PRINCESS MARIE, painted in front in large black letters. By their greeting they seemed to be saying "Welcome! Whatever your color and your origin, we are in the coming struggle together, as equals."

"We will devour the French as fire eats up the dried sugar cane," I replied in my mind. But all this failed to completely relieve my suspense. The belly of the ship where I would have to live and sleep, if only for a day and night, awaited me.

To enter this large vessel with its bulging wooden sides, I first had to climb up a ladder made of long and wide pieces of wood nailed fast to the timbers. Side ropes of hemp ran alongside the ladder. These, I noticed, had been worn smooth and shiny by many hands. After a short climb made difficult by all the tools of soldiering hanging from my body, I reached the door of the ship where I encountered a large and solemn marine sentry in a red coat like my own. I had heard much about these tough sea soldiers who, I was told, were as much a fighting force against the French as they were a barrier against mutiny. Lowering my head I passed into a strange wooden kingdom.

Below decks the air was close and stuffy. The low ceiling and the big, black guns cramped life. But no recognizable landscape of fear confronted me. No wails of those about to die greeted my ears. No stench fouled my nostrils. No, I found the situation aboard this big war canoe agreeable. Aside from the rocking and pitching motion, which I knew to be an essential part of life on the sea, there was no other source of distress visible to my eyes. It is true that the inside walls of this ship were painted blood-red like that of the belly of some gigantic beast, but this, as I later learned from a buckra sailor, was done to hide the blood of his mates which was often spattered there in battle.

We were immediately shown racks which had been fitted up to receive our flintlocks. Our accouterments were stowed near our berths. The berths were a surprise. We were to sleep in clean hammocks, in the manner of the native Caribs of Dominica. They were of a dull brown color, like the color of the Mandara Hill during the dry season. They were hung from the deck beams between the guns. Sleeping in this way pleased me since it was much better than a handful of straw strewn on a damp, cold floor. (Later, when we drew near St. Martin, our hammocks were brought up from below and then lashed up into long-shaped rolls by the sailors, who then placed them about the decks as a sort of barricade against small arms fire.)

As I moved about the canoe, I noticed an activity carried on by each and every sailor: the drinking of rum, or "grog" as they prefer to title it. Each sailor received a great quantity of this fiery drink every day. Once they swallowed it they become happy and delighted with everything. Thus, this ration was always eagerly expected. I was told that sailors often injured themselves while under the influence of this evil spirit. Many received bad head knocks from running against the overhead beams while caught in the spell of this potion. Still others became ill from drinking too much of it and never recovered their health. Yet, the ration was never cut.

"Why is yo' officers so blind as to continue dis rashun?" I asked a short but powerfully built black sailor.

He looked startled. "Yuh are mad, " he cried, "de rashun of rum spirit is a tradishun in the King's navy. It be how we handle bot' stress an' triumph. It be how we rules the seas. Dem may water it down like Admiral Vernon did in the long ago. But dem dare not cut de rashun. Take it away an' yuh hav mutiny. What is more, did not Solomon himself advise, 'Let 'im drink, an' forget he poverty, an' remember he misery no more'?" He then stalked away on some mission with a puzzled look upon his features.

"SHOVE OFF!" someone shouted. We were finally on our way. From where I stood on the canoe's deck I could see several sailors grappling with the thick ropes which bound the big canoe to the wharf. At the same time the gigantic iron hooks that held the canoe fast to the sea bed had come roaring up from the cloudy water like a captured sea animal. This was accompanied by the harsh grinding noises of the lifting machines in the forward part of the canoe. After what seemed like a long wait, the canoe began to drift lazily away from the wharf. And then she stopped dead in the water. The big white cloths on the three tall wooden poles hung limp. Under the Cabrit hills and Devil's Mountain there was no wind to move the canoe. A glance at the shifting shapes of the clouds behind Devil's Mountain showed that the winds on the other side of Dominica, where the tall waves sweep in unbroken lines from the coast of Africa, were working as usual. The wait was maddening. The breeze remained scant and the water flat like a Margi metal mirror. Then the wind suddenly picked up. And just as suddenly the canoe's cloths stretched out with a snap and the canoe began to slowly pull away.

Clear of Prince Rupert's Bay, we slid past the Cabrits headland, with deep blue water right up to the base of the Outer Cabrit. As we did, the cape of clouds covering the top of Devil's Mountain parted to reveal its majestic shape. Having seen her naked once again, I was reminded why the Caribs called the island, "Tall is her body."

I leaned over to Pedro who, like me, was purchased at Portsmouth by the army. "Do yuh remember," I said solemnly, "seeing de Cabrits fuh de first time?"

A long pause, much too long. I wondered if this was a painful thing for him to remember, which would explain the delay in answering my question.

"Very well," he whispered.

"Where was yuh stolen?" The manner in which we soldiers were kidnapped from our loved ones and our homes in Africa was a subject often discussed in our barracks during quiet reflective moments. Once he got used to military life, each new recruit was eagerly questioned about his own experience. It was a way of getting news about our families and villages, particularly if the new soldier was a member of our own nation. Truth to tell, I had forgotten to put this question to the Yungur-speaking Pedro until now.

He appeared to be far away in his thoughts. "In Kodosim, my village, during de harvest season. It happened at a time when de evil bush spirits were bent on murder. I should not have gone out to de farm dat day."

"How many died in yo' ship?" I pressed him.

" 'Bout half."

"Have yuh family?"

Another long pause.

He spoke without feeling. "A wife an six children."

"Are yuh not sick at de heart fuh dem, Pedro? How it feel, mon?"

"Yungur people have little interest in life after dis one. What is important fuh we is de here an de now of dis life. An since most of dis life is not happy, me have learn' to embrace what me have become. Dat makes life easier fuh livin'. Me is now a British soldier livin' a life on dis side of de big salt water. Nevah no more will I see me homeland an' all dem me once love. All dem now belong to de long ago an' nevah me hold on to dat."

I was stunned by this burst of openness. How soon are sorrows forgotten.

Just then the sun came out from behind a cloud cover like a carnival, throwing out dancing golden rays of light everywhere. Nothing retained its true color. Everything became molten metal. The water turned a rare shade of blue. The blazing sun made Dominica even more beautiful.

This day, filled with so many new experiences and painful memories, left me fatigued. Thus did I welcome sleep when it sealed my eyes. Soon even the snapping sounds of the wind beating into the large, white cloths and the rhythmic slap and rush of the waves against the front of the canoe faded into silence. As I drifted off I remembered an event in the long ago, when I was a little boy. A Margi memory man had playfully asked several of us children which animals sleep well. "Those who work hard and hunt hard and become tired," we boldly replied, certain in our innocence that we had provided the right answer. "No, no," cried our memory man, much to our great disappointment, *"it is those who can afford to be unafraid."* We children sat in stunned silence sensing that we had just heard very wise words but not knowing why. Why had those words lodged in my memory and why did I remember them now? I began to nod off. My last memory of that night was looking through the canoe's four-sided window from my hammock and seeing a bright moon turn the drifting clouds silver against the night sky.

Twenty-third March 1801 began for me a few minutes before four o'clock in the morning. The morning watch! The shrill sounds of pipe calls followed by hoarse shouts of "Starboard watch ahoy! Larboard watch ahoy! Hey! Out down there!" thundered through the bowels of the canoe and tore me from my dreams. At four o'clock, with a bell clanging on deck, we were mustered. A few moments later I joined the larboard watch.

With the ringing of the bell the canoe instantly sprang to life. By the light of the moon I witnessed a scene of orderly hurry and activity. The men of the middle watch went happily below to their waiting hammocks, as the men of the morning watch ran on deck. The cook lit his fires. Carpenters and their mates began their work of repairs. Sailors of the watch took off their shoes, rolled up their pants over their knees and commenced to clean the deck: wetting, sanding, drying. Brass was cleaned. Steel was polished. Ropes were coiled.

Suddenly, the young marine drummers beat to quarters. The drum roll to quarters was short, fast and determined. Something serious had happened or was about to. The roll was repeated two more times. Directly the drumming stopped, the entire company of the ship ran to their duties. We went below and quickly returned with our muskets and sidearms. The carpenter and his mates disappeared below. Iron swivel guns were loaded. Heavy battle lanterns were secured. Strong rope nettings were hung over the decks and under the tall wooden poles. A wall of dull brown, rolled-up hammocks ran around the upper deck. Buckets were filled with water. Wet sand was sprinkled over each deck. Wetted blankets were thrown over doorways and the magazine hatches. Marines fell in with us with their muskets and sidearms. Sentries were posted. Down below the guns were made ready. The four-sided canoe's windows were thrown open. The sailors were in a fever of excitement as the canoe was made ready for battle. And it all took but a few minutes.

Now many of the crew gestured violently, pointing ahead. An enemy canoe? I searched the night for some sign: a light, a white cloth, a gun flash, a bow wave.

"LAND! LAND! ST. MARTIN! DEAD AHEAD!"

At last St. Martin was in my view. The island was difficult to pick up in the darkness. But then she rose higher and higher every moment as the canoe advanced. As we bore down upon her from the northeast she appeared as several sharp rocks jutting out of the dark water. As we neared I could make out some main features: it was a long island with jagged hills from one tip of it to the other. Nearer and I could clearly see water creaming against the rocks and reef at its base. A small spot of calm water amidst the boiling surf indicated the passage or channel into a grand bay through the reef.

St. Martin was now rising fast and purplish. Still nearer and I could plainly see a small town with many wharves at the top of a large bay. At the entrance to the bay, away on the left side on a low-lying point of land, was a fort. I then observed yet another fort, this one higher up the bay, commanding the town. Both forts were large and in good repair, and I could picture soldiers rushing from their barracks to man the guns at our approach. The dangers that the forts represented gave an edge to my life, a sharp sense of urgency.

We paraded at 5:30 in the morning. Orders were given for us to turn out in our light marching order. This news was cheered wildly. Here was proof that our officers expected us to defeat the enemy quickly. It also meant that we would not have to move against the French heavily laden with equipment. Our light marching order included our greatcoat, water canteen, eighty rounds of ball cartridge, and biscuit for three days. When the French turned and ran, as we were convinced they would, we would not be impeded in closing with them by equipment hanging all over our bodies. No, we would be among them in an instant, each of us transformed into a lion capable of extraordinary things.

We made a very soldier-like appearance in our light marching order this early morning. It is true that we were all uncomfortable in our tight white breeches, thick woolen clothes, and high stiff collars. But never did eyes behold the sight of ranked humans more splendid. Standing is not a simple, passive act. No, human standing is an art. It can be a form of strength that involves the whole of a person. And the way one stands discloses character and how he relates to the world. In this way did our phalanx stand still, a perfect and vigorous solid mass. We conveyed male strength, pride and discipline. We were the image of martial order. We looked like the rock-steady British soldiers that we were. We felt invincible and we communicated this in the manner in which we stood, even on a rolling deck.

A sharp splash caught my attention. A seaman had thrown the lead to sound the depth of the water. The thick rope attached to the long lead weight raced through the seaman's hand and plunged down into the water. After a few moments the rope ceased its downward movement. The same seaman quickly hauled it back into the canoe and carefully studied the red bit of cloth attached to it. "Ten fathoms," he cried. The operation was then repeated, followed by a different shout: "Nine fathoms with a sandy bottom!"

I knew well the changes in the color of water when land was coming up fast under a canoe. It starts with deep blue, then a lighter blue, then deep green, and finally light green with a visible bottom. At that moment the water was still a strong green color.

We were the first ship to enter the bay, and still the French forts did not fire on us. Suddenly we had the island on both sides of us and straight ahead. Just as suddenly the wind ran out and the small swells disappeared from the water. We had entered a still, watery valley and I felt imprisoned by the mysteriously quiet hills that looked down upon us. It was a large harbor, good for canoes both great and small, but not a one was to be seen.

We came to anchor but two pistol shots from the shore. At a distance the island had no attractive appearance, but once inside the bay it was more agreeable. The ground was uneven but not as high as Dominica or even the Mandara Hills. These hills were well cultivated with sugar plantations. The tops were covered with wood. Every now and then, through the foliage, I saw a well-built planter's house, encompassed by the familiar mean huts of the field negroes.

However agreeable this scene might have been, the situation was far from pleasant. Nothing moved on the shore. No human could be seen. No cattle grazed on the tough grass that grew along the bank. No birds flew out to perch on the masts and dazzle us with their beautiful feathers. In truth there was no living scenery. It was as if nature had died or was in hiding.

But where were the enemy buckras? Had they lost their nerve upon observing us? Surely they intended to defend this rich land. They seemed to have hidden their slaves and run in their cattle. Did they plan to attack us at our most vulnerable moment when the landing boats were bobbing up and down in the surf? That would certainly be their strategy if they knew that our muskets were unloaded and would remain so until after we had landed. What wisdom lay behind that order to load with ball only after we had formed up on the beach? How were we to defend ourselves before that time? I felt that behind each tree was a watching enemy who eagerly awaited the right moment to shoot me.

"READY THE BOATS!" A command.

A long pause.

"BOATS AWAY!" A reply.

Our little army was on its way. It seemed so puny when matched against that fatal shore and the phantom soldiers who lurked there. The canoes carrying us skimmed over the still green water like so many water striders. As we neared land the wind suddenly blew very hard against the boats. The spray of the sea beat over me, soaking my tunic. Was this a sign, an omen? Was that land to be fatal shore? Did the sea spirit wish finally to claim me before the enemy did? At that moment I recalled a Carib saying that when one died at sea it was because the sea was hungry for meat. I feared for my life.

The canoe crunched into the sand. We were there. I leaped from the boat as if it were a prison whose doors had been suddenly thrown open. I quickly formed up with my comrades in a long line, two ranks deep, then immediately loaded with ball and snapped my wedged-shape bayonet onto the muzzle of my flintlock. We all were silent, but I did overhear Sergeant Major Bostonian warning Lively in a hushed voice that since we were near the enemy, he should be careful and mind what he was about.

With my musket now armed, I no longer had that cold and naked feeling. With the soothing ramming of the ball and the snapping into place of the bayonet, my courage instantly returned. Once again I thought of the sheer love of meeting the enemy and the excitement of battle. Not a single thought was given to the possibility that I might be destined in a short time to die.

"LIGHT COMPANY TO THE FRONT!"

Our light infantry, called Light Bobs, quickly fanned out in front of us in a long, irregular, red line.

"FORWARD!"

In a flash they bounded up and over the high bank that rimmed the shore. Quickly they disappeared from view. The last sight of them was a long line of dark green helmet feathers bobbing up and down just over the crest of the bank. Only the creaking of stretching leather and the clatter of accouterments marked the passage of these men. Soon these sounds faded into an uneasy silence. They had vanished.

Still no signs of the French. Where were they? The cannon of the forts could easily have sunk us in the harbor. Why did they not contest the landing? This quiet made no sense. It seemed that we, the attackers, were being stalked. I wanted this terrible suspense to end—now!

We stood in the sand and waited. We watched Captain Cameron atop the bank. All eyes had turned instinctively to him. We hung on his every movement, his every gesture. He looked intently ahead, in the direction taken by the Light Company. What did he see? What sign was he looking for?

As I stood there, straining my ears to pick out some unusual sounds that would tell me something—anything— of the fate of the Light Company or the whereabouts of the enemy, my imagination once again saw my family, just as it had on my landing in Dominica. I could see my beloved mother, my father, and my sisters and brothers. Again and again I attempted to hail them, to get them to take notice of me so that I might tell them that I lived, that I was a British warrior, that I was finally honorable. But no, they kept low to the ground, bent over double, engaged in some unrecognizable task. They never looked up.

Stirrings on the bank broke the spell of this bitter vision. Captain Cameron had suddenly turned toward us and solemnly pointed his bright and gleaming sword forward. With that simple gesture, away we all went up the high bank.

In our eagerness to catch sight of the French we scrambled up the incline in disorderly haste. Once we had gained the crest of the bank we were ordered to form into open columns. Commands flew fast. "HALT! DRESS! STAND SQUARE! SUPPORT ARMS! RANKS ONE PACE

APART!" The jostling mass of soldiers quickly composed itself into orderly formation as though on parade.

To our great disappointment the enemy was still nowhere to be seen. Ahead was nothing but trees and grass. Overhead the sun saluted me with brightness. No steam as yet frowned on the early day. No unwholesome damp: the air was cool and refreshing.

"FORWARD—MARCH!" We stepped off in the deepest silence, our muskets in the crook of our elbows. We moved onward, marching from one ground to the next, past lofty coconut and cabbage trees and across wide open areas in a high state of cultivation.

It was at this moment that I saw my first living creature. It was a beautiful bird, dark green in color. It hovered in midair, the quick motion of its wings producing a kind of humming sound as it attempted to insert its long beak into a red, trumpet-shaped flower. I watched it as long as I could.

CRACK! CRACK! A few sputtering musket shots announced the opening of a battle up ahead between our skirmishers and theirs. The sounds were quickly followed by the crash and roar of continuous musketry. Wild ringing yells and huzzahs could be heard between the rapid "crack! crack!" of muskets. Bullets began to hiss through the air overhead.

We marched straight toward the sound of those guns. We gave no hint of haste but simply marched into battle as if on parade. Ahead, behind a line of coconut trees, I could now see a growing cover of smoke and dust hugging the crest of a low hill. At that moment several more bullets whistled through the air close by. Next a black speck arched high in the sky and plummeted toward us. I followed its flight with interest. The speck turned into a cannon ball that hissed angrily as it appeared to pass within a few feet of my head. It crashed with a loud bang into a line of trees behind.

I closed my eyes, held my breath, and ducked instinctively as it shrieked past. "Yuh der, Private Jack," cried Sergeant Major Bostonian, "keep dem head up, dat was a cannon ball not a flyin' turd."

Another solid shot plowed into the earth off to my right. It had come howling in like a destroying evil spirit. The desire to duck was almost overpowering. The sound was so great and the collision with the ground so violent that my heart pounded, and I fully expected it to burst in my chest. Up ahead, atop that low hill shrouded with thick smoke, I could see darting figures and musket flashes. I could now hear the voices of individual men cheering and shouting with mad excitement.

Over the growing din of the battle I heard the order to wheel into line. Instantly, non commissioned officers darted out of the columns to give the points for wheeling and forming. Again commands flew at us. "HALT! DRESS! KEEP SHOULDERS LEVEL! REAR RANK KEEP LOCKED UP!"

Bullets now began to hit around us like a shower of rain. Then a bugle sounded one of our calls, the "Fire and Retire!" The signal was repeated. There were again a few sputtering shots and directly the Light Company emerged from the cloud of smoke like phantom spirits and passed through our lines in good order. Several men went limping and crawling to the rear. When our Light Bobs retired, I noticed that the front of their clothing, their hands and faces, were blackened by the exploding powder at the lock of their muskets. A buckra sergeant had his eyebrows dyed black by the frequent flashes from the pan. "We have driven in the French skirmishers upon their main body, sir!" I heard a Light Company subaltern tell Captain Cameron excitedly.

We moved on a short distance to our front and came to a halt atop the low hill where our Light Infantry had only recently engaged the French and defeated them. What I saw of the field shocked me. The ground was covered with smashed and abandoned things: muskets, helmets, dead and wounded bodies, blankets, greatcoats, canteens, a dead horse, caps, belts, epaulettes, knapsacks, bundles of cartridges, shoes. And all over this wreckage, like a white carpet, were the folded ends of the cartridge papers. "So this is the bed of honor our officers speak of," I thought.

Not all the wounded could carry themselves to the rear. Here and there in the tall grass, stained red with blood, were men—comrades and enemies—waiting for the coming of death. We rested on our arms and avoided them as ordered. We tried mightily not to let their agony affect us. But their shrieks, calls of despair, demands for water, hands waving as if calling for assistance, and death rattles were hard to bear.

One of our wounded caused me to weep deeply and the sight of him I will carry to my grave. Dying though he was from a horrible wound, he could not cry out and give voice to his agony. We were halted and I saw him propped against some ammunition boxes and looking over at me. He sat there, not more than four musket lengths away, and looked steadily at me. A cannon ball had struck the lower part of his face and carried away his tongue and jaw. Even at that distance I could plainly see the white powder from the round shot on his black skin around the hideous wound. I was horrified, but said nothing. He sat there and looked at me steadily, his black eyes bursting with a longing for help and an apprehension of fatality. Oh, those eyes. What his misery must be, silenced yet alive to unbearable pain. I wept for him since he could not. I turned away, no longer able to endure his silent suffering. Stretcher-bearers came and took him away.

So this was the glory of war!

This was supposed to be an inspiring moment, a thrilling hour. The contested field belonged to the regiment. We had met the French and bested them, at least for the moment. But no man who stood on that field could send forth a cheer from his throat and heart. No! There was no glory to be had in the tempest of death that had just taken place.

Next, the thundering fire of two cannons rolled across to us. A few seconds later two great solid shot rushed in, hissing past high over our heads. The smoke that had hung over the battlefield was lifted by the wind, and across a wooded valley floor, atop a low hill, *I saw the French!* I could see two groups of men dressed in blue rapidly working their guns. The cannons were hauled back into place by dragrope-men. The long, black muzzles were pointed at us hardly above the level of the ground. Reloaded, they came into action, first one, then the other, but the range was too short. The balls fell to earth bouncing and ploughing up the ground each time they landed well in front of us. The gun-ners stopped to watch the flight of the solid iron shot, whereupon they went back to their cruel work: reloading, ramming, aiming and firing again at us.

All the while we stood there in the open, like cane wait-ing to be cut down, our flintlocks in the shoulder arms position.

The shot shrieked in as before. I know it was considered cowardly to duck, but I could not bring myself—no matter how hard I tried—to watch those balls of death coming straight at us. And so I ducked, waiting for a blow that would kill me. While in the act of bowing my head I heard a strange noise. It proved to be the sickening thuds of shot striking flesh. Away across the valley defiant cheer on cheer rang out like bells. I turned in the direction of the sounds. Both balls had struck men in the next file. I saw three of our men in a row with their heads clearly knocked off as if severed by a sword. Crimson pools formed on the ground from the rivulets of blood that squirted from several severed tubes in their battered neck-stumps. A few paces beyond was a soldier in five pieces. Both legs and an arm had been blown off. His chest, head, and the other arm made up the fourth piece. The pelvis was the fifth.

Again and again the lethal shot flew at us. Every ball seemed to hit something. From left to right the shot tore instant bloody gaps in our thin red lines. I could see our officers and sergeants pushing and shoving those still standing to close the bloody holes. What a terrible mixture of sounds this scene produced: the roaring of cannon; the hissing of round shot; men yelling, groaning, cursing, screaming, cheering, and orders to "CLOSE UP! GUIDE RIGHT! STAND FIRM! STAND FAST!"

And all the while we stood there, in silence, without firing our muskets, fully exposed to death. This way of soldiering was madness, standing still in the open and dying. "Have I come here only to die like this?" I thought. "This way of death is without reason."

The power of the cannon was not in the number of men it killed and wounded. It was in the horrible way it accomplished this. A solid shot did not simply kill or wound. It smashed a man to pieces!

Thinking that we were about to break, Captain Cameron ran up to speak to us. Calmly turning his back on the enemy guns, he addressed us. We were not about to break and run, but the truth is we all wanted to get out of the way of those guns. That was only human, wasn't it?

"Soldiers," he shouted over the din of the cannon fire, "you have been conspicuous by your daring bravery in the face of those guns. Cannon fire is the hardest thing for the soldier to bear since he cannot strike back. But remember, the cannon is doing what it was meant to do. Its horrible work is intended to destroy your courage before the infantry of the enemy attacks. In that, the enemy has not succeeded. It has been sharp work, but you have this day earned the honor to take the King's pay as British soldiers. Remain steadfast and the day will be yours."

We greeted these inspiring and refreshing words with a roaring shout. No sooner had the huzzah cleared our throats when we straightened up and shouldered arms once more.

The cannons boomed and shrieked again, then fell silent.

A strange hush had fallen over the battlefield.

Then I heard new sounds from the bottom of the wooded valley. Enemy drums beat to arms. After a long pause the drummers switched to a new and distinctive measure— *rum dum, rum dum, rummadum dummadum, dum, dum,* followed by shouts of *"Vive l'Empereur!"* Over and over they beat it without stop. We stiffened up to the color line.

"Dat be de *pas de charge* of de French," said Sergeant Major Bostonian dryly. "I remember it well." He pointed the spearhead of his pike toward the valley. "Dat is where dey will attack us from." My eyes swept the scene before me, back and forth, yet I saw nothing. But I did hear the steady tramp of a large body of men, *rum dum, rum dum, rummadum dummadum, dum, dum,* of the imposing drum beats, and growing shouts of *"Vive l'Empereur!"*

Then, without warning, a mass of marching men in column formation spilled from the trees in the valley cheering and shouting. This huge, solid block of men marched slowly up the slope to the drum. Here and there in the column flags fluttered and arms gleamed and flashed in the sun's rays. Beyond them a few skirmishers ran forward and stopped to fire upon us and ran forward again. Just then a bullet whistled passed my head. Our Light Bobs came on quickly and drove the enemy skirmishers back and away from the immense column, which continued its slow and steady march up the hill all alone.

Never before had I seen such a large column of men. The French were coming on in ranks of at least thirty men abreast! The enormous column stretched from the foot of the hill upon which we stood, back to the trees and within. It looked invincible. It seemed as though its sheer weight of numbers and forward motion would drive it with a power that could not be opposed through our slender red lines. I could not restrain my admiration of their imposing method of attack. It was a grand sight as ever a warrior looked upon. But that array caused fear to eat at my soul. It ate at the souls of my comrades, too, for our lines began to waver as if struck by a powerful wind. Shouts of "STAND FIRM! STAND FAST!" were heard up and down our lines.

The enemy column continued to advance in magnificent order to that unpleasant drumbeat. As the range decreased, I could plainly see them coming on in blue ranks, carrying their bayonet-tipped muskets at the port, and their officers in advance of them, some waving swords, others flourishing helmets.

In the very center of this enormous mass of men was a small open space. In it I counted three files of little boys marching in perfect step and beating the charge furiously. Up and down went their hands in perfect unison.

The column drew nearer and nearer. I was an eager witness to this magnificent spectacle. Yet at the same time I knew too well what its approach foretold. Involuntarily I put my hand on the cartridge pouch to assure myself that it was unfastened and completely filled. Next I thrust my fingers into the pocket of the pouch flap to determine if the spare flints, turnscrew and worm were where they should be. Victory depends no less upon these simple items than upon my own courage as a warrior. But all the while my gaze was clapped on the advancing column.

Small gaps appeared in the column as its inmates stepped over and around the remains of their own skirmishers slain by our Light Bobs. The obstacles passed, the gaps closed; the column never wavered.

Suddenly, the head of the column crested the hill eighty paces away. At this point the leader of the column put his hat on the point of his sword and waved it at his men. Again and again I distinctly heard his shout: *"Vive l'Empereur!"* And so did the entire column.

"Now's the time, Eighth West India Regiment!" It was the voice of Captain Cameron. "The fatal field is before the enemy. Remember, aim low." A few second later —"MAKE READY!" We were now a long, red wall of leveled muskets. "PRESENT!" I clutched my flintlock more firmly and braced myself to receive the shock. "FIRE!"

The crash of muskets was deafening. There was a brilliant explosion at the lock. A sheet of orange flame leaped forth from the muzzle of my musket. My head and face became enveloped in a thick, greasy smoke from the priming powder and the charge that obscured my vision. All around the air filled with smoke and dust. All was turmoil and confusion. I reloaded my weapon in an instant and awaited the results. The smoke slowly lifted off the ground. As it did, I was astonished to see that the front ranks of the column all lay in a writhing wall of dead and wounded, including the officers who moments before had been urging their men forward with raised swords and hats and shouts of *"Vive l'Empereur!"* It was oh, so quick; one moment these men were alive, the very next they were either dead or wounded. Among the prostrate mass I could see the pitiful motions of those attempting to crawl away and those in the final struggles of the agonies of death. Behind this gruesome wall of dead and dying the column seemed staggered by the volley and shook violently like a wounded animal.

"MAKE READY!" Someone shouted behind me. Again I aimed my trusty flintlock with deadly accuracy upon the mass of blue-clad soldiers before me. "FIRE!" Another sharp rattle of musketry issued from our ranks. Another sheet of orange flame erupted from our muskets. Our fire was marked by yet another wall of dead and dying Frenchmen. I could see streams of wounded men peel away from the front of the stricken column and stumble back down the slope to the rear. The column remained rooted to the spot as if frozen with fear. It seemed to be imprisoned, trapped by the walls of dead men before it and pressed by the living behind. We reloaded and fired again and again with the same effect. Oh, how fast they crashed to the ground. Rank upon rank were laid down in heaps by our musketry. How easy it was to kill and maim at that distance. The fire from our guns was too heavy to stand and live. It was so mechanical, so impersonal, so easy.

The column seemed to be breaking apart. The front remained halted, the middle part tried in vain to surge forward into the front ranks, and the rear sections seemed to be turning about.

Just after our last volley, while we were in the act of reloading, several of the files wheeled out from the middle of the column like a bird extending one of its wings. They rapidly deployed into line and fired on us. I saw a flash. I heard the unmistakable thud of bullets striking flesh. I saw comrades fall, some never to rise again. I heard large, strong men moaning and crying out for assistance. There was wreckage everywhere. Our own killed and wounded were scattered all along the line, but mostly on the left wing and the center, which were opposite the head of the column.

Captain Cameron saw the enemy's movement and decided to redeploy the regiment. The left and center wings were ordered to mark time and the command "Right shoulders forward!" came down the line from Captain Cameron. It was repeated over and over again by the other officers and sergeants. The right wing, where I stood proudly, wheeled smartly to its left until it faced the flank of the enemy wing, which had detached itself from the column. At the order, we in the front ran, fired and half-halted to reload, while the second rank passed rapidly through our line to fire in their turn. In this way we kept up an unrelenting fire while we closed the gap between us and the enemy toward the point of a bayonet attack. The enemy, their once-imposing formation now on the verge of crumbling, returned only a few sputtering shots, whereupon we fixed bayonets and charged, cheering wildly as we did.

Before we closed with them we had to pass over their wounded and dead. They lay thick on this field of mutilation. Here death presented itself in many terrible shapes: a private soldier, his lips moving in death; a little drummer boy with a large hole in his breast; an old sergeant, his face covered with blood and a blood froth squirting from his mouth; a dead soldier in a kneeling position; an officer, his blue tunic riddled with bullets.

When we finally came up with them they offered little resistance in defense of their lives. I slaughtered six men with my bayonet and stove in the head of a seventh with my flintlock. They then broke and ran. We charged after them huzzahing, shooting, and stabbing as we went. I pierced three more and left my bayonet stuck in the chest of a fourth. We pressed them so closely that many threw away their knapsacks and muskets. Flushed with wild excitement we chased after them in the manner of a leopard that has cut a goat out of a flock.

With the retreat of the enemy, their artillery began again to play upon us. The cannons boomed and the balls shrieked in. As we neared the valley floor in our pursuit of the French, the gunners on the hill above loaded their guns with case shot and let fly at us. Several of my comrades were instantly cut down. The order to halt and retire checked our advance and we fell slowly back to the top of our hill in good order. Upon looking back down the slope, I saw a crowd of soldiers disappear in confusion into the green woods out of which they had emerged but a short time before, so certain of victory, so menacing.

The guns, those terrible guns, also withdrew. I saw them limbered up and the gunners dash away into the green. Nothing pleased me more than to see them go, for nothing frightened me and weakened my resolve more than the sight of solid shot hopping into us or the sound of balls whizzing by overhead.

It was now strangely quiet after what had seemed like many hours of constant noise. I had the feeling of emerging from a slow eternity of flashes, explosions, crashes, screams, hissing bullets, shrieking balls, smoke, shouts, commands—and into a calm. The peace of the outer world was matched by the peace I felt withinside myself. Slowly my sense of time and place returned. With that came a rush of physical sensations. The air was heavy with the sharp smell of powder and saturated with the reek of fresh blood. My hands, face and tunic were black with the greasy remains of the powder smoke. My lungs were filled with smoke. My eyes burned. My head ached. My right shoulder was nearly jellied from the many violent recoils of my flintlock. My mouth was begrimed with gunpowder giving me a raging and tormenting thirst. The faint drone of mosquitoes and whispering voices were drowned in ringing ears. My whole body was heavy with fatigue and I felt as though I was about to drop down in a stupor. All discipline was now forgotten. I let fall my musket and sank heavily to the ground. Absorbed in these feelings I took no notice of the main wing of our division as it approached and passed through our lines on its way to seize one of the enemy's forts. Now drained of all strength, I passed into sleep.

Jubba Lily:

Death had changed you, Jack. When I first saw you upon your return from St. Martin I became absorbed in your face. It was as though I was looking at you for the first time. For a brief moment I tried to look away but those large, deep, black eyes attracted me irresistibly. You immediately noticed my inquiring gaze. As if to hide something, you forced a weak smile and tried unsuccessfully to look away. But you could not avoid my fixed gaze. As always, you stood out handsomely in your flashy black, red and white uniform. You were the same size and shape. And you sprang forward and snatched me up when you saw me waiting for you on the wharf. So you were still young and lusty. But you no longer looked young. Your gaze was now hard and you stared at everything, even me. The look was both wary and scornful. Suddenly I caught my breath. You had the eyes of an old man! The killing had changed you forever. That night I cried for you and what you had lost. Was the loss of your youth, your innocence, worth what you saw and did at St. Martin?

Jack:

That night I waited until everyone in my barrack was fast asleep. I lit a candle and looked into Pedro's mirror, which I had hidden under my crib. She was right, my eyes had indeed changed. They were no longer soft and empty with a child's brightness. They stared back at me. They were hard with faint lines spreading out from the corners. I tried to wipe them away with a smile, but the hard eyes still stared back at me. I turned my head this way and that way to allow the candlelight to strike my face from different directions. Perhaps the look had something to do with the light. It made no difference. The hard eyes stared back at me. The sad truth was that I was no longer the same, I was no longer young. I did not feel any different. Except for a few bruises, my body was the same. No matter, she was right. A few hours of war had changed me and my eyes registered this passage like my Margi facial marks. If one battle had robbed me of my youth, what would the next battle forever steal from me? My soul? My life? I had seen enough of this different me. I blew out the candle.

Chapter 13

The Trial: Puxley's Testimony

Since the start of my trial the world had changed for me. I now had a better understanding and appreciation of qualities and factors I had taken for granted. Colors were more intense with sensual energy. Instead of the subtle movement of minutes and hours, time stood still one moment and then leaped ahead suddenly the next. I saw for the first time the wonderful forms of balance that every living thing achieved, whether in motion or in standing. Order and destruction, although opposed forces, *could* be held together in harmony. As I faced the possibility of death, a veil parted, allowing me to see the essential balance, harmony, patchwork and primary vitality of life. A feeling of great joy swept over me, for the secrets of the sweet aliveness of life were uncovered for me to see for the first time. Thanks to the approach of death I better understood life.

Dark as my fate seemed, I believed firmly that truth and mercy ever triumph over injustice and evil. Yet now, in the third day of my trial, I dreaded this court of sitting white men. *See them!* It is not that their gaze is always straightforward. No, any other focus would be a bad sign, even an omen of death. Imagine the man who judges you looking down at his feet or turned sideways looking out through a window at the form of a pretty maiden! As a Margi I understood this. Seated persons of authority *must* show an awareness of themselves as individuals of power and must present a fitting image to those watching. But what troubled me were the cold, fixed expressions on the faces of the judges. The brilliance of their red uniforms merely charged the intensity of the vacant silence on their faces. It was that utter lack of humanity that troubled me. "I want this over now," I said quietly.

The scraping sound of a chair dragging across the rough wooden floor suddenly broke the spell of my thoughts. The judge advocate had pushed his chair back from his table and gotten to his feet to present the testimony of the ill Captain Puxley to the court. It sickened me that I would be forced to listen for a second time to evidence that could be the death of me. The judge advocate nodded silently to the court and began:

"It is my sad duty to have to inform the court of Captain Puxley's untimely death early this morning. This gallant officer is but the latest victim of the all-devouring jaws of the West India plague. His death was unexpected, as he appeared to recover from the ills of the climate.

"Still, this sad picture is not without a bright spot. It pleases me to advise the court that Lieutenant Wills and Markland have been successful in obtaining the whole testimony, in writing, of Captain Puxley before his death. Captain Puxley's evidence having been judged to be material in support of the charge, permission to question him on his sickbed was sought and received from the court. It is intended to have this evidence read to the court. The judge advocate wishes to thank the court for this special exemption, for he is ever mindful that no witness or his substitute is ordinarily permitted to read his testimony to the court, for this may well give room for the subornation of evidence, against which all courts are most anxious to guard. The law is precise on this point."

The president responded, his voice unusually warm, "Captain Puxley took a leading part in the enterprise to take back the Cabrit from the mutineers, and the service is ever grateful to him as he knew the fortress and its localities well. The court is saddened to learn of the death of Captain Puxley. I remember him well. No officer's character stood higher than his. He was a most agreeable Englishman. His loss is a staggering blow to His Majesty's service." Silence reigned for a moment, except for the buzzing of a few hungry mosquitoes.

"This wicked climate will never cease in its efforts to destroy us." The tenderness in his voice had yielded to harsh, chilling sounds. "These islands are nothing more than magazines of nastiness . . . Will you, Captain Mapp, mention to the court the name of the officer who will read Captain Puxley's testimony?"

"Lieutenant Markland, sir."

As the officer prepared to read the testimony, a deep silence returned to the room.

"Intelligence of the tragic circumstances of the mutiny, as well as the state of matters at the Cabrits, was received at Roseau by Governor Johnstone by express at gunfire, that is, five o'clock in the morning of 10 April. By ten o'clock that morning the Sixty-eighth Foot, then doing duty at Morne Bruce, the St. George's regiment of militia, and a small detachment of the Royal Artillery, were all put on board vessels with supplies of provisions and ammunition.

"This force got promptly underway and arrived at Portsmouth the same afternoon. Governor Johnstone and his staff embarked in a man-of-war, which was then on its way to Guadeloupe, but volunteered to assist in the operations. Two British ships-of-the-line, the *Excellent* and *Magnificent*, each of seventy-four guns, happened fortunately to arrive at Portsmouth for wood and water the very night of the mutiny. Being fired on by mutineers, these ships immediately landed their marines to the north and south of the Cabrits and thus severed all outside communications with the mutineers.

"As soon as Governor Johnstone arrived at Portsmouth, which was late in the day of 10 April, he dispatched the *Magnificent* to the Iles des Saintes for some of the troops of the Royals which were in garrison there. This detachment, which was subsequently placed under my command, arrived at Portsmouth early the following morning, on 11 April. At that moment Governor Johnstone's command consisted of not more than 1,000 bayonets.

"In the early morning hours of 11 April, at eight to be precise, a flag of truce carried by Captain Marlow, one of the prisoners of the mutineers, arrived in camp. The mutineers proposed to surrender the fortress on the condition that their lives would be spared. The Governor rejected these terms, whereupon the mutineers then agreed to lay down their arms, to surrender the post at four o'clock that day, and to throw themselves on the clemency of Sir Thomas Trigge, Commander-in-Chief. With that, the column got immediately underway and marched straight for the Cabrits with Governor Johnstone at their head. The column moved cautiously along the access road leading into the Cabrits past the swamp on our right.

"Upon gaining the barrier gate, I saw the mutineers up ahead on the esplanade immediately before Fort Shirley. They were drawn up two deep, with their uncased colors in the center and several bound officers directly behind the colors. I also observed that they had manned those guns in the fort that could be trained on the forward part of the esplanade, the very ground we intended to occupy. As the column arrived at the bottom of the sloping open space before the fort, we quickly formed into line opposite them and they presented arms once we had executed our movement.

"The Governor then proceeded to address the mutineers, in the course of which he ordered them to ground their arms. At that moment I observed a great unsteadiness in their ranks. It was as though the mutineers were at odds with themselves. Only a few of the mutineers obeyed the command to lay their muskets on the ground. As I was standing now more than thirty paces from them, and directly opposite the Grenadier Company, I observed a lone grenadier suddenly step forward from their front rank. Upon stepping forward this man cried out that they must not ground their arms and he then pointed his flintlock at us.

"Then without warning he fired his musket, whereupon the whole Grenadier Company fired a volley into us. We, however, immediately returned their fire and then charged, whereupon they dispersed in disorder and in all directions. The chief part of them made for the top of the Outer Cabrits. We followed them so closely that their gunners were prevented from firing their guns on us, fearing that they would strike their fellow mutineers.

"With the idea of a truce now completely swept away, the red flag was hoisted, which indicated that no quarter would be shown to any still in mutiny. For about six hours they were hunted down by the troops and fired on by the navy. It was only the next day, however, that the red flag was taken down and a white one displayed. Those in hiding then came out and surrendered. Captured mutineers, after being disarmed and stripped of all but the barest essentials of their regimentals, were herded together on the main parade where they were kept under the watchful eye of the troops. Their dead numbered about 200.

"This testimony I do solemnly swear to be the whole truth. Signed this fifteenth day of April 1802 — Captain Alexander Puxley, First Regiment of Foot"

"Ha! That officer has failed in his mission from the grave," I thought. "The clay pot of my life will not be broken by that testimony." I believed, no, I was certain, that the judge advocate had no case against us. The pitiful evidence of the two officers was clear proof of that. Everything the judge advocate had done was so contemptible I wanted to burst into laughter. But I dared not and instead bit my lip to fight back the grin that tried to escape from me.

At that moment I felt a soft hand on my shoulder and turned to see Hussar's handsome face. A big, toothy smile covered it. Without saying a word to each other, I sensed that he and I silently shared the same view of the dead officer's testimony. *The judge advocate does not have a case against us.*

The outward appearance of the judge advocate suggested a man in trouble. During the reading of the testimony he moved his head back and forth in a helpless gesture. His expression was one of alarm. I also noticed that his forehead had suddenly become wet and beads of sweat ran down his temple and disappeared inside the collar of his tunic.

By these signs he admitted that he did not have evidence to send us before a firing party. He was squirming inside and it amused me to watch him suffer. I could read his thoughts. "What should I do?" he kept saying to himself. "What should I do next?"

"Guess wrong!" I said to myself, hoping, somehow, to force my thoughts into his mind and thus completely confound him. "Guess wrong, you pissing she-goat! Guess wrong!"

Still, I had to look at the danger of my situation in cold, hard terms. Someone—the army? the buckras? evil spirits?—badly wanted our deaths to atone for the mutiny. I glanced over at the judge advocate. He sat still and stared into the air as if to gain time. He was still a clever creature and as slick as a wet bayonet.

So there could be no wavering on our part. Souvarine Petro would have to be protector at every instant. There could be no rest, no pause since our very lives depended on his success.

By now it was becoming very familiar. Souvarine Petro leaped to attack the dead officer's evidence in his customary ways. But first he dazzled his onlookers, including us who knew of him. I say *of* him because none of us ever truly knew or understood him. And it was calculated. He knew instinctively the power of physical impression and he missed no opportunity to play on his own qualities. He was invested with an aura of importance. One could see and sense this in his attitude. It was enlivened with honor and authority. Even when standing still he radiated active potentiality. He was like an African dancer caught for a moment in arrested motion. Was this a burden for him? I think not, for he bore his regality easily and with conviction. Here was the very reason for his posting to the Grenadier Company. Although he was well under the six foot mark, it was his natural ability to stand and move with power and authority that made him seem taller and larger than he really was.

Under the full panoply of his enlivened spirit he set upon the testimony of the dead officer. He dismissed it as mere circumstantial evidence. The testimony was, as he put it, "nothing more than attendant circumstances used as evidence to *imply* the proof of a fact." He also referred to the objectives in the opening speech of the judge advocate as absurd and not capable of being proven. He had succeeded in turning things around, becoming the accuser.

But he avoided the matter of the "lone grenadier" who fired the fatal shot. Why? Was it a delicate point for him? Was *he* the lone grenadier?

Chapter 14

The Trial: Enter and Exit Hamlet

Now it was the turn of that damn negro, Hamlet, to give evidence against us. *Hamlet*. What a peculiar name for an African; and it was the name he was apparently given at birth, as he answered to it even when he was alone with Africans! What is more, two names, not one, give Africans particular identity. And African names have real meaning: names in honor of esteemed ancestors and friends, or of God, or of special events. All blacks born in the West Indies lack true African names. What they answer to are buckra names and labels for pet animals and trinkets, slave names one and all. How eagerly he approached the witness chair, like a mongoose who has caught the scent of snake eggs. Look again: that thin-lipped, smug grin. He could barely hide his glee to do us harm. He was much too impatient and that was not a good sign for us.

He took no notice of us as he sat in the witness chair. The judge advocate then appeared and began to swear in this cowering dog as he sat on the edge of the chair, nearly tipping it over.

"Are you the negro known as Hamlet?"

"Yas, sah."

"Do you solemnly declare to tell the truth, the whole truth, and nothing but the truth in so far as shall be asked of you?"

"Yas."

With my attention fixed on that cringing Hamlet, I failed to notice that Souvarine Petro had risen from our bench until he cut the negro off.

"I object to this man being called to testify."

"Private Petro, I do hope this is not an attempt to delay or to tease the court." The president of the court spoke slowly and carefully in a heavy, flat voice.

"No. It is not."

"What reason, then, do you offer in support of your objection to this man as a witness?"

"The man Hamlet is a . . . a slave." Souvarine Petro's voice faltered for a brief moment. It was as though the words he spoke pained him. He continued. "The British army, in conformity to . . . to West Indian legal custom, has never permitted a slave to give evidence at its court-martial."

Conformity! West Indian legal custom!

With those surprising words Souvarine Petro sat down. His face showed no emotion. But a slight twitching in the corners of his mouth revealed that there was a great struggle going on withinside of him. A puzzled look swept across the faces of my comrades. The members of the court spoke to each other in low tones. The judge advocate seemed momentarily absorbed in his own thoughts, as though he was searching for the words with which to reply to Souvarine Petro. The court waited for the judge advocate to speak. The judge advocate waited for the court to respond. A long, uncomfortable stillness prevailed.

Finally the judge advocate broke the heavy silence: "The view expressed by Private Petro is a tropical truth and a tropical truth only. In English law His Majesty's army takes its *own* law overseas. This law has a statutory basis in the annual *Mutiny Act* and therefore overrides law made by West Indian legislatures. British military law, the law that regulates the army's courts-martial, is therefore not, insofar as it is based on English statute, governed by or subservient to local law or custom.

"Private Petro has introduced the legal status of the negro Hamlet into this proceeding. This is not a point under military authority and, thus, is not a matter for the court to consider. What *is* important is the credibility of the witness. The negro Hamlet is a slave and I do not question that. But he is also a man, and as a man he is incontrovertibly capable of stating real facts. The state of slavery, in my view, does not incapacitate one from being a credible witness in a court of justice. And since Private Petro has not raised any direct objection to the competency of the witness, I am forced to conclude that he, too, is satisfied with the witness on that account.

"The negro Hamlet should be allowed to give evidence before this court. His ability to do so is in no way infringed upon by legal conventions. To do otherwise would represent a high invasion of the prerogative of the Crown and the rights of the imperial Parliament."

The judge advocate, who until then had been speaking to the court, turned slowly toward Souvarine Petro and asked confidently, "If, as you claim, slaves are not permitted to give evidence at courts-martial, in deference to local conventions, does not your argument apply with equal force to the prisoners, who, I am told, are considered slaves by the law officers of the crown?"

"I had not considered that question," replied Souvarine Petro, "as I saw no need to call any of my comrades as witnesses."

Another heavy silence prevailed in the room.

The judge advocate looked pained and frustrated. He clearly had not expected Souvarine Petro to answer as he did.

I was stunned by Petro's words. I had expected to testify and tell my side of the story to the court. I looked around me and saw surprised expressions on the faces of my comrades. Why has Souvarine Petro kept us in the dark about his plans? Our lives were at risk and we deserved to know. And what made him fear Hamlet's testimony so much that he would shame himself by recognizing the authority of the evil slave system in order to silence Hamlet—*and us as well?* No wonder he choked on his own words. How strange, how distressing, considering his hatred of slavery.

"The objection to the credibility of the witness has been stated." The voice of the president of the court broke the silence. It was firm and showed no emotion. "As His Majesty's courts-martial never deliberate with doors open, the court will now be cleared in order to weigh the import of the objection. Once the court has arrived at a resolution, that decision will afterwards be communicated in open court to all concerned. The court is hereby adjourned until two o'clock this day."

I could not make up my mind if I wanted Hamlet to testify or not. Part of me wanted him silenced since he clearly intended us harm. But that would mean acknowledging the tyranny of slavery. (I was beginning to sound like Souvarine Petro.) Another part of me wanted to know what it was he knew and wanted to say. But to let him give this evidence might destroy our chances to live and to soldier again.

It is said around the Cabrits that Hamlet hated all black soldiers because one of them had prevented him from enlisting in the regiment. He had been identified by a black soldier in the recruiting party and sent back to his owner, who flogged him before returning him to the cane fields. He also hated me personally because I had taken Jubba Lily away from him. No. This creature was consumed with hatred and vengeance. I was sure of it. No. It would be dangerous for him to testify. His mouth must be sealed even if it meant acknowledging the tyranny of slavery. (Those words again.) That was my wish. Death was always hungry for the flesh of the living. Why stick our heads into his mouth?

From withinside the courtroom came the heavy sounds of shuffling boots and chairs being pushed about. The court had reassembled. A command rang out and we were marched back into the room. Its members were already seated when I entered. They sat there as before, stone-faced, eyes flat and hard. What decision had they reached? Would Hamlet give evidence or not? My eyes searched theirs for some sign. Nothing.

"The court has been applied to for our opinion upon a question of evidence," the president proclaimed. His voice was indifferent as before. "That question is whether or not the evidence of a slave can be offered in proof of a charge before a court-martial sitting in Dominica. Anything that is likely to raise the political expectation of the slaves, which might prove to be incompatible with their status as slaves, must be avoided at all cost. To permit a common slave to participate in the solemnity of a military court would, in fact, raise the expectation of all slaves. To do this would weaken white rule. The calamity in Haiti is further proof against tampering with the social order in these islands. It is, therefore, the considered opinion of the court that the evidence of a slave is strictly inadmissible upon a British army court-martial. Such evidence must be restricted to those special forms of trial reserved for slaves only. The negro known as Hamlet may not give evidence at this proceeding."

For a very long time there was an uneasy silence in the room. It was a few moments before I realized the consequences of the court's decision. Hamlet would not testify. Although I did not know all the complexities of our case or of military law, I knew that the judge advocate had been defeated. His pitiful efforts were meaningless thrashing. He had failed utterly to show that we were mutineers. A flush of excitement swept over my body. I would live. I was certain of that. I would go free and once again be an honorable person.

But there remained a curious, nagging question: Souvarine Petro had smashed every attempt to make us into mutineers, but had he proven to the court that it was not possible for us to suppress the mutiny or to give immediate information of it? The *Articles of War* were clear on this part: accessories to mutiny could suffer gruesome death or such other punishments. I could not see into Souvarine Petro's mind, but I felt certain that he would similarly destroy any attempts to picture us as furthering the mutiny.

Hamlet slowly rose from his chair. But he bent low, the way all slaves stand when in the presence of whites, clutching at his cap. He looked hard at me with narrowed eyes and his lips drew back in a bitter smile that came direct from the depths of his injured soul. He turned by degrees, as if wounded, and dragged himself out of the room. I watched him leave with inexpressible pleasure. His efforts to make war on us, and particularly me, had failed. Still, he was a turd, a shit of slavery, a man-animal guided wholly by the passions of jealousy, bitterness and revenge. "May it be your fate," I thought, "to pay in days of bitter sorrow for the few hours of pleasure the thoughts of my death at your hands gave you!" He was gone, but I felt I had not seen the last of him.

The judge advocate then rose from his chair to address the court. The decision of the court had caused his face to redden to the color of the frangipani flower. His face sagged as if pulled down by invisible weights, a look of embarrassment and defeat. "Gentlemen, I . . . I do not plan to call any more witnesses in support of the several charges. It is my intention . . . to sum up." His voice was at first unsteady. It faltered. It was also raspy as if the back of his throat was dry. Quickly, however, his voice regained that air of authority that awed me at the start of the trial.

"You have no doubt that all the prisoners were with the Eighth West India Regiment on the evening of 9 April 1802, when the said mutiny occurred, as mentioned in the indictments. It is equally evident that it cannot be precisely ascertained if any of the prisoners initiated the mutiny or if any of them killed those fallen comrades mentioned in the several indictments. However, gentlemen of the court, permit me to make four important observations. First, it is the rule of law, is it not, that when the fact of mutiny is once proved—indeed, it was never questioned—every circumstance excusing, alleviating or justifying in order to lessen the seriousness of the crime must be proved by the prisoners, for the law, which is precise on this point, presumes the fact malicious until the contrary appears in the evidence. Secondly, gentlemen, there is another rule that states that it is immaterial, where there are several prisoners concerned, who actually initiated mutiny, for *all* who were present are in the eyes of the law principals. This is a rule that was settled long ago upon solid arguments and by the wisdom and policy of ages.

"Thirdly, honorable gentlemen, it is the bounden duty of every one of the King's soldiers to check the spread of the dreadful evil of mutiny in its earliest stage by giving *immediate information* of mutinous purpose that may come to his knowledge. Inactivity or silence in the face of mutiny is a breach of the soldier's solemn duty. And this breach will be justly held to be an approbation and acquiescence in this criminal design. Such misbehavior is declared to be punishable in the same with the actual crime. Thus, according to Section two, Article four of the *Articles of War,* it is enacted that 'any officer, non-commissioned officer, or soldier, who, being present at any mutiny or intended mutiny, shall not without delay give information thereof to his commanding officer, shall suffer death or such other punishment as by a general court-martial shall be awarded.'

"Lastly, honorable gentlemen, I need not remind the court that mutiny is the highest military crime of which a soldier is capable, for it strikes at the life's blood of the state itself. Such mischief *cannot* go unpunished, lest it encourage the enemy in our midst who plot serious injury to the realm and to British interests. Given all this, gentlemen, I do rest the case as it is. And I doubt not but on the evidence as it now stands, that the facts, as far as we have gone, are fully proved. And by the force of that evidence you must pronounce the several prisoners *guilty* of mutiny."

Words. Truth is never enough to win an argument. For truth to prevail the speaker must have a mastery of words. First, he must be a sensual man: one who feels words, one who is ever alive to the sounds, the texture of words. Then he must know the many shades of meaning of words. This is an acquired skill, but an important one nonetheless. A sense of timing and effective delivery are yet additional weapons he must possess in his arsenal of speech-ways in support of truth. Joining all these things together is the love of words and language. Finally, dramatic use of all key body parts—eyes, mouth, legs, head, feet, hands, fingers, torso—must be joined to this dominion of words. This, then, is truth fully armed and invincible. Without this art, truth is disarmed and abandoned, made powerless and pitiful like an old lion deprived of its teeth and claws.

Words. The judge advocate understood all of this. His words were like a weapon drawn and sparkling. Because of my training as a Margi memory man, I was instantly alert to what the judge advocate had done. I would not pretend that I was not impressed with what I both saw and heard. It was evident that care had been given to the selection of words he used. And they were carefully delivered for effect; his voice rose and fell like swelling, crashing waves, a device used to ensnare the listeners. Another fact. His words were so high-sounding. Although he used the word "gentlemen" much too often, to the point of irritation, he spoke in an arresting way.

But enough of that. His words and gestures had a deadly purpose—*my death*! I felt an overmastering desire to jump to my feet and challenge this man who would have me murdered. But the mere thought of organizing a reply in English quickly discouraged me and only served to remind me of the New World me: *pidgin me.* Unless something dramatically changed the course of my life for the better (and that seemed most unlikely), I was doomed to exist in the silent world of my Margi thoughts. Here was a world known only to me, a world that would end without a trace when I died. No. I could not address the court. That was fantasy. Only Souvarine Petro could match the clever words of the judge advocate with his own clever words. But he *must* succeed in driving out any doubts about our innocence from the heads of the court.

It was time. Souvarine Petro pushed his chair back from the long, bare table behind which my comrades and I sat. He stepped slowly and deliberately to the front of the table, turning as he did to face the court. He struck what I thought was a defiant pose. His legs were apart with the right leg pointing away at an angle with the rest of his body. The left hand rested on his hip while the right hand was coiled inside his tunic ready to spring forth to stab at the air whenever he stressed a point. His bold attitude was most strongly communicated, however, by his face. His eyes bulged and shone in an insistent gaze, directed at the court, while one corner of his lip rose slightly. "The following will serve both as my opening as well as my closing remarks." His voice was sharp and clear as it ever was.

"My brothers stand indicted for murder. To these indictments they have pleaded *not guilty*. By this plea they throw the burden of proof as to the facts of mutiny upon the judge advocate. This ancient rule is also based upon solid arguments and wisdom.

"It is not contested that a number of unfortunate people were killed at the time the indictments charge. Thus, this trial naturally divides itself into three main questions. One—did any of these men aid and assist in the deaths of those people cited in the indictments? Two—is there any evidence which in any way implicates these men directly in the mutiny? And three. Were these men accessories to mutiny?

"Before I enter upon these questions, let me remind you of a notion that is foreign both to truth and law. It is an idea that has been universally adopted throughout these islands. It demands our attention because it may well have a bearing on this case. It is the view that the life of an African is of little value, of much less value than that of a white man and on par with that of an ox. *This is a very great mistake, a cruel mistake, one which has poisoned the very air and land of the region.* Let me remind you that military law, unlike the laws of this island, puts the black soldier and the white soldier under equal restraint. Military law, unlike the slave laws of this island, knows no distinction of persons. What will justify and mitigate the actions of a black soldier will do the same for a white soldier. *Military law is precise on this point, is it not?*

"As I have suggested, the army and its law exist side by side with a larger society, planter society. The two societies are not strangers to each other, are they? Over time the army and the planters have developed many common interests, have they not? In view of this community of interests between the army and the planters, how do the colonists view the daughters and sons of Africa? The black color of their skin, the toil of their life on the estates, the ignorance and hatred of things African, the severity of discipline to which they are constantly exposed, the precarious tenure by which they are generally believed to hold their lives, have all conspired to propagate a sentiment against Africans as punitive as it is untrue.

"These cruel notions, as steady and constant as the winds and tides, inexorably seep into the minds of *all* who live in these islands. They spare no one: planter, merchant, soldier, seaman, officer, black man, white man. But by recognizing that this pernicious prejudice flies in the face of all facts, we can—with the assistance of the human heart—dissipate these false and demeaning ideas. *My brothers must not fall victims to this evil.*

"As for the charges, they were falsely sounded against these men, and those who brought them must have known it to be so. To refute these charges it is no more necessary than to declare the simple truth.

"First, there is no evidence, direct or circumstantial, in support of the charge of murder. The judge advocate has admitted this, has he not, as he never attempted to prove the charge. The inescapable conclusion to be drawn from the evidence he himself introduced into the record brings out the simple truth: *these men are innocent*!

"Second, unable to pin these deaths on the prisoners, the core of the judge advocate's plan was then to link my brothers to the mutiny conspiracy. He failed for all to see, did he not? His own witnesses were unable to link my brothers to the mutiny in any way. In fact, the questions put by the judge advocate to his own witnesses merely brought out the simple truth once again: *my brothers are innocent*!

"And three. Are these men accessories to mutiny? Once again the judge advocate failed to introduce any evidence that they were. His own heavy silence on this question brings out the simple truth yet again: *these men are innocent*!

"It must be clear from the evidence that none of the actions of these men were in breach of the *Articles of War*. Therefore, to find them guilty would be contrary to every principle of justice and humanity. Finally let me remind you of the importance of this trial to these men. IT IS FOR THEIR LIVES!"

Souvarine Petro's words ended suddenly, as dreams do. A heavy silence followed.

Souvarine Petro glared at the court. He seemed bent on provoking them. What sense was there in making enemies of these men of authority? Had his rage gotten the best of him? The court looked back. As hard as I tried, I could discern nothing on the faces of those stern face men. Their feelings and opinions were hidden.

"The court is now in possession of the whole evidence." The voice of the president rang in the long room. "It will now deliberate upon the judgment in the return of a solemn verdict on the innocence or guilt of the prisoners. The court will adjourn until tomorrow, 17 April, at the hour of nine of the clock in the morning, at which time it will make known its judgment and pronounce sentence. The parties and all indifferent persons are ordered to withdraw!"

The setting sun was in my face as we were marched back to our cells.

As I looked out my cell window I suddenly had a new feeling about the island. I looked in surprise at all the tropical growth. For the first time the luxuriant foliage was no longer just a brilliant garden of flowers and trees. It seemed oppressive. It gave a sense of crowding, of struggling to recapture what man had dared to take. Nature, cheated and wounded by the hand of man, wanted to restore its paradise by shoving man and all his polluting machinery off the land and into the deep sea where all would be swallowed up and forever lost. Then the majestic rain forests would sweep back down to the sea triumphant and cover the scars that had disfigured the landscape: the plantations, great houses, slave huts, forts, wharves, towns, roads. Once again the island would be covered to the water's edge by great trees whose lower trunks had never known daylight or the evil touch of greedy, insane man.

Chapter 15

A New Life

Quite suddenly, as things happen in this world, I knew I would live. *I would live.* It was instinctive, but it was characteristic of me to trust instinct. The decision of the court was yet to come, but I was certain that I would be declared blameless.

How could it be otherwise? Souvarine Petro had demonstrated our innocence over and over. Had he not? And St. Martin. Did we not prove that we soldiers were necessary to the British by our great victory over the French, a victory that Sergeant Major Bostonian predicted? Facts are stubborn things; they cannot be ignored.

It was suddenly like springtime after a long, withering dry season whose terrible excesses of gloom and despair now seemed almost dreamlike, shoved far back into the long ago. It was like the first spatters of the early light rains that soften the sun-hardened ground, laying the terrible dust and freshening the stagnant air with the sweetness and vitality of nature. All that could live in the world came joyously alive.

I felt excited, intense. I felt free; despite this narrow cell, my spirit was no longer imprisoned and carried along against its will. *I would live.* I felt my power again, and never was the vital power that exists only in youth more evident than now.

The way lay open to a new earth and new heaven. There was to be a new day for me, a precious time of life continued. The old heaven and the old earth had passed forever away. Intensity, excitement, aliveness and love would mark my new day. I would live and love as never before. This I promised myself.

Where would I begin? One thing came first before all others. I would start my new life by loving my Jubba Lily, by *truly* loving her.

Of all that was necessary to make one happy, love was the most important. It was pure. It awakened. It mattered. It was giving. It was knowing. Most important, it offered oneness and an end to separateness. I had failed so utterly to love Jubba Lily in the right way.

Oh! Yes! Our love was passionate. We craved each other. We were intimate in a moment. I was bold and would plunge into her. She would open her legs wide apart and arch her body up to meet mine. As we moved together her fingernails would cut long bloody trails in my back and shoulders as she tossed her head from side to side. And all the while she would drive me to wild excitement by her frenzied calls to thrust harder and faster. These were precious hours when she was mine, when I possessed her.

But I discovered, when I stopped to think and admit the truth, that I was merely a sense slave, a man unable, at least unwilling, to master his lust. The thought of nightfall and our coming meeting out there in that sensuous garden was ever haunting me. I would lay awake at night, savoring the inexpressible pleasure that would come and taking satisfaction in the certainly that it *would* come, for I had the power to make it so. When we embraced I thought I would die of excitement. Hungrily, I sought the sucking mouth of her young, unlined face, her high, firm breasts, her all-capturing, moist woman-parts. Rather than take possession of her in stages, I sought her body in all ways at the same time. I could not separate one action from another. Such was my craving for her. With all her soul in her eyes and on her tongue, she yielded. With my body strengthening, we locked.

I was swallowed up in an ecstasy of throbbing, straining, passion. But that alone was not loving. Emotions quickly collapsed when I pulled myself from her wet core. There was no sweetness and sweet memories. What passed for loving was only the contact of flesh with flesh. And she, so far beyond mere sense and contented to give without receiving, became a machine for my thrusting. No, it was not loving. It had little to do with love. I was sated but I was still alone and separate, still trapped in the prison of my aloneness. No, my love called forth no love. Physical, sexual desire did not give me what I desperately needed.In my intense awareness of the flesh, I knew instinctively that I was not fully alive and engaged in true love.

Jubba Lily:

Yes. Our fire was a hot one, of sweat, heat like a living thing, moans and sucking noises. Oh, those times when we coupled. You possessed me. I took you. When we had finished making love I would smear my fingers with the warm love sauce between my legs. I smelled it, and the deep, primitive odor was strangely comforting.

You were always so hungry and robust to have me. Making love merely provoked our appetite for each other further. And when done we had carried pleasure to its fullest bound and exhausted it. Yet we were never weary of it. No, there was never a reverse to this sensuous picture.

And your absence did not diminish my pleasure. Our passion carried over into my dreams. On the night of the day you left with your regiment to go to St. Martin, I had the most sensuous dream in my lifetime. It was so real. I had fallen asleep on my belly and I dreamed that I awoke and you were here, stroking my naked back and buttocks and legs, first with your warm wonderful hands and then with your mouth— exploring, tasting, bringing me to ecstasy I have never known. And, then, at a point where I thought I would go mad, you crawled on top of me and entered me from behind. Oh, God, how my whole body shuddered in ecstasy. And in my dream, Jack, I turned to look at you over my shoulder and I asked you if it was really true, were you really here and you said yes. Then I realized I was sleeping. I did not want to be asleep while you were here. I wanted to be awake so I could hold you, grab you and leave trails of our passion on your back. I made myself wake up so I could be with you, see you, hold you. So I woke up and I think I even rolled over immediately to grab hold of you, but you were not there. I started crying, my love. It hurt so much to be teased that way by my own mind. I have never had a dream so real in my lifetime. Never have I wanted so badly for a dream to be true. Somehow I believe you were here with me, making me alive and thus brightening up this dreary slave hut.

Although it is not easy to explain what happiness is, what we had made me happy. I love you with my heart and mind as well as my body. I wanted our souls to blend into one and in the end I wanted to carry our child and to cry out one day in that ancient pain of childbirth. But I hungered for two things—you alone could not satisfy my hunger for freedom.

I will begin by entering into unconditional oneness with Jubba Lily. With the power that is love I will call forth love. I will stop being afraid to give of myself. I will come to know her as I know myself. There will be no lacking in my caring for her. I will be ready to respond to her needs. I will encourage her to grow and unfold like a beautiful flower, just as the Great High God meant her to. All of these things can be by becoming one with her, by escaping from the cell that is myself. *This is loving.*

These simple yet powerful thoughts brought great comfort to my heart and led me to recall something else I wanted so very much to experience. As a boy I used to watch the Margi women leave the village in the early morning in long single files to visit the dense, lush forest world. They went to those parts of the forest where food was plentiful. They returned at dusk with their carrying baskets and calabashes balanced atop their heads, heaped with all sorts of good things to eat: nourishing roots, wild fruits and berries, green leaves, small bulbs, even small animals. The forest is generous. It is both the father and the mother.

The forest nourishes in yet another way. There where mighty trees soar upward to the sky and seem to touch the clouds, man finds his original unity with nature. We humans instinctively identify with this world of the trees. We court the forest, do we not, when we dance there alone and make love there in the moonlight. *The forest is home.*

For these reasons, I thought I would carefully explore and come to know the lush garden forest of the island. I had always been too busy with regimental duties to take the time to discover the forest and its all-nourishing power. Even in my homeland, my duties as a *mafa* prevented me from following the forest trails taken each day by the Margi women. Now, there would be no wavering, I would make time to travel the forest.

What would delight me even more would be to make this journey in the company of the first people of the island, the Caribs. I had come to know one of them. He was in the habit of coming to the Cabrits to watch in amazement as the regiment drilled under arms while clothed in our brilliant red uniforms. The name he was given was Hiali. He was called after the founder of the Carib people: Hiali, the Man in the Moon with the Genip Stained Face. I saw in him a man who was not young, not old. He was a transitional man, a man in the middle of his span. Like the other Caribs who came from the forest to watch us drill, he used the red seeds of the annatto tree to draw beautiful and mysterious designs on his light brown skin. He bore the other distinctive marks of his people on his body: oiled hair, the color of the darkest night, kept long and straight, and a flattened head which had been fashioned when he was a baby. I was able to speak to him in my army-taught English. I discovered that he was not just a man like the rest. He was the source of much wisdom, like the Margi memory men. Like them, he knew all the tales, legends and place names of his people. His beautiful eyes twinkled like stars when he proclaimed that he spoke the two languages used by male and female Caribs. It greatly depressed him, however, that with each passing day a piece of the Carib way of life vanished from the minds of people. He reminded me that Uyuhao was the *Karina* name for the village of Portsmouth. "Yes,

Karina!" he cried. "*Carib* is what de white people call us. We name weselves *Karina!*" In a soft voice full of pain, he would add, "Der is little time lef' fuh Karina. Each day we stay close to white men, each day is we closer to disappearing."

One evening, while sitting in the lengthening shadow of Devil's Mountain, he offered to take me to the hidden side of the great forest. All I had to do was to follow his way. My journey with Hiali would ease my trip, as the forest was his home. He knew its every secret. We would make this journey together during my favorite time of the day, high morning, when the sun had almost burned its way through the gentle misting rain, leaving the air still fresh with newness. From what I know of the Caribs they, like us Margi, express an attitude of love and dependence toward the forest. To them, like us, the forest was protective, not hostile. They had learned to live from the forest without changing it. Hiali would be the perfect companion in this journey back to nature and the bonds of soil and blood. I looked forward to this trip.

In my new life I would also plan how to return home with honor, so that when the time came I could lay my bones in the land of my mother and father. My parent's love ever haunted me, as did the memory of the Mandara Hills. And although it had been many, many revolutions of the moon since I was stolen and carried over the great salt sea, still there was hardly a night that went by that tears did not streak my face and home memories make sleep impossible. I would return home. *I deserved to return.*

No, this was not grasping at the air. It was rumored that the war against the French would end soon and that some of those born in the land of Africans would be sent back across the big water. This made sense. The British would have no need for all of us when peace came. I would continue to be a good soldier, loyal and brave, so that when our officers chose those who would be permitted to return to the lands of our ancestors, I would be among them. I *would* return to my homeland with honor and with my Jubba Lily. An inner voice kept telling me this. Dominica was a garden, but to return to Margiland was my dream of dreams.

My imagination saw all this becoming true before it. The picture was bright without shade. To suppose all lost was the way to lose all. My heart and head would not be conquered by evil and lies. My courage would rise with misfortune. This I learned from my mother.

Chapter 16

The Trial: Conclusion

Despite a clear blue sky and blazing sun, this day began badly. A rumor had raced through the Cabrits like a raging fire that the revolution in Haiti was dead! The fort negroes and the white soldiers, who usually lined our route of march to the court in order to gape at us, paid little attention to our party this day. I shot a look at them as we passed by. They were, as usual, in groups according to color. The negroes appeared shaken and depressed. Some seemed to be staring horribly. The buckras, leaning on their bayonet-tipped muskets, whispered to one another and smiled confidently. It was said that a large French army, many thousands strong, had landed in Haiti two revolutions of the moon ago, in February. The mighty Toussaint, unable to stem this tide of Frenchmen, was forced to abandon his cities and retreated into the mountains. The soldiers of the great Napoleon poured ashore in a torrent at many points from a crowd of canoes. No sooner had they landed when they began to fall dead to the fever. Their naked bodies, wrapped in white sheets, were dumped in great trenches cut into a hundred fields. Nonetheless, within a few days those that lived had captured the whole of the northern part of the land of Haiti. It was further said that many of Toussaint's black generals had abandoned him and gone over to the French, which led to the surrender of Toussaint himself but a few days ago!

Was this rumor alive with truth? How could it be? It must be an evil trick set loose by the buckras to discourage those who looked to Toussaint and Haiti as the savior of the black man. Souvarine Petro had led us all to believe that Toussaint was god-like, invincible, and the revolution to end French rule and slavery unstoppable. I had secretly come to admire this man Toussaint for his courage in standing up to the whites and for his power in getting worldly and smart people, like Souvarine Petro, to believe in him. Night after night Souvarine Petro would sing the praises of Toussaint and his revolution.

With eyes darting fire and his soul aflame, Souvarine Petro spoke of Toussaint as an unmixed negro with not a single drop of white blood in his veins. He described Toussaint as the man who had foiled the greedy British when they tried to crush the revolution in order to gain for themselves the great riches of Haiti. Shaking with excitement, he called Toussaint the fighter of liberty, a man of action, the sword of the negro, the destroyer of slavery, the creation of nature. According to Souvarine Petro, Toussaint was fond of reminding his followers, "This island is ours, not a white foot shall touch it. I will plant a nation so deep that no one in the world will be able to root it up." How could this revolution be over? How could the mighty Toussaint submit? If true, what did it mean for me and my comrades? Souvarine Petro! What could he tell us?

At last he was in my view. I was not able to get his eyes to make four with mine, but I felt that something was very wrong with him. He always moved nervously, restlessly, even when sitting. He had the habit of picking at the skin along the edge of his right ear. This was very noticeable; it was not something he could hide. The ear was often raw and bloody. Now he sat listlessly. His hands were motionless. He merely sat, solid and silent like a stone, his shoulders dropped heavily as if abandoned by life.

Gone was that constant flame and the showers of sparks it gave off. Without that fire he looked so pitifully small, fearful, so human. He seemed to have given up completely for his regimentals were oily and dirty. In truth, his clothes stuck to his skin like bark to a tree. As I leaned forward in my chair to get a better look at his face, I saw that his eyes were swollen and filled with tears. All the muscles in his face sagged. As I looked upon Souvarine Petro in this condition, all I could think of was that a man does not founder like this upon nothing. So the rumor *was* alive with truth. The revolution *was* dead. And the once mighty Toussaint was now no more.

I looked round me at my comrades. Their faces were stunned as if by a blow. They too had come to believe in this place called Haiti and this man known as Toussaint. What black man could resist believing in what Souvarine Petro said of both. Here were Haitians, black men and women, fresh from the lash of the whip and the hot sweat of the cane fields, driving the French into the sea. Here were black men and women taking their own freedom. But it was not to be. The first nation of black people in these parts was not to be. The bright sunshine on a landscape of fear was no more.

As I looked at Souvarine Petro, my heart grew heavy and an uneasiness filled me. We needed him to be alert and alive to anything that might happen in the court. We were lost

273

without him. What would cause him to catch fire again? What would give him back his fierce heart again? There had to be be some reverse to this terrible picture before me.

I turned away from the pitiful scene. My eyes swept the room and I saw the judge advocate rising from his chair to speak.

"It is important that rules governing His Majesty's military courts be observed. Any deviation from these regulations may well derange the chain of evidence and thereby introduce confusion and perplexity into the record of court-martial proceedings. The judge advocate is aware that the evidence on both sides of the charges is closed and that the court is about to exercise its judicative function and return a solemn verdict on the guilt or innocence of the prisoners. All this notwithstanding, the judge advocate respectfully seeks the consent of the court to briefly reopen the prosecution in order to introduce vital new evidence in support of the charges. The judge advocate hopes the court will not view this unusual request as a dangerous innovation. He fully and properly understands his duty to accommodate himself in the forms and practice of military law and court-martial proceedings. What motivates his actions is the atrocious nature of this case and the fact that this material witness was prevented from making himself known until after the conclusion of the evidence, both for the prosecution and the defense. It is the hope of the judge advocate that the court will approve this request and permit a most material witness to be examined."

How high-minded he sounded. If this was the first time you heard him speak, you would easily conclude that he labored to protect the future of humanity itself. But no such noble cause lay behind his neat words. Only death was on his mind, my death and that of my comrades. Who was this mysterious "most material witness?" Why should he be allowed to give evidence at this time? I had already begun to spend my freedom in my head. "If dis trial dem go on, me will look death on de face," I heard myself say in English.

Poor Souvarine Petro. His body was there, but his heart was still.

"The judge advocate is quite correct when he observed that the established rules governing the procedure and forms of military tribunals should be strictly observed." The sharp voice of the president of the court floated down the long room to me. "Adherence to this immemorial usage has placed court-martial proceedings on a solid foundation. To do otherwise would heap inextricable embarrassment upon the military tribunal. This is best obviated by following the established regulations. This is the *private* feeling of the court. Feelings of private concern must give way at times to the great ends of public justice, however. Thus it is the view of the court that such evidence as the judge advocate wishes to introduce would benefit the court and would not be prejudicial to the public service. The court would like to make it known that this decision is an indulgence granted only from necessity. The request is therefore approved. You may call your witness."

A pause . . .

"Sergeant Major Bostonian, freedman of the Eighth West India Regiment, is called to testify."

Hardly had the thin voice of the judge advocate reached my ears when the Sergeant Major came striding into the court. He was dressed as if on parade. Every strap and every button was in place. He glistened and gleamed like a snake. His red tunic and white pants were cut smooth of every wrinkle. The long silver-tipped cane, which he was never without, was tucked inside his sergeant's sash. He swaggered to the witness chair as a man sure of his welcome among friends! Curious. He never once looked at us as he passed by. We were invisible to him.

Here was our father, who we soldiers would march day and night for, yet make it a matter of honor never to mention our fatigue or pain. At this man's command we were instantly ready to die and let our bodies serve only to manure the fields. Our service as British soldiers required our submission as individuals. And so he demanded our immediate subordination. Thus we assigned to him the twenty-four hours use of our minds and bodies. We gave it quickly without the slightest objection. In return for our subordination we asked for nothing more than his approval and bits of painted cloth nailed to a wooden pole.

Each of us had felt the weight of his silver-tipped cane and coarse fists when we were put through our first drills. He cuffed us about the head if we looked to the left instead of the right. He or his corporals would rap us with a piece of shingle if our bodies did not maintain the military square. One time he thrust a rough piece of wood between my naked ankles and wrenched them apart when I failed to place the heels of my feet at the proper angle when standing at attention. Drills were so constant as to keep us in permanent motion. And all the while the Sergeant Major pushed and pulled and cuffed us about our bodies. He never let up until we got our drill right.

If a man grumbled we soldiers took it upon ourselves to silence him. At night, in the secret world of our barrack kingdom, we made that man obedient. Even when bruised and battered, we never blamed the Sergeant Major; he was only trying to make British soldiers of us. His sole wish was to teach us how to out-fight and out-suffer the French. Our awkwardness, our uncouth gestures, were our own fault, not his. He was our father, and we admired and loved him as any loving son would a deserving father.

Yet there he sat pledged to destroy us. At that moment I thought of an old Margi saying that evil does not always appear as a demon, dripping blood, long-tongued with claws. No, evil often takes the shape of a trusted friend, a brother, a revered king, *a father.*

We had been betrayed. *Betrayed.* The word stabbed me like a hot knife and the pain burned in me. Why did he, of all the men, want us dead? It made no sense: a father killing his obedient sons. *It made no sense.*

I stared at him as a hammering hatred began to pound in my head. "So the lowly negro in my dream was the Sergeant Major," I heard myself say. My gaze was intruded upon by a stream of memories of him . . . *curses . . . blows . . . extra drill . . . "in de regulated way" . . . survival! . . . survival . . . it is a question of survival . . . .*

Just when I thought I had the key to the Sergeant Major's betrayal, a stirring broke my thoughts and I heard the familiar voice of the judge advocate.

"To which company of the Eighth West India Regiment do you belong, Sergeant Major?" There was a greasy sound to his voice.

"Captain Cameron's, Number Four Company—sah!"

"How long have you served with the regiment?"

"Since de year 1798, when de regiment was raised—sah!"

"Of what country are you a native, Sergeant Major?"

"I believes I was born in de big state of America—sah!"

"You may relax, Sergeant Major, no need to be so formal."

"Sah? Yas, sah."

"Tell the court, please, how you came to serve in His Majesty's Eighth West India Regiment."

"My master's name was Colonel Alexander Boston. De Colonel 'im made me free in 1783 wen de British dem leave America. I go to mother England wid' de Colonel as he man-servant. In 1793 war breaks out wid' de tyrant French in Flanders, which place I goes wid' de Colonel. Den George de king 'im sends de Colonel to serve in Dominica, which place we goes in de year 1797. Since I am master of meself, I takes leave of de Colonel 'im, and join de Eighth West India Regiment on de occashun of de 6th of October 1798, sah."

"What was your rank in the regiment at the time you enlisted?"

"I was a private soldier on dat occashan, sah."

"How much time elapsed before you achieved your present rank, Sergeant Major?"

"What yuh mean *elapsed*, sah?"

"Eh, how long did it take you to earn your four chevrons?"

"Ah! I sees. But three short years, sah!"

"Is it true, Sergeant Major, that you are the senior NCO in the regiment?"

"Yas, sah!"

"And is it also true, Sergeant Major, that your rate of promotion through the ranks from private soldier to senior NCO was the fastest in the regiment?"

"Yas, sah!"

"Thank you, Sergeant Major."

"Sah!"

"To the best of your recollection, Sergeant Major, were the *Articles of War* ever read aloud and most carefully explained to the troops of the Eighth West India Regiment?"

"Yas, sah, at least once in every two months as required by de King's regulashans. Sah!"

"What proof do you have of this, Sergeant Major?"

"I was present on doz occashans, sah!"

"Were *all* the rules read and explained to the troops, including those pertaining to mutiny?"

"Yas, sah!"

"Were the prisoners present on those occasions?"

"Yas, sah!"

"Now then, Sergeant Major, relate to the court what you know of the late mutiny."

"I should be much pleased to, sah! It was de evenin' of de 8th of April an' I was returnin' to my quarters on de Outer Cabrit from Fort Shirley. I had gone to de fort to get de company books ready for de comin' inspecshun. As I was passin' Number Three barrack I hears a commoshun inside. Since tattoo had been beat an' de troops was supposed to be asleep, I decides to investigate. I approached a slightly opened window at de rear of de barrack. De light inside caused me to recognize a number of soldiers talkin' 'bout mutiny. Dem says, in so many words, dat de time has come to leave death an pass into life. Man after man gets up an' says how deh are oppressed by de laws of de army buckras— what I knows to be untrue. Finally dem all jumps up an' in one voice cry out for de deaths of all buckra officers as de only way to breathe de sweet air of freedom, as deh terms it."

"You have testified, Sergeant Major, that you recognized the mutineers in Number Three barrack."

"Yas, sah!"

"Look at the prisoners attentively, Sergeant Major, and inform the court if you are perfectly convinced that they were among the persons you observed in a mutinous state."

"I perfectly recollect each an' every one of dem as mutineers, sah!"

I perfectly recollect each an' every one of dem as mutineers. His words hissed at me. There was no hint in his voice that he realized his evidence doomed the lives of seven good men. No. In fact he seemed to be enjoying what he was doing, like a snake basking in the sunshine. Then he smiled.

It was the first time I had ever seen him do this. It was a crooked, twisted grin that gave a clue to who he really was behind that unperturbed expression. Now I understood his evil. He turned and glared at me with eyes filled with pure hatred.

"Lies!" I screamed. Then I exploded in rage. I leaped to my feet, knocking over my chair and the table in a mad rush to get at him and rip the foul tongue from this shit-eating son of dirt. The guards were taken by surprise by my sudden move. I cleared the table in a flash and was about to strike the Sergeant Major with both fists when I was grabbed from behind. Just before I was thrown to the floor, I looked up, and saw him afraid for the first time. A pained look shot across his hideous face.

I fell hard to the floor face first. Wooden splinters tore my nose and jaw. I was dragged back to the prisoners' table battered and bleeding. But I was pleased. I had frightened that shit-eating son of dirt. For a moment his whole face had been covered with animal fright. For a moment he feared *me*.

I began to laugh uncontrollably. My hysteria mounted higher and higher until I began to shake violently. Then, just as suddenly, I dropped my head into my hands, where it remained for what seemed like a long time. A worn-out feeling swept over me. I fell backwards in my chair. My limbs felt like iron weights. I had a feeling of wanting to escape myself. When I finally looked up, everyone in the room, even my comrades, were watching me warily, like men who had seen an evil spirit. But Genus, as quiet as ever, welcomed me back with a smile.

"Eh . . . what was the general conduct and character of the prisoners during the time you have known them, Sergeant Major?" A question that had not been rehearsed. So the judge advocate intended to turn my sudden explosive actions to his advantage.

The Sergeant Major looked triumphant, like a hawk with a rat in its mouth. "As certain as it is dat one day I will depart from dis life, I can say dat dem all was troublemakers from de start of dere service in the King's army."

"Finally, Sergeant Major, why did you not raise a hue and cry immediately upon learning of the mutiny?"

"It was my intenshun to do so, sah! I looked for a chance to make my way to de nearest officers' quarters. But I was discovered by a guard posted by de mutineers. Dem took me to de dead house where dem ties me up an' leaves me widout food an water. When I was discovered an' set free I was near death from want of someting to eat and drink. I was taken to de hospital where I was restored to health. I was lets go from de hospital on 16 April when I contact you, sah!"

"Eh . . . yes. Thank you, Sergeant Major. You may stand down unless the prisoners have questions to put to you."

"Yas, sah!"

He has pissed over me with his words, was my first thought. Everything he did tore at my heart: the honeyed tone of his voice, his mocking grin, his pompous manner. I felt locked in the coil of his evil. How could the court not see what I saw, not hear what I heard? How could they let him sit there and tell all those lies? How could they fail to see that the judge advocate spoke through the willing tongue of this son of dirt? Were they so stupid?

My hatred grew with each of his greasy words. It swelled until I thought I would go mad with rage. Then in an instant my anger was gone. Like smoke scattered in a wind, it lifted. I was left numb. I looked over at him indifferently, too tired to hate. Still . . . his words were my death. Here was proof of the old saying that life lives on life. A man cannot live without causing destruction of life somewhere. The fact of *his* living required *my* death.

I was suddenly aware that Souvarine Petro had stood up. I edged forward in my chair in expectation of a flood of biting, stinging words that would destroy this last evil effort of the judge advocate and his whore. But my heart broke as I looked across at him. His eyes were blank. His face showed no emotion. His body sagged. As I watched him he held on to the edge of the table for support. He seemed old, small. Gone was the grand beginning that marked his speeches. Gone, too, was the vision of him in triumph. No matter, he was on his feet ready to do battle. Some part of his spirit had survived the blow of Toussaint's fall. He was ready to speak.

"I will formally not challenge the validity of the evidence of Sergeant Major Bostonian. It would be useless to do so as the judge advocate has seduced the court into believing the Sergeant Major to be a soldier of respected character and rank. But it is clear to me by his testimony that he is engaged in a plot to entrap and destroy us by giving false evidence. He will *never* escape the dreadful reflection that awaits him for having tried to shed the blood of innocent men whose only crime was to blindly place their trust in him. No, I will not challenge the evidence of the Sergeant Major which serves only to establish him as a perjured, debased creature. I do, however, question the authority of this court! I declare this, this *trial* to be illegal since it is not consistent with military law and practice!"

So the fire in him had not died out. His words still had teeth. They told me that his heart was still fierce, that fire still raged in his blood.

I looked around at my comrades. They, too, looked surprised. I had expected Souvarine Petro to challenge the evidence of the Sergeant Major. This line of attack was a complete surprise to me, albeit a most welcome one. My mind leaped at it because I sensed that Souvarine Petro's challenge questioned the very existence of the court. If the court were destroyed, I would live.

Petro's unexpected move also caught the court by surprise.

"Not legal?" the president blurted out. "How so?"

"It is an established principle of military law, is it not, that *before* a prisoner can be called before a tribunal to answer a charge, a court of enquiry must *first* declare that sufficient grounds exist for bringing him to trial. To my knowledge, no such court of inquest has met. As a consequence, this . . . *procedure* is not legal."

The court was silent. I could read their thoughts so easily. They were thinking, *We had been told before going out to the West Indies that negroes were savages, the product of heathen conditions. How could a man of such obvious intelligence emerge from an uncivilized state? Were there others like him? How did he know so much about the law of the army? His type bears watching for they may make it difficult for us to continue our rule.* I felt like telling them that Africans did not lack in civilization. I felt like telling them that my homeland was filled with men like Souvarine Petro who lacked neither knowledge nor spirit. I felt like telling them that many plantation negroes possessed special talents and even read buckra newspapers. But even if I did tell them these things it would not change them. They were rooted in the belief that Africans were not men but—

"Is there foundation to this charge, Captain Mapp?" The agitated voice of the president broke into my thoughts.

"Eh . . . I believe so, sir."

"Are you quite certain, Captain Mapp? Are you quite certain that this, this . . . *matter* is nothing more than *busyness?*"

"Eh . . . it is not uncommon for courts of inquest to go . . . in advance of general courts-martial. But may I suggest to the court that it take the opportunity afforded them by this challenge to . . . clear up any . . . ambiguity surrounding the established usage of courts of enquiry."

The face of the president glowed like a fire. "The court will adjourn for one hour to consider this matter."

Court of enquiry. Why did the officers of the court not know about it? It was their duty to know. My life depended on their knowledge and honesty. Was I not entitled to both as a British soldier? And the judge advocate. He knew of that kind of court all along. Yet he never shared this with the court until now, until he was forced to! He was a clever man, so he intentionally failed to tell the court that it might be in error. What lies he told us prisoners. He said he was guided in his position as judge advocate by what he called a just sense of duty. He also told us that one of his duties was to assist us in our defense. He disarmed my comrades with his greasy words for when they heard him they expressed confidence in him. But not me. I saw into his true nature. And now I had proof of his treachery. I felt anger rising hot through my face. I fought it down. I could not lose control of myself as I had done when the Sergeant Major testified against us. To do so would only hurt our chances.

And Souvarine Petro. He knew about courts of enquiry. But when did he first learn about them? Did he possess this information at the start of the trial? If so, why did he wait until now to reveal this knowledge? Strange . . . .

The heavy storehouse door leading into the courtroom swung open, pushed by unseen hands. For a brief moment what remained of the brilliant morning sunlight flooded the long room through the opened space. The glare of light was impenetrable and prevented me from seeing beyond it. The air that rushed in with the light was cool, earthy and damp.

The whole was like liquid sunshine and it brought back tender memories. I imagined the lovely colors of the flowers and the birds that hovered in mid-air. I wondered if the mighty mountain revealed her awesome top this day, or was it wrapped as usual in a cape of piled clouds. I thought of the immense trees of the rain forest whose lower trunks had never been touched by daylight. All this and more—much, much more—lay just beyond the wall of blazing light in the doorway, just beyond . . .

The return of the court quickly scattered the shreds of this dreamy vision. One by one, the officers stepped into the courtroom through the blaze of yellowish light framed by the doorway. They looked like travelers returning from a visit to another world. The last to enter was the judge advocate. The heavy door closed shut behind him, pushed by those unseen hands. At once the sweet, ripening day turned stale. At that moment I heard an inner voice in me saying, *Life is a clay pot—it breaks where you take it.* The fragile clay pot of life is carried through birth, childhood, maturity, old age and, finally, death—wherever it may happen. Did this mean that I was going to die? Was it an omen? No! No! I must stop this. Hope lives. I closed my eyes and concentrated on specific objects of life. I imagined my beloved uniform. I could see it in detail, from its tight white pantaloons, to its red tunic with gray facing, to its tall, shiny black helmet which dazzled the eye when licked by the sun . . .

"The prisoners will stand." There was something foreboding in the voice of the president. I tried to convince myself that all was well, that we would triumph in the end. But something felt wrong.

"The prisoners have challenged the legality of this, His Majesty's tribunal. They have charged that the manner in which this case came to trial is not consonant with British military law and established practice since a court of enquiry did not first determine that there was sufficient ground for bringing the accused before a court-martial. This is a most serious charge. Not only does the accusation strike a blow at the legitimacy of this court, it also calls into question the integrity of the individual members of the tribunal. Were it not for the very grave implications of the charge, I would have dismissed this calumnious and frivolous action with the contempt it so deserves. That cannot be done, however. Sworn as we are to try this grave crime with a free and unprejudiced mind, the court have taken the matter under advisement and have determined that the actions taken by this tribunal were perfectly legal and in strict conformity with the established practice of British army courts. *The law is clear with regard to this question.* Courts of enquiry are *not* obligatory.

"Certainty as to whom charges of criminality *ought* to be chiefly attached is sufficient ground for bringing the accused to trial before a court-martial. In those cases when certainty is lacking, a court of inquest should take the matter under its consideration and determine whether there is or is not enough ground for bringing the accused to trial. It was the opinion of an assembly of senior officers in this command that there *was* certainty on whom the charge of mutiny should be affixed, namely the prisoners. The objection of the prisoners is hereby denied."

Somehow, I had already known what the decision of the court would be, even before the president announced it. Still, I groaned when I heard it. I heard moans from my comrades around me. I turned to Souvarine Petro. He took no notice of anything. Once again he was swallowed up in some misery, no doubt the defeat of his General Toussaint. I had the sense that life was moving faster and faster to some . . . end. End. I dropped my head in despair. For the first time I felt that hope was dead. Dead. Death of hope is the true death. The death of the body merely confirms what had already taken place.

My legs suddenly gave way under me and I fell backwards into my chair. My arms hung lifelessly at my sides.

No sooner had I fallen into my chair when the president ordered me to get back on my feet. He then motioned to the guards who moved toward me, but I managed to get back on my feet before they reached me. The president's next words were a hammer blow. He announced that the court was ready to return a decision in our trial! So soon? I knew a decision was coming, but I did not expect it now. It was all too quick. There was something indecent in the way things were coming to an end.

The court was cleared of all bystanders. The doors were slammed shut.

We stood before the court. The president spoke. His voice sounded deeper than usual. His words seemed to float in the air like bodyless spirits.

"As the court is now in possession of the whole of the evidence, which has been carefully put into writing by the Judge Advocate, we are now ready to render a solemn verdict on the guilt or innocence of the prisoners.

"At this general court-martial, held at Prince Rupert's Point, Dominica, on the 12th of April and continued by several adjournments to the 17th instant, Privates Manby, Lively, Genus, Jack, Cuffy, Pedro, and Hussar, all of the Eighth West India Regiment, were tried for the following crimes: for exciting and joining in mutiny on and between the 9th and 10th instant, and for aiding and assisting in the murders of Captain Cameron, Lieutenants MacKay and Wastenays, Sergeant Major Broughton, Sergeant MacKay, Private Gill and Commissary Lang.

"The court having maturely and deliberately considered the whole evidence for the prosecution, together with what has been advanced for the defense of the prisoners, do adjudge as follows: that the prisoners are *guilty* of the whole crimes contained in the charge, being in breach of the *Articles of War*, and do therefore sentence them to suffer death before a firing party composed of loyal men of their own regiment. The sentence will be carried out tomorrow morning at the hour of eight of the clock in the Cabrits Valley."

Dead silence. Silence for a dozen heartbeats.

So there it was straight and plain. The word I dreaded so much: guilty. It pierced me like a bayonet. *Guilty. Guilty. Guilty.* I said that word again and again to myself as the consequence enveloped me. Just like that and the trial was over. Just so simply and I was to die. Die!

I glanced around at my comrades. When I looked into their faces I saw by the fear etched in each the confirmation of my own feelings. Only Souvarine Petro was unmoved.

A file of grim-faced white soldiers led us out of the courtroom and back to our cells. A crowd of people were waiting outside. They had gathered to stare at us. Hamlet was there. He grinned widely and gestured at me. "Dem high-up soldier man goin' to he death," he shouted. "'Im mek pretty corpse." The sullen crowd heard him and burst into wild laughter. I marched along in silence, weighed down by shame and the lusty laughter rising in the warm air.

When I reached my cell, I stretched out on my cot and stared at the ceiling. I tried to think of anything—anything except death. But it was no use. The reality of death and dying crowded out all other thoughts from my head. *Shot to death by a firing party.* What would that be like? Would I behave firmly, calmly and die like a British soldier? Or would my courage desert me, causing me to flinch or worse?

I remembered a white deserter who was shot some time back. He did not wince or cry out. But such was his fright that his entire hair slowly lifted off his scalp and stood straight out from his head like needles.

And how would it feel to be blindfolded and left alone, kneeling atop of my own coffin, a few paces from the firing party? What would my last seconds be like? Every sound would be intensified as I imagined the movements of the firing party preparing to shoot me. They had better not bungle it. They *must* kill me outright. They botched the execution of that white deserter. Every ball struck him and he fell hard to the ground. But his hands waved in the air like the fins of a dying fish. Finally, four men stepped up to him and fired their pieces into his head, ending his misery. I did not want to die like that . . .

The sun began to set. Evening drew on quickly. The stars that would powder the night sky were just coming into view. As I began to drift off into my last sleep the wind suddenly picked up outside my cell window. "The spirit of death is on the move," I thought. And in that wind I could hear the beating of his wings as he hovered.

Chapter 17

An Offer in the Night

Crunching footsteps approached the door of my cell. There was a momentary pause. A loud insistent thud on the door convinced me that I was not dreaming. Before I could get up from my cot I heard a key digging into the lock. The large studded door creaked open. Two guards framed the doorway. I glimpsed a movement beyond. The judge advocate emerged from the shadows and walked quickly past the guards into my cell, bowing as he did to clear the lintel. His face was visible only in the brief flashes of light from a torch held by one of the guards. He stood there for a moment looking uncomfortable in the chilling gloom of my cell. Finally he raised his hand to me. In it was a piece of paper covered with writing in great black boldness.

"This paper contains the orders for your immediate release, your immediate freedom. All you have to do is cooperate." His voice was calm. It wasn't a sham. He meant what he said. But he smiled blandly. My mouth fell open in amazement.

"Our investigations have discovered that Souvarine Petro has plotted the destruction of British rule on this island. We have proof that he is a Haitian agent whose mission is to rouse our loyal negroes to open rebellion. We have further proof that his actions helped to ignite the mutiny which was to serve as a signal for a general slave insurrection. It is an injustice, would you not agree, that you face imminent death for mutiny while he goes free? We must put an immediate end to this troublemaker and the menace he represents.

"We know that you have only hatred for this man. Unlike him, you have devoted yourself to honoring the uniform you proudly wore. He sickens us all." He moved closer, his lizard-like eyes reflecting the torch light.

"You have only to give evidence implicating him in the mutiny and you shall go free at once, as stated in these orders. All we need to make matters right is a simple statement from you." Again he raised his hand so I could see the paper.

"Join with us!" he exhorted. "Join with us and together we shall defeat Souvarine Petro and the other Haitian devils who threaten the peace and security of these islands. This paper is a special hand from George the King. Clasp it and be free: free to return to your native Africa, free to sleep every night with the slave woman Jubba Lily. All this can be yours!" His smile then faded. "Refuse . . . and you will suffer the penalty of your actions as well as those of Souvarine Petro. I shall wait outside for your answer. The door will be left ajar. Push it open and step forward a free man; close the door and die. The choice is yours."

He turned and walked toward the door. Without looking back, he added, "You have one hour to make up your mind."

In a few moments the judge advocate had vanished into the darkness beyond the flickering light. An unseen hand pushed the door until it was nearly closed.

Shaking, I sat down on my cot. I was stunned. Suddenly the air reeked of my sweat. I could feel a trickle snake down my back. I had already begun to feel I was living among the dead, and suddenly I had the chance to return to the living. The miracle which I had hoped for was here. It seemed so simple. Just walk through the door and I would be free. Just walk through the door and I could be in the sweet embrace of Jubba Lily! All I had to do was to make war on Souvarine Petro. But to do that I needed the living flame of anger and revenge against him. I called it forth like some lurking beast . . . I waited and waited and waited but it wouldn't come. There was no answer. I searched my soul for any anger that would make me want to send him to his death. Again it wouldn't come forth. I did not have it in me. Then it hit me. The answer had been staring me in the face all the time. The judge advocate was wrong. I had no hatred of this man. How could I stab the man who had only tried to help me? He merely spoke the truth. No wonder they wanted him dead. All along I refused to admit that I was drawn to him because he spoke the truth and had a vision, whereas I had none. Truth is seldom gentle. It arrives one day in your life like a storm, an unpredictable force, like Souvarine Petro. We don't like the truth because it has power, like a raging storm, to upset the climate of our false lives.

I had spent my time on this island rooted in the here and now, in the service of the white man. Souvarine Petro's truth exposed the falsity of my actions as a soldier. And still he tried to save me! Until now I was unable to see that a part of his message included the great promise of truth: it may race in like a ferocious storm but it leaves in its wake fresh air, a rainbow of hope, peace. Souvarine Petro never failed to remind us of that fresh air. His rainbow words tore into my thoughts: "Action is dignity . . . There are chains to be broken . . . Become your own authority . . . Power is limited *only* by your imagination . . . Whatever you think you can do . . ." I wept at the thought that I had been deaf so long to these liberating words that came up from the depths of truth, and I ached for the missed opportunities they represented.

Souvarine Petro was right: I was as much a slave as any negro in the field. Only I had refused to see what I was. I had let the red cloth on my back and the musket in my hand blind me to the truth that swirled round me. But the facts were these: like the slave I was powerless; like the slave I was cut off from my ancestors and descendants; like the slave I lived in the margin between life and death.

The door. To pass through the door would mean that I would live . . . but as a slave. I heard an inner voice saying: *You can bear that no longer. Break this bond.* The voice was insistent. *Break this bond before it is too late!* This was the truth to which I had been so blind. Still I was divided. Life meant Jubba Lily . . . and shame like a suffocation. I felt confusion and despair come over me. It was hard to resist the temptation to live. My usually stubborn resistant mind now bent under all these claims. I began to shake like a man in a nightmare. I splashed some water on my face hoping somehow it would slake my agony.

The thoughts that held me captive suddenly vanished. I felt a cooling calm in my person. Now, calmer, everything became clear. The army was not my tribe. Its cause was not mine. My true comrades were those I had been taught to despise: my African brothers and sisters who labored in the hot fields under the lash (and was not Jubba Lily one of them?). I had falsely considered them too ignorant and too enslaved to worry about, let alone join their cause. Not surprisingly, they responded with candid hatred of me.

Souvarine Petro had been right all along. My enormous envy of him prevented me from hearing the truths that flew off his tongue like shots out of a cannon. Despite their eloquence, I thought of them as brave but empty words. I laughed at them. That was then. *That was then!* Now I saw how correctly he explained things with his art of language. "Forgive me," I heard myself say over and over. It was Souvarine Petro's mission to end the abomination of slavery. Of all of us, only he possessed the ability to accomplish this task. The enemy was stubborn and clever, and there were many traps ahead. But he could outthink them. Freedom was not possible without him. He must live. *He must live!*

In Margiland a person is released from slavery when he is marked with chalk, the symbol of death, by his master. In that way the redeemed slave gets his authority from his former master. If I learned anything from Souvarine Petro and Jubba Lily it was that one should become their own authority, the source of their own power. I will redeem myself! I will serve no more masters but myself! Honor *is* stronger than death . . . I grasped the door and slammed it shut.

It was over. At last I was really going to die. This earthly adventure was finished. But what would I really lose? Somehow I felt my coming death was merely the death of my past and the way I had formed my past. I felt this coming death was not the end, it was not oblivion. I felt a new light, a new beginning dawning in me. I didn't fully understand this strange feeling but I welcomed it. If there were things I didn't completely fathom there were things I did. At last my troubles and pain were over. Finished the doubts. Finished the lying. Finished the pretense. Finished the shame. Finished being shunned by those I loved—*even in my dreams.* Now I was in a world of peace. I dropped down on the cot, floating in a sea of relief.

Jubba Lily. Jubba Lily. Necessary, nurturing, life sweetener, bed sweetener, maternal, earthy Jubba Lily, goodby, goodby. What gifts you gave me. *Jubba! Kind dreams to you . . . my beautiful, strong, wise companion of my sojourn in this land of wet mountains and senseless butchery.*

With a deep sigh I tried to sleep myself into my last day.

Chapter 18

The Dwelling of Iju

It grows light. Soon it will be day and hot with the rays of the sun. I can hear the rustling of the land crabs among the leaves on the ground as they scurry for their holes to escape the coming sun. But for the moment it is dawn, beautiful dawn, the only bearable time of a West Indian day. The air is cool and once again scented with the smell of hot cassava cakes, fried ripe plantain, and coffee. This morning is beautiful to an extent which no morning has been before. How, how can this morning be my last? I want to see and smell a thousand mornings. Enough. Why do I torment myself with such thoughts? This is a day for dying, not living. Still . . . I must pretend . . .

Where are my boots? *This white execution uniform mocks me.* It is important that I be clean shaven . . . Why should I? That's stupid. Every nick in my skin will only sting in the heat. Why should I primp just to be shot? . . . No I will not shave! There I go again, thinking about . . . it. I must find something else to think about before I fall apart . . . What was that story grandfather used to tell about . . . Iju . . . Mptu . . . Yes. The dwelling of Iju, the great High God, was in the sky. In the beginning, it was so close to the earth that men could touch it with their hands. *I can hear the steady tramp of soldiers' feet.* In . . . those days men were like gods. They . . . lived forever. *Now I hear the muffled drums of my own regiment.* They . . . they did not have to work, they had only to leave their clean calabashes on the platforms outside their houses and Iju would send his children of heaven to fill them with food. *My guts are tightening. This is a dream.* One day this . . . this . . . happy life came to a sudden end through the sin of a woman who set out a dirty calabash which caused a swelling on the finger of one of the children of heaven. *"Private Jack!"* In his anger Iju withdrew his dwelling far into the sky, away from men who, unable to find food, raided the farms of Mptu. When Mptu objected to Iju of the ways of men, Iju made a compact with him, that the raids would continue but Mptu could . . . take the lives of a few men each year as compensation. *"What me fe deserve dis, Jack?"* In this, this way men obtain corn but . . . death enters among them. When Mptu took the, the life of his first victim, the brother of the man saw this and followed Mptu to . . . kill him. *Rude stares.* But when he overtook Mptu he found him bathing in a lake of liquid fire and fled in terror. Another brother resolved to kill Mptu. He persisted in his hunt and, and one day discovered Mptu bathing in fire and cut off one of his legs which is why Mptu is lame. *"Souvarine Petro has disappeared. He turned himself into a white bird and flew away to the north."* Angry that men were taking the law into their own hands, Iju stained the eyes of men with dark coloring so that they could not see Mptu. *The band has begun playing the "Dead March."* As more and

more continued to die, the men sent a turtle to Iju to determine why Death was in their midst. He told the turtle to
tell the men that the dead would be restored to life if the
living threw hot porridge on the bodies of the dead. *I can
see three sides of a square up ahead.* But as the turtle, being a
slow mover, had been gone for a long time, the men decided
to send a lizard, for Mptu continued to take fresh victims.
*His drawn back arm and upraised sword was a single gesture
that held the soldiers to attention.* Angered at this second
message, Iju told the lizard, to tell men to dig a hole in the
earth and to throw the bodies of the dead in it. The lizard
returned to the men before the turtle *"You have been found
guilty of"* and delivered the message from Iju and the bodies
were buried. *Hussar refuses to kneel.* But when the turtle
finally arrived with his message from Iju and the grave was
opened so that baked porridge could be thrown on the
bodies, the bodies were no longer there . . . *A volley! Bright
red blood spurting with his last heartbeats!* And so it is that
men can no longer be restored to *Me! Me*! Heart pounding.
Body no longer has feeling . . . yet I am aware of possessing
it . . . Jubba . . . Elana . . . Sweet Mother . . . action is dignity . . . whatever you can think you can do . . . whatever
you can—

Sometime later

Hamlet:

Jack? That dirt who used to soak up the sun like a lizard in his fancy red coat? That filth who stole my woman? I hated him. I hated him with a hatred so pure it made me weak. I am happy he is dead, dead! I walked all the way from Calibishi, on the other side of the island, just to watch him suffer and die. He thought he was better than us because he carried a gun and because he could sit in the shade in his red coat while we negroes toiled in the heat of the sun. He looked so pleased with himself when he walked about in his fancy dress and went calling on my Jubba Lily. Him and his red coat and his too-bright smile. He thought he was above us but he wasn't. He was a slave, too, only he was the ultimate slave. Yes, the ultimate slave! He lived totally apart from everyone that mattered, from his ancestors and from those who could give him offspring. He was an outsider who lived in a narrow, dead middle ground between the world of the buckras and ours. Even though he carried a gun, to whom could he pass on this power? No one! His life was a lie. But he was still dangerous to us who toiled in the stinking fields. As long as there were slaves like him slavery would live.

The British know how to torment a man about to die. First they terrorize him and then they shoot him. I have seen every black soldier shot at the Cabrits and they all died that way. They were all shot but only after a long ritual carried out to a steady drumbeat and dread music. It was meant to fill those about to die with fear. That was how Jack was supposed to die. But he didn't. I looked forward to seeing him and all the other pretty soldier boys squirm before they were shot down dead. But that's not how things went. That overbearing bull Hussar, Jack's friend, was nailed first. But he refused to kneel on his coffin so they shot him while he was on his feet looking quietly up into the sky. What a great pity he wasn't crying like a baby as I was praying he would. Jack's death disappointed me even more. No grisly fear covered his looks. He was so calm, so peaceful, so unafraid. He never wavered once. In fact, he seemed to be far away and in deep conversation with himself when they shot him down. I cannot believe he would die so bravely and thus cheat me of my just deserts. I walked a long way that day just to see that he-goat shit in his pants. How dare he deny me! Since the others were likely to cheat me as well, I dropped a few tears of rage and walked away in disgust.

Souvarine Petro:

Private Jack? Oh . . . yes, Private Jack. *Congo Jack.* He saved my life . . . I underestimated him. I truly thought he would go to his grave believing all that cow shit his officers fed him about him being better than the slaves and about the need for men like him to hold the line against us Haitians. Everything he did indicated that he thought he was a man when in truth he was a slave. He struck me as one of those Africans who fought desperately for acceptance and would do anything to win the approval of the white enslavers. But he surprised all of us. People do strange things when they look death in the eye. He died a man of us, bone of our bone, didn't he? But only just. Only at the last moment did he see the need for fighting for the freedom of black people. I wonder what it was that made him gather his senses. I remember him always looking at me intently. Could it be my words finally penetrated his thick African skull? When, I wonder? Certainly after he made that shameful speech at the palaver about the regiment being his new tribe or something. Still, it was a damn close thing.

But . . . when will the accommodationists in this world stop deceiving themselves that they can live unsullied with the tyranny of evil? When will they learn that their lives count for nothing to those who wield power? When will they learn that they live only so long as they are useful to those who dominate them? Congo Jack found out just in time.

Private Jack reminds me of the old African fable, "How Do You Catch A Monkey?" To catch a monkey, a gourd with a small hole cut in its neck is attached to a stake in the ground. Bait is placed inside. The monkey thrusts his hand through the narrow hole and grasps the food. But in holding on to the bait the monkey cannot extricate its hand and thus traps itself. Jack was that monkey. The bait? A bit of red cloth and a gun he did not own. Only until the very end did he let go the bait and thus free himself from those who controlled the gourd.

Like I said, Jack died a man of us, bone of our bone, but he threw away his golden chance to do more, to march hand in hand with us Haitians on the field of battle against the white enslavers. It is true that General Toussaint was captured and died a wretched death in a French dungeon. But one of his officers, General Jean-Jacques Dessalines, continued the struggle and Haiti finally took its freedom in 1804. If Jack had acted sooner Dominica might have been a second Haiti. But Jack failed to understand that he lived in an age for breaking rules, not preserving rules. Only at the very end did he understand that a man is defined by his actions.

Jubba Lily:

Oh, Madu, I knew the moment they shot you down. I was hoeing with my gang when I heard the second shot and immediately a cool wind blew for a long moment across my face. It caressed my body in the way only you could. Was that you, Madu? Was that your spirit saying goodbye to me before flying home to Margiland? At the moment I felt a great lostness and a heavy ache in my heart. I felt you bleed and die. Oh, Madu, I never wanted you to die. We had so many things to look forward to. I only wanted you to see the truth and to look in a common direction with us negroes. Those things I said were never meant to hurt you. I would have gladly taken my place at your side. There was a part of me that wished that. That way my spirit would have traveled with yours to the Africa I heard so much about. But I understand that this was something you had to do. It was something I expected you to do. You always said that each person has one big thing to do in their lifetime before time made dust of them.

Tears came to my eyes when I heard that horrible sound. For days I felt trampled on. I felt alone and wanted you to protect me. After a long while my spirits picked up again and immediately I thought of the wonder of you, Madu. You were the bearer of something honest and good and all-enduring, and because of that it was to you that I gave my first free rush of love and passion and I am glad of it. I am glad I had the chance to know that love did not have to be ugly. Our passion was so different, with no reminders of the past. I was happy with you, Madu, as happy as a kitten stretched out in the morning sun. Only stroke its fur and feel its deep contentment as it wallows completely in the present moment. That was me, Madu.

Sometimes when I want to recapture the magic of our first meeting, the high moment of my life, I go to the coffee-drying platform, and there I can feel that moment when our hands first touched. I do this when things wear me down. Then the memories of you and me make me happy and I feel strong again.

No heart had more feeling than yours, Madu. Your memory is still warm on my mind. I love you, Madu.

And in my next life, which you claim awaits me, I will look hard for you—look for me. You will find me dancing, this time alone. I will love you Madu, long after I am dead, long after I am clay.

AFTERWORD

In a novel, characters and situations are usually invented. Although my imagination was clearly at work in *Congo Jack*, much of the story is rooted in truth. Authentic information about Jack, the mutiny, and the military history of the West Indies comes from Colonial Office Papers and War Office Papers located at the Public Record Office just outside London at Kew Gardens. Jack's name as well as the names of his comrades are all recorded in these official papers, as is much of the quoted trial testimony.

Also found in the official record is Souvarine Petro's statement regarding the legal status of African soldiers serving in the West India Regiments at the time. His statement is, in fact, the opinion of the British Law Officers of the Crown who, in 1801, ruled that West India soldiers were subject to the same hated police laws that governed the behavior and movements of plantation slaves. It is rather likely that this opinion helped spark the mutiny, since the men of the Eighth were proud of their status as British soldiers and thus determined to avoid any connection with the evils of plantation slavery.

Much of Jack's African environment is similarly authentic. It is based on scholarly studies of the Margi and other tribal groups of northeastern Nigeria. For example, facial and body decorations, which were recognized tribal badges, and which distinguished one group from another, are based on ethnological investigations. Chief among my sources were the works of C.K. Meek, Carl Hoffmann, L. Lewis Wall, and Robert Farris Thompson.

Congo Jack is thus in many ways a true story. Most important, the principal character was a real-life stolen African about whom some things are known with certainty. "Congo Jack" was, in fact, the protagonist's British army name. The name Congo Jack was one of a strange medley of names given to blacks by their white masters. This new identity was part of the process of transforming a kidnapped African into a New World African slave by a series of shock experiences, one of which was the loss of one's name and identity.

In 1798, Congo Jack was recruited into the British Eighth West India Regiment. Twelve in number, these regiments were formed largely of African slaves by order of the London government to lessen the British army's dependency on European troops, who died in appalling numbers from disease. Three years later, in March 1801, the soldiers of the Eighth sealed their comradeship in blood when the regiment bore the brunt of the fighting against French troops on the tiny Leeward island of St. Martin. The British commander of the expedition did not stint in his praise of the soldiers of the Eighth. He wrote in his battle report:

"They behave[d] in a manner that would do honor to any Troops."

Except for his short stay at St. Martin, Private Congo Jack spent virtually all of his short career as a British soldier on the lush island of Dominica, among the sprawling complex of barracks and forts and other buildings on an extraordinary site known as the Cabrits. And then his world ended abruptly. The tragic unraveling of Congo Jack's life began on the evening of April 9, 1802, when his regiment mutinied. The rebellion was quickly crushed. A few days later a general court-martial was convened. As officially reported in Colonial and War Office Papers, Private Congo Jack and his comrades, Privates Manby, Lively, Cuffy, Genus, Pedro and Hussar, were found guilty of "exciting and joining in Mutiny . . . and . . . Murder" and sentenced to death.

Having found Congo Jack and his comrades guilty of a capital offense, the army moved with what seems like indecent haste. The day following the tribunal's decision, Congo Jack and the other prisoners were put through the ritual of execution, a ceremony as terror-filled as British military justice could contrive. The morning after the executions, a court of inquiry was convened. It came to the conclusion that the Eighth had mutinied because of the fear among the soldiers of being sold into slavery.

My principal object in writing *Congo Jack* was to look into the heart and mind of a stolen African and, in the process, to meet him in person. Another reason was to explore the African warrior class, arguably the most favored and unique group in the black community in the West Indies during the slave era. To accomplish this I read extant official records. I also visited the Cabrits and saw the scenes Congo Jack saw so I could recreate some of his experiences.

Finally, the idea to write this story came to me in London, in the Public Record Office, when my eyes first clapped onto the name "Congo Jack" in the court martial proceedings of the mutiny of the Eighth West India Regiment. It was an unusual name, I thought, and I became fascinated with it and the man to whom it was forcibly given. Indeed, the name and the man took on a special life in my imagination. I hope I have done justice to Congo Jack who, in the name of progress and discovery, lost his world while being driven to create a new one.

R.N.B.

GULF OF

MEXICO

FLORIDA

C. Canavera

Rolls Town

St. John

Apalache

Tampa

Bay of Espiritu Santo

Bleach Yards

Charlotte Harb.

C. Sable

Gulf of Florida

Chatham Bay

Dry Tortugas

Martyrs Reefs

Florida Straits

Key Sal

C.

Colorados

Havanna

Matanzas

ISLE of

C. St. Antonio

L. of Pinos

Jardinas

Lagua Bay

Que

Mouths of the Mississippe

Serpent pt.

Passo del

Carcallo

Rio Bravo

Rio Palmas

Panuco

Taminague Lagoon

R. Cazones

P. Delgado

Vera Cruz

MEXICO

GUAXACA

Cayuca

S. Anns I.

Cryalva R.

Tabasco

Chiapa

Cojuca

Alvarado

Trist. I.

VERAPAZ

G. of Dulce

Palacca

Placentia Lagoon

C. Catouche

P. Piedras

Merida

BAY of Campeche

CAMPECHE

Campeton

YUCATAN

False C.

Cozumel

Ascension Bay

R. Nova

Amber I.

Key Channel

Turnell I.

Rattan

Bonacca

BAY of HONDURAS

R. Belize

Nicalanga Lagoon

Triumpho

Omoa

Trivello

C. Honduras

Pateok P.

Swan I.

Serranilla

Pearl

Cayman

Caymanbr

P. Neg

C.

NEW

SPAIN

HONDURAS

MOSKITO SHORE

Black R.

Brewers

Cape R.

Brammon Bluff

C. Gracias a Dios

Devils Key

lo Ventosa

Gulf of Teguantepec

Guatimala

Estapa

Sensonatear

la Trinidad

Valladolid

R. Leon

R. Roca

Tongulaw

Great R.

Man of War Keys

Old Provi

St. Andres

Gulf of Fonseca

Reolego

Leon

L. Lindiri

NICARAGUA

Nicaragua

Lake Nicaragua

Pearl Key Lagoon

Gyn I.

Blewfields Lagoon

Three Brothers

Gulf Papagyo

COSTA RICA

Fort

R. St. Juan

C. Blanco

G. of Nicoya

la Caldera

Cartago

Fort Cartago

Monkey Pt.

Bacalena

Fort Bello

Burica P.

VERAGUA

Conception

Pan

Bay of Panama

Quicara

Coybo

P. Mala

B. St.

P. Ipuna

C.A

NORTH

PACIFIC

OCEAN

B. of